Also by Pico Iyer

Falling Off the Map

The Lady and the Monk

Video Night in Kathmandu

THESE ARE BORZOI BOOKS PUBLISHED
IN NEW YORK BY ALFRED A. KNOPF

CUBA
AND THE
NIGHT

A Novel

PICO IYER

Alfred A. Knopf   New York   1995

THIS IS A BORZOI BOOK PUBLISHED
BY ALFRED A. KNOPF, INC.

Library of Congress Cataloging-in-Publication Data
Iyer, Pico.
Cuba and the night : a novel / by Pico Iyer.—1st ed.
p.   cm.
ISBN 0-679-44052-6
1. Man-woman relationships—Cuba—Havana—Fiction.
2. Photographers—Cuba—Havana—Fiction.
3. Havana (Cuba)—Fiction. I. Title.
PS3559.Y47C8 1995
813'.54—dc20   94-31104   CIP

Manufactured in the United States of America

FIRST EDITION

For Carlos, Peter, and, of course, Lourdes—and all those who smile through suffering in the Cubas of the world

And with deepest thanks to Hiroko Takeuchi for sustenance; to Astrid Golomb for inspiration; to Michael Hofmann for penetration; to Kristin McCloy for particular fierceness; to Mark Muro for unfailing support; and to Lynn Nesbit, Sonny Mehta, and Charles Elliott for making the words, so to speak, flesh.

Rápida, como un reflejo,
Dos veces vi el alma, dos:
Cuando murió el pobre viejo,
Cuando ella me dijo adiós.

Two times, in the flash of an eye,
Two times, I have seen the soul:
Once, when the old man died,
Once, when she said goodbye.

—José Martí

I

I think I'll always remember the first time I saw him, in the bar of the old Nacional, on one of those messy Carnival evenings in July, the temperature about 120, with the blare of the floats and the trumpets carrying across the lawns, and the dancing young boys on the Malecón jiving over overflowing cups of beer, and the whole city kind of strutting its stuff and shimmying in the tropical night.

Things were pretty much the same as usual in the bar: a couple of Mexicans smooching in the corner, acting as if they were on their honeymoon, or their second honeymoon, or the honeymoon they'd never have; a mulatta at the counter, making time with Boris and Ivan; some Italian girl pressing the Wurlitzer and getting her boy to slow-dance with her to Pablo. Alfredo over by the register, taking it all in, and dreaming of Asunción.

I thought the pasty-faced guy in the gray sweater must be a Bulgarian at first, he dressed so stylishly. Then I was put right.

"Excuse me. This can't be right."

"*Qué?*"

"Well, I don't want to make problems for you, but I'm sure . . ."

"What's the problem?" I asked.

"Well, you see, he claims he's got no change for five dollars. And earlier, they told me they couldn't accept my pesos because I don't have my passport on me. And now they're saying I've got to give them five dollars and they can't give me any change."

I took the guy in again, and turned to Alfredo. "Look," I said, "this man is a journalist. *Periodista, no?* A very important *periodista.* CIA, M.I.5, all that stuff. You make problems for him, and his friends in the government make problems for you."

Alfredo looked sullen and went back to his stool.

"Thanks so much. Awfully kind of you."

"Not at all. What are you drinking?"

"Oh, a beer would be fine."

"*Dos,*" I said to Alfredo, and then turned back to the Englishman. "Are you here for the party?"

"Well, in a manner of speaking."

"And what manner would that be?"

He looked back at me blankly. People say that Americans don't have a sense of humor, but the Brits, I can tell you, are no barrel of laughs.

"Your first time down here?"

"It is, actually. I usually go down to Greece for the summer holidays. With my friend—and colleague, actually—Stephen. But this time there was some kind of balls-up, and the travel agent told me she could get me onto a cheap flight to Havana."

"And now . . ."

"Well, now I'm just pottering around, really. Looking at a few churches. Visiting the museums. Engaging in a little private research. My uncle used to be posted here."

"After the war?"

"Right. During Batista. He'd been in North Africa during the forties—something in intelligence, I suspect—and somehow he ended up over here."

"Protecting Western interests?"

"I suppose that's what they call it." He looked into his drink for a moment, as if to cut the conversation short. "In any case, when I was growing up, I was always hearing about this very grand house of his in Miramar."

"Not so grand anymore."

"No, I suppose not. But anyway, that's just a diversion. The main reason I'm here is for the jazz bars. They're my great passion."

"Of course," I said, wondering whether I'd really flown two thousand miles to make small talk with a Brit.

"And you?"

"Oh, the usual. Making a few photographs. The Rumba-Revolution-comes-of-age kind of thing."

"You're a journalist?"

"Yeah. If a journalist is someone who makes his living off other people's misery."

"No. I believe that's what they call a schoolteacher."

"That's what you do?"

"In a manner of speaking."

"In London?"

"No, Winchester, actually. Where Malory found Camelot." He smiled at me, not very convincingly, and then fumbled around in his pocket and pulled out a yellow piece of tissue to wipe his glasses. His face had gone an unhealthy kind of red in the sun, and even with the fan going behind the bar, he seemed to be sweating. It felt kind of weird, to tell the truth, to be wasting time with a British schoolteacher while the mulatta was pressing her claims on the Soviets and there were pantings from the corner. The Mexicans looked as if they were inhaling one another.

"It *is* fascinating, though, don't you think?" he started up again. "This place. I mean, you really feel as if you're seeing history in the making."

"Or the unmaking. It's like history's on the pause button here. Everywhere else in the world, everything's either on fast-forward or rewind. This is the only place I know where everything's moving and nothing ever changes. It's like instant replay round the clock."

"Very good way of putting it."

"Well, I'll be seeing you," I said, feeling that life was too short for more of this.

"I do hope so. The name's Hugo. Hugo Cartwright." He extended his hand in what he probably thought was the American way.

"Hugo. I'm Richard."

"Very good. If ever you find yourself in Winchester, do look me up. It's not exactly Havana, of course, but it's not without its charms. There are some tremendous wine bars. First-class churches. And the Quiristers, of course."

"Of course. Take it easy now," I said, and put my pesos on the counter and went upstairs before Alfredo could ask me why I wasn't paying in dollars.

. . .

It was a funny thing, but every time I stepped out of my hotel in those days, on another bright and windless morning, my heart just felt like singing. It was like being in love, I guess, though it's even easier to be in love with a place than a person. Whatever, I felt wide open and alive, as if anything could happen. And after I'd left, I'd find myself haunted by the memories: just the way the battered buildings followed the beautiful curve of the bay, and the blue sea sat before you in the brilliant stillness of the morning, and when you went out early you could see the first boys gathered in the shade for a bus, and hear the day's first music coming from some upstairs window. The woman at Black Star used to say that it was like being back in high school for some of us, and I guess she was right. All these lush sixteen-year-olds feeling the power in their smiles, and the handsome boys strutting around like roosters, and the sense of music and rum in the air, and a few unsmiling monitors waiting to report you to the teacher. And everyone living in the moment: no thought of tomorrow, just a blurry haze of past and present, and trying to find a way to get a car for the night, or hustle some cash or some nooky.

I was on assignment for *Stern* that time—the Europeans never could get enough of all that Mulatta Marxism stuff—and I was also shooting for myself, using Fuji for rich colors and editing in the camera. Mostly, though, I was just happy to be away from Nicaragua for a while: after a few months of bus rides to Jinotega, and roundups of guerrilla movements in the hills, I would have given anything to get back to Havana. It was one of those places that just brought a smile to your face, even when your heart was breaking. And it always had the magic of the unexpected: at two o'clock, you never knew what you'd be doing at two-thirty. You could be in a fight somewhere, or making some girl, or on your way to prison.

I got up early the next day and went out to Vedado. I'd got most of the bacchanal stuff I needed already, and all I wanted now were some cut-price ironies: the old Mafia hotels with pictures of Che beside their entrances; the Communist Youth halls with cartoon characters outside, advertising videos and discos; the old women with their heads in their hands, under signs that read: NOBODY SUR-RENDERS HERE.

I began with the Cuba Pavilion, the weird monolithic hulk on La Rampa that looks like some once-futuristic spaceship left over from an ancient world's fair, and I was just trying to gauge the light while pretending to read the plaque in front of it, when I heard a voice at my side—"Excuse me, you know the time?"—and I turned to see this young guy smiling at me, slim, with narrow Chinese eyes, the usual Cuban mix of slyness and good nature.

I flashed my watch at him so I wouldn't have to speak.

"Thank you," he said in English again. "You American?"

I guess he could tell I was a foreigner from the fact I was reading the slogans. Usually, I tried to pass myself off as a Cuban down here, by dressing down and talking only in monosyllables. This guy, I guessed, made it his job to spot the foreigner.

"In a manner of speaking." I'd learned something at least from Hugo.

"Great. Me too. I love your country," he said, and then reached into the bag he was carrying and pulled out a small rectangle on which was neatly typed:

> *José Santos Cruz*
> *Translator-Facilitator*
> *Calle J 410, (Apto. 7, 3er piso),*
> *e/t 19 y 21,*
> *Vedado, La Habana*

"Thanks," I said. "If I need any facilitation, I'll get in touch."

"So you are a photographer?"

"*Turista.*"

"Tourist. Great. You have seen the Hemingway house? You know the home of José Martí? You know Graham Greene?"

"Not personally."

"Look, I show you. That book *Our Man in Havana*, it was written on the veranda of the Nacional. Every day he comes and drinks coffee at this place. How about I take you there, I buy you some coffee?"

"How about I take you there and we buy our own coffee?"

"Sure. Is better," said José. "I want to talk with you. Who is your favorite writer? You know William Saroyan? Oh, I love him. That book *Papa, You're Crazy*. And Steinbeck too. You know Hemingway . . ." And he went on listing his enthusiasms while we walked back to the hotel. I might as well see where this would lead, I thought: in my job, even a bad time is better than no time at all.

In the lobby of the hotel, a few girls were already working the phones, hanging around the reception desk and catching the names and numbers of unattached men, then calling up to them from couches, while a Dominican student was standing by the cashier, dialing for dollars, and the elevator boys were cadging for Chiclets. Everyone was looking at everyone else as if they were all targets or spies.

Out in the garden, it was just another Havana morning: blue sea, blue sky, stationary cannons in front of the wall. The whole city as motionless as if it were posing for a still life. We took a place on the veranda and waited not to be served.

"*Mira,*" said José as a couple of girls walked past, letting the straps of their blouses fall off their coffee shoulders. "You like?"

"*Más o menos.*"

"*Más o menos,*" he said. "Is good."

"So what do you do for a living, José?" I thought it was better for me to be asking him questions than for him to be asking me.

"A little this, a little that."

"I'll bet."

"Sometimes I translate—you know, the Top Forty Countdown from Miami. Sometimes I read the people's future from their photographs. Sometimes I teach English, French, Italian."

"And sometimes you just drink coffee."

"Sometimes I just drink coffee," he said with a broad smile, and then his eyes lit up, in a lazy kind of way, and he started making the hissy-kissy sound that Cuban males use when they want to get a girl's attention. To my surprise, the girl in question turned round, and it was a girl with honey hair, golden skin, golden bracelets and necklaces around her white pantsuit: gold on two legs, she seemed, on her way to the runways in Milan. *"Oye, oye! Pilar! Ven acá!"* he said, and then she was coming over to us, there was kissing on both cheeks, and exclamations of surprise, and a long golden arm, under a golden Rolex, extended toward me, and a pretty *"Encantada."*

"So when did you get here?" José asked as she sat between us, crossing her legs.

"Sunday. Just for business."

"How is it with you now? You are in Ciudad Mexico?"

"Cuernavaca."

"Ay!" José turned to me, impressed. "Pilar is married with a Mexican. Doctor, right?" She nodded, and flashed me a smile. "Very old, very rich. They meet here one year before. Is good there, no?"

"Claro. We have a swimming pool, a tennis court, a *casita* for the weekends. Is good."

She had practiced her nonchalance, and he responded on cue, showing her off to me like a prize. "For girls here, it's easy. They find a man, they make magic with their eyes, they get out. But for me—what do I have? Only my mind."

"And your *pinga!"* said Pilar, reaching for his thighs.

There wasn't anything in this for me, so I got up and told them I was going back to work.

"Okay, Richard," said José. "I'll catch you later. Maybe we go to Tropicana? I get some girls, we buy some rum, we have a good time, okay? You have my address? Or maybe I find you? What is your room number?"

"You can find me."

"I can find you," he said, and turned back to his latest project.

T hat night, I walked in and out of the crowds along the Malecón, underneath the viewing stands, past the teams of boys in polka-dot shorts, past the cries of *"Mira," "Digame," "Orlando!,"* past the lines of gyrating men in top hats. At one point, I met José and a couple of other guys, checking out the action. A girl came up to me in feathers and a kind of rhinestone minidress, and I recognized a woman from the hotel reception desk. Sometimes black kids in wild Pierrot masks danced over and began saying things I couldn't understand, and sometimes I heard fierce whispers in the dark, and once, between the bleachers, I found myself next to a Soviet, a doctor, he said, who was looking at the dancing girls as if he were dizzy, his eyes out of focus, his face transfigured. "Fantastic, no? For me, this is a dream! A dream!"

A dream of incitations, I thought, around the clock, around the country, in every nook and shadowed cranny. Everywhere you went, it felt as if you were passing through an echo chamber of hisses, a tunnel of whispers. "*Ven acá, mi amor. Mi vida, mi alma, mi corazón.*" "*Ven acá, por qué no?*" "*Por qué no, mi amor? Por qué no?*"

I left the Russian to his dreams, and wandered around groups of people sitting in the streets, while dancers like parrots and toucans fluttered all around them.

"Excuse me?" called out a woman from the blanket where she was sitting. "You are from America?"

"No."

"Tourist?"

"Yes."

"Here. Sit down. Meet my brother." She motioned to the blanket, and the man who was with her—her brother or her boyfriend—made a space for me and handed me a bottle of rum.

"You study in America?"

"Sometimes."

"I think so. I see from your shoes. Maybe you come to my store sometime. Behind the cathedral. I show you the plaza, Habana Vieja, everything."

"Sure, great."

"Maybe tomorrow? What is your plan?"

"I don't know right now. I'll look in on you, if I get the chance," I said, and got up: she was moving way too fast for me. Besides, if I was going to get a guide, it might as well be someone who would shoot well. This woman was too sophisticated, had too much of the *hacienda* in her already. I needed someone fresher, more like an amateur: a girl alone on a bed in a broken-down hotel and, in the distance, a man along the sea, pointing his son's gaze out to the horizon. "The Permanent Revolution," they could caption it, and it could run in any kind of story. Even get resale rights in Spanish *Playboy*.

Around Coppelia, the kids were sauntering about like queens waiting to be defrocked, and on the Calle 21 side, near the Vita Nuova, the girls looked so gorgeous I figured that most of them weren't girls at all. Look for the Adam's apple, I told myself, and remember why it's called that. Check out the size of their wrists. In a culture where women had cornered the biggest market, everyone wanted to be one.

After a few minutes of cruising, I decided to cut into Karachi for a drink. The place was dead tonight—who wanted to dance in a bar when there was an all-night orgy going on in the streets?—and there were only a couple of pros there, watched hungrily by some boozy spies from the Ukraine.

A girl came up to me, in that slow, hip-swinging way they have, with memories of their grandfathers and hot days in West Africa. She had a big gap in her teeth, but when she didn't smile, she looked fine. Silvio was singing on the jukebox—"La Prisión"—and we moved around a little in the dark while one of the bartenders slept in the corner and the other changed his pesos into dollars. I had nothing to lose, I figured, and anything was better than returning to my hotel room alone.

After we'd danced through a couple of slow ones, I bought her a drink at a table in the corner, and she told me how she had a kid, how she lived with her mother, how her boyfriend was in Angola and her brother was in Miami. A millionaire, she'd heard. How she'd had *esposos,* but nothing serious. I returned the favor in kind— told her I was Robert, from Toronto, a tourist here for a month, and poor, very poor—and she took it all in like it was holy writ, looking at me in that bright-eyed, teasing way the Habañeras have, and I figured I might as well go for it: the night was getting on, and nothing else was developing.

"You want to go somewhere?"

She nodded.

"Round here?"

"Not here. Habana Vieja."

"Okay." We walked back to the Capri, and found a Turistaxi, and I stuffed five dollars in the guy's hand. We drove down backstreets—the Malecón was closed tonight for the party—and then Neptuno, and we got off near a place she knew. We went up some creaking stairs and came to an empty reception desk. Past it, there was a door that led out onto a half-lit terrace. A few girls were sitting there in demure white dresses as if lined up at some debutantes' ball, and the guys beside them were staring at their feet as if on their way to war.

My girl—she told me to call her Célia—knocked at a door, and it opened, and there was a shout of surprise, and some tired blonde who was in there with an even older guy came out and started babbling.

We tried the next door down, and it gave pretty easily, and we were alone in a bare room, with a shelf and a chair. There was a naked lightbulb, and a towel at the foot of the bed. There were two pairs of cartoon slippers from Shanghai.

"You want a shower?"

"Okay," I said, and then we went into the bathroom, and it was bare too—just one worn faucet in the wall, and a trickle of cold water. I decided to take a rain check on the shower—a rain check on the whole thing, in fact: she'd taken off her clothes and folded them as neatly on the chair as if she were a schoolgirl, and I saw raw bruises on her side, and scars across her belly, and one of her breasts looked kind of lopped off. It was no kind of body for a girl of sixteen.

"Look, Célia. This is fine. Enough. How about we talk for a little, and then I take some photos, and we go?"

"What's wrong? You don't like me?" She came up and began kissing my neck.

"I like you fine. It's just that I've been drinking too much."

"No problem. I can help. We have to make love. We cannot leave until we have done it." Plaintively almost, she moved her mouth down my stomach.

"I can't."

"*Qué pasa, mi amor?*"

"*SIDA*," I said.

"*SIDA?*"

"*Soy americano.*" And then she nodded respectfully and backed off.

I didn't have the heart to take any pictures of her then, and just as I was reaching for my pants, the light went off, and she gave a little gasp, and then I heard her sniffling and felt her shivering beside me.

"It's okay," I said. "It's a blackout. It's nothing." But she was shaking now, and I could tell she had closed her eyes, and a sad kind of terrible moan came up from her. "It's okay," I said, "don't worry," and I reached out to hold her, and she grabbed at me like I was a life jacket, and I thought of nights in Aranya, and the shelling overhead, and some fourteen-year-old in my arms, more scared of me than of the war.

Célia was helpless in my arms now, just a trembling, terrified bundle of nerves, and I fumbled around for a candle and couldn't find one, so I got out my lighter and struck a light. From outside, there came the sound of footsteps pacing back and forth.

"Come on, Célia," I said. "You can dress by this light," and I smoothed her hair, and held the lighter out while she put on her clothes, hands fumbling.

When she was through, I did the same, and we walked out into the street. Kissing her on both cheeks, I pressed a few notes into her palm.

"*Gracias, muchas gracias,*" she said, smiling back at me. "You want?" And handed me in return a stick of gum.

The whole thing had left a kind of sour taste in my mouth, and I knew there was no way I could get to sleep. I needed to talk to someone, to get the whole thing out of my system. I needed to erase the night from my memory. Another romance that fizzled was the last thing I needed.

So I headed back to the Nacional, and when I went in, Alfredo gave me his usual terse nod and poured me "the usual": some concoction he'd learned down in Asunción.

"Your friend?" he asked, and motioned to the other side. It was the Englishman again—the only other single man in Havana—and he was sitting next to some Spanish kid in glasses, who was telling him about Bilbao and the death of Franco and the importance of the Basque struggle, while Hugo was responding in that classic British orchestral tune-up of "Quite so"s and "Really?"s and "Is that right?"s.

I figured it was time to rescue him again.

"Hugo." I raised my glass. "Come and join me for a drink."

"Think I might, actually," he said, getting up, a little unsteadily, and almost bowing to the kid. "Very good to have met you. Do hope we'll meet again soon," and then coming over to the stool next to mine.

"So what's up?"

"Not a great deal, really."

"What's your poison?"

"Tropicola '76. Quite a good vintage, so they say."

You couldn't exactly wet your glass with him, but the guy was better company than none.

"Seen anything interesting?"

"Well, I went down to this thing they have called the Humor Museum, but it was closed. 'For repairs,' the sign said. Took a few snapshots of the old *palacios* for the boys—best-preserved colonials in the Caribbean, so they say. And I did come upon a very pleasant jazz bar. Célia Cruz sort of place."

"Met any girls?"

"Cubans, you mean?"

"Well, they are usually the ones you meet in Cuba."

"Can't say I have. They're not that easy to meet, are they?"

"No. Not unless you go out of your hotel. Or walk down any street."

"So you do have a local involvement, I take it?"

"Naw, I'm married, as it happens. We're separated right now, to make a long story nonexistent, but we haven't got divorced yet because of the alimony payments."

"Oh, I'm sorry."

"Don't be; she isn't. Photographers aren't the easiest people in the world to be married to."

"Yes. Must be terribly consuming. I suppose you rarely get the chance to spend time at home."

"Rarely get the wish to be at home. Home for me is a hotel and an expense account."

He looked down at his drink, and I could feel the conversation beginning to flag.

"Anyway, it's a way to keep things safe. Anyone starts getting too friendly with you round here, and it's fifty-fifty they're playing footsie with Fidel. Look,"—I could see how Alfredo was listening to us, and I knew he could speak as much English as he needed—"how about checking out somewhere else? Have you ever been up to the Capri at night?"

"Can't say I have."

"Let me take you there. If you're into ancient history, it's sure to be your place. Hasn't changed since George Raft was running the casino and Sinatra was headlining downstairs." We headed out then, leaving Alfredo muttering in the corner, and wandered down the long avenue of palms, past a couple of soldiers necking in the bushes, and a boy in a leather jacket working undercover, and a few girls on the lookout for foreigners, on their own behalf or someone else's. As usual, half the people here looked like they were in the slums of Lagos, and half looked as if they were on their way to Vegas, with golden handbags, and scarlet earrings, and eyes glittery with excitement.

We took the elevator up to the eighteenth floor, and when we walked outside, the place was almost empty: just a couple of fat Colombians in the pool, and the yellow streetlights of the Malecón below. The Capri kept the rooftop bar open round the clock, but the action only started when the other places closed. I loved to come here at one, two, when it was still quiet, and shoot the nightscape from this angle, with the pool eerily spotlit in the foreground, and the grand, lonely towers of the Nacional behind, and the deck chairs lined up, ghostly, in front of the blue-tinted glass, the whole white city receding into darkness.

"You know," I said, "it must have been really something in its prime. Going to be something too, after they've done some reconstruction."

"Deconstruction seems to be more the Cuban way."

"Meaning?"

"Meaning that it's such a hard place to make out, don't you think? Everyone here seems to spend half his time complaining about Castro, and half his time glorying in the country's autonomy."

"And half their energy planning to go to Miami, and half their energy bad-mouthing the *yanquis.*"

"Quite so. And not many of the people one meets seem to have anything good to say about the Revolution."

"Maybe a function of the people you meet. The only ones who hang out with foreigners are the ones with complaints or agendas. The ones who are happy have no need of us."

"I suppose you're right."

"I know I am. It's the same anywhere. I hate my wife, but if you say anything against her, I'll punch you out."

"The wife in this case being the Revolution?"

"Right. Fidel's aging lover."

We took the scene in without talking for a while. One of the Colombians got out of the pool and toweled himself dry. A Frenchman came up, looked round, snarled, and went down again. It was like being on a film set after they've wrapped for the day and everyone else was off at some party or watching dailies, but the soundstage was still lit up, waiting for a scene that's already gone.

"You know, sometimes I think Fidel is really on to something here." He looked at me as I spoke. "I mean, if there's anywhere that's crazy and passionate and reckless enough to make a Revolution work, it's here. And he just plays right into that whole Spanish thing of holding hands and swearing eternal love and promising to shoot the stars down from the sky. You should see some of the other Communist dumps—Beijing or Moscow, even Prague: they'd kill for even a small piece of the energy they have here. Because they've got nothing going on there except gray buildings and cold offices and dead slogans. But Fidel, you know, he's just like this sultry crooner who knows the people are in love—crazily in love—with wild gestures and poetic dreams and love songs. So he just sings them all these pretty melodies that stick in your head like jingles. "Until the Final Victory." "Ready to Conquer." "We Will Prevail."

I'd had too much to drink, I knew, but I wasn't in a mood to stop. And I certainly wasn't in a mood to talk about myself. "And you know the craziest thing?"

"What's that?"

"The people love it. It's almost like they want to be conned: they want to be wooed with false promises and poems and pretty lies. They want to be given a line, to be told that they'll be held till the rivers run dry and the moon falls from the sky."

"I should have thought they'd much rather have bread."

"Sure. But that's the beauty of it. Making them forget the things they haven't got. It's like, who thinks of food and money when he's on the beach with his girl? Who worries about human rights when he's singing a love song on his guitar? Who gives a fuck about anything when he's in the middle of making love?"

I thought about what I wasn't talking about, and all the false promises and lies I'd seen in my time. But that was beside the point, I thought: you could help people most by not giving them the burden of your heart.

"Anyway, if you want to get a feel for this place, you should go to Nicaragua sometime. The whole country's just like this huge black hole. The main cathedral's just this big gutted place with crows rooting around in the grass. The capital's nothing but an empty field. But you read the newspapers, and you think it's the last frontier of the cold war. East against West, Marx against Ford. And the truth of it is, the whole place is just a few *campesinos* with shy smiles, sitting around in empty huts and asking how Dennis Martinez is doing with the Expos. That's the craziness. The contras want dollars so they can get cable TV. The Sandinistas want cable TV so they can learn how to get more dollars. And all the while the people are going down by the handful."

I was talking too much, I knew, saying things I wouldn't believe in the morning. But Hugo was more generous—or polite—than I'd imagined: he just sat there, taking it all in.

"So it sounds as if you're on a mission against politics."

"Oh, I don't know. Anyway, politics is kind of beside the point when half the people round you are starving. Listen"—I stopped for a moment, and looked at him—"I've been talking your ear off. I'm sorry, my friend. You get so whenever you see someone who speaks English, you go crazy."

"That's fine," he said. "I know the feeling. Still, think I might be shoving off now."

"Okay, you shove off, then. I'll see you later."

"I do hope so," he said, and left me to my drink.

In the morning, I felt better: hell at first, but at least Hugo had helped wipe out the memory of the girl and the hotel. That was the great thing about hell: it made it good to be in purgatory again. And the other thing was that it was always good to shoot in Cuba: it must have been the easiest place in the world to make pictures. You just got off the plane, and you were in the thick of it. One guy was making some girl, and the others were trying to swim out, and a woman was weeping for her son in New Jersey, and the guy over there was trying to sell you a pigeon. Everywhere you turned, everything was happening, and everything that was happening took you away from all abstraction and into something human, where answers weren't so easy.

I guess the other reason I was happy to be here, if I stopped to think about it, was that it was good to be out of myself for a while. After the separation, things hadn't been too easy on the home front. I figured the thing to do now was just concentrate on the pictures. Play the part of the photographer that everyone expected; focus on the job and work out the angles. Live by the book for a while. If I had to choose between a partner and a job, it made more sense to choose the one I could make a living out of.

Besides, I knew it was better not to get too hooked on things. That could only lead to heartbreak. When I was a kid, I'd believed in everything around. Politics and revolution and even love eternal. But after the breakups and the wars and the long nights in Taipei, I'd learned a safer rule of thumb: people let you down, principles don't. People tell lies, images never do. The first time you come into a foreign country, and everyone looks the same to you, and there's fighting all around, there's no way of telling right from wrong. The only thing to do is get out the lens and catch the ambiguity; and when it came to ambiguity, Cuba was the leader of the pack.

I'd got most of what I needed from the present trip, in any case, and the only thing I needed now was some more intimate shots—the inside of houses, the texture of hopes. So I decided to take José up on his offer and track that crooked wire to wherever it would take me.

So I followed the instructions he'd given me, walked past Coppelia—it looked kind of hungover this morning, with an after-the-party feel—and down 23, where a few old men were buying the day's copy of *Granma,* and the kids were talking about how they'd spent the night, and the housewives were calculating lines and quotas. I went down a side street, and up some narrow stairs, past two apartments open, with little boys watching me from the sofa, and up to a floor where an old woman was on the telephone, with the door open. CDR, I figured: the neighborhood spies making sure that everything was peachy. I knocked on the door that said 7, and heard a dog barking, and then it sprung open, and there was José, a big black boy behind him. "Richard," he said, "meet my brother," and the big smiling boy extended a hand. I followed them in, through a small room and into the kitchen. I figured there was no way this guy was really his brother—the only thing they had in common was two eyes and two legs—but distinctions were all dissolved here. In fact, it looked like half Havana was in the kitchen: kids with university manners, and three boys gathered around an English grammar book, and some girls huddled over *Playboy* in the corner, and a few shirtless teenagers sprawled out on the floor in front of a boom box on which you could catch the stations from Key West. Another Havana slumber party.

Around me, on the living room wall, there was a cross, and rows and rows of books in every kind of language: worn old orange Penguins of Somerset Maugham and Raymond Chandler; Martí, Gogol, Spinoza, Wilde, *The Gulag Archipelago*, something called *The Book of Knowledge*. A rooster was strutting around the room, and I could see the mangy white dog who'd greeted me at the door slurping up water from the toilet bowl. There was a photo of the Beatles on the bathroom door, a couple of postcards of the Yucatán on the wall.

"Too many books, eh?" said José. "It is my love. Books and friends. I have books from every country. Friends too—in Barcelona, Lima, Paris. But I cannot see them. My books I can always see and hold. Hey, Richard. This is Myra and Osman and Reynaldo," and I smiled at them all, and they smiled back, and then went back to Cyndi Lauper and discussing whether Jesse Jackson was a Communist.

"So how is it with you, Richard? What can I give you?"

"Suffering. I need suffering. Images of pain, of desperation."

"No problem," he said. "You come to the right place. You can take pictures of my apartment and my friends. What else?"

"I need to see despair."

"Okay. Later, I take you to a typical house. But first you need something else? Some cigars, maybe? The cigars with Shakespeare on the box. Maybe the ones with that English place—the House of Kings?"

"House of Lords?"

"Sure; House of Lords, anything: my friend can get you. Five boxes, ten. Usually, they are fifty pesos. I can get you for twenty U.S. Just tell me how many you need. Then I visit him, get the boxes, and we go to Capri. I get some girls, we have a party. What do you say?"

"Maybe."

"Sure. No maybe. This is better. You stay at the Nacional now? Okay. Maybe I give you ten dollars. You buy some food, some beer in the Tiendas there, and after, we go to the show." Better that than another night with Hugo and Alfredo, I thought: better that than another night with a Célia.

Just then there came a knock on the door. The dog barked, the rooster cried, and José went off to look out through the keyhole. The knock came again, more insistent.

"*Quién e'?*"

There was no answer.

"Manolo? Eusebio?"

Nothing.

José pulled back the lock and opened up. It was a Minint man—from the Ministry of the Interior—and a guy in a white shirt and gray slacks. I figured there was safety in numbers: just sit in the kitchen and blend in with the crowd.

"José Santos Cruz?" the man said, while his friend cast his eye around the apartment.

"Yes."

"It is time to help the Fatherland."

"I am helping the Fatherland already."

"You can help it more. You do not want to go to Angola?"

"*Compañero,* I want to go. But what can I do? My mother is sick. She is in Camagüey, she is a widow. I think she will die soon. Have some feeling, *compañero.*"

"So what do I tell my boss?"

"Tell him I will join you as soon as my mother dies."

The man wrote something down. "Okay, *compañero,*" he said, and patted José on the shoulder. "I hope your mother has a good long life."

His usual bravado back in place, José came back into the kitchen, all smiles.

"Okay, Richard. Let's go. I take you to Centro."

"Those guys were cool."

"Cool? Sure. They know it is not good to make problems for other Cubans. Come on, I introduce you to my mother."

I wondered what kind of mother this would be: A teenager? An Eskimo? A man, perhaps?

We went back out into the blinding sun, and José hailed a gasping old *colectivo* that was on its way downtown, and there was some heartfelt pleading and shouting and numbers flung back and forth, both parties trying to keep the smiles out of their voices, and then we were bumping down La Rampa, toward the sea, and turning toward Centro, and then José was leading me through a rectangle of dirty streets to a house with an old wooden door on Virtudes. He knocked and pulled at the door—no bells here, and no telephones, so every visit was a surprise—and there was no sound for a long time, and finally a frightened-looking woman, in a soiled white nightdress, came out on the balcony above us.

"*Ay, mi vida!* José, why do you come now?"

"To see Lázara."

"Okay, come in. She is with Lourdes and Caridad. *Ven, ven!*" The door swung open before us, pulled by a thin blue string that ran along the whole length of the stairs, and we scrambled up to the room. It was empty, except for some framed Spanish banknotes on the wall, and a set of lottery tickets posted up, and an old black-and-white picture of Fidel. Beyond, there was another room, even darker, with no lights and no windows.

"*Ven, ven,*" said the woman as we walked into the farther room, where three girls were sitting on a bed, sorting through old post-cards.

"Lázara," said José, and the youngest of them, dark-eyed, with long curls—she could have been Miss Havana five years from now—got up and kissed him on both cheeks. "This is Richard. He lives in New York."

Her eyes brightened, and she gave me her prettiest smile. "You know this street?" she asked, and then went over to a dresser, and got out a letter, and handed it to me. It was addressed to someone on 179th Street in the Bronx.

"Sure," I said.

"You can send it for her?" asked José.

"No problem."

"*Mira, un momentico,*" said another of the girls, a big, buxom blonde, with blue eyes that looked like they were going to tear. "I have a letter for my father. In New York. Wait here, I will go and get it."

"Me too," said the third.

"Sure," I said, "but in return I have a favor too. Let me get some pictures of you."

The girls giggled and all but clapped their hands, and José led me back out to the kitchen. Ten minutes later, the three of them came out, ready for prime time: red lips, and loosened hair, and mascara, and perfume, and their flashiest, low-cut numbers. All at eleven-thirty on a hot morning in July. "Okay," I said, and calculating the light in my head, trying to make it seem casual, I told them to go out on the balcony, with the dilapidated houses behind them, and then to come inside, under the picture of Che, and then in the door-way, where you could see Che and Michael Jackson and Jesus on the Cross all at once. I reeled off about fifteen, twenty frames like that, real fast, with no film in the camera, to get them relaxed, and then a few more in the same way, till they were getting bored and forgetting their poses and coming into focus—turning into them-selves again—and then, just about the time they were getting fed up, and forgetting I was there, I put some film in and clicked off a couple of fast rolls, shot after shot after shot, of Lázara in her Chanel shirt, the mother at her empty table, the three budding beauties wilting in the Havana sun. Sex appeal and political irony all in the same pretty frame.

When we were done, José completed the introductions. "This is Lourdes," he said, pointing to the smallest of the girls, who had dark hair below her shoulders, and olive skin, and a kind of ironic gleam in her eyes. "Very pleased to meet you," she said.

"You speak English?"

"A little. It was my subject in the university."

"Great."

"So you will deliver this note for me? To my aunt in Miami?"

"Sure," I said.

"And this is Caridad," said José, and the other girl, the light com-ing through her golden hair, sweat making circles on her tight turquoise top, said, "Maybe later I will give you my letter."

"Fine."

"Vamos," said José. "Listen, tonight we go to Capri. You want to come?"

"Sure," said Lourdes, again in English, and Caridad gave me her teary smile, and Lázara was told she was still too young.

"Okay, you come to my house at nine o'clock, *m'entiendes?*"

"Nine o'clock, boss," said Lourdes, and smiled an ironic good-bye.

So later, when you go to New York, you can give these photos to Lázara's mother, okay?" José said as we walked past construction sites where workers sat on bricks all day, whistling at girls. "She works in New York. Big house and everything: three cars, color TV. I think she has a good life there. Maybe she can help you with your work. She left in Mariel. But now, seven years, she cannot see her daughter. Her son went to America too, on a tube, and now he is a *mafioso*. Listen, I give you some other letters for New York, okay? What you want to eat?"

"Is there anywhere good in Havana?"

"Sure. La Torre. Is only for the Russians."

"Like the whole country."

"Sure. Why not? You know what they say: the Russians sneeze, and we get a cold. Everything is for the Russians here. Everything. Just like Cubans in Angola. You know, in Africa, only Cubans can go into the clubs? Only Cubans can use the beaches. Only Cubans can buy the girls. The Russians in one world are the Cubans in the other."

"You ever speak Russian these days?"

"Never. We learn Russian in school. But now everyone wants to speak English. It is like our girlfriend. Our dream of crazy love." He smiled with his crinkly slyness, and we stopped outside what looked like a high school cafeteria—a beaten old building with a long line of people snaking around its walls, and bright pictures of smiling hamburgers and dancing milk shakes above the bodies. "Okay, Richard, now you give me your passport, and we go in."

"No. I hold on to my passport, and we go together."

"Sure," he said. "Why not?"

We went to the front of the line, I flashed my passport at the woman, and she waved us in.

José hadn't missed a trick. "So you are Italian? Not American?"

"My mother is from Italy. That's why I look like this. Anyway, it's easier to travel as an Italian than an American."

"Sure. Look, Richard, I want to help you. But you can help me too. If I give you two hundred dollars, you will lend me your passport?"

"Great. And stay in Cuba the rest of my life?"

"No. For you is easy to get another. Then I use your passport, go to the Dominican, then give you your passport again. Then you have two."

"Thanks but no thanks, José."

"Okay. No problem." He took everything in his stride. "So what you think of the girls?"

"Cute."

"You don't need a Cuban girlfriend?"

"Look, I've had enough girlfriends to last me a lifetime. That's what I'm trying to get away from."

"But which one you like?"

"Any. They all look fine."

"I think they like you."

"Sure. Who wouldn't like a ticket to New York?"

"Okay. Anything is okay. But let me give you this. It is from Lourdes. She keeps these things—these underground papers—and one day, when things are different, she will show them to the world. Maybe you read it, then you can understand our country."

"Okay," I said, and glanced at what he'd given me: a yellowed old scrap that said: "Martí the Lover."

"You know this man?"

"Of course. The only guy in the world that both Washington and Havana have the hots for."

"Sure. I love Martí. You know what he says? What is that line? It is my favorite." He paused for a second. " 'Dos patrias tengo yo: Cuba y la noche.' Two fatherlands I have: Cuba and the night."

By then our lunch was over, and it was getting late, and I told him that I had to get back to work, so we hopped a car back to Vedado and walked through the quiet streets together. We could have been walking through a pleasant town in Oregon then: the shady parks, the old women on their rocking chairs, swinging back and forth, the little girls skipping rope outside the dancing schools. But there was a buzz to the air, a sexual charge that they'd have outlawed up in Medford: there was the sound of drumming in the distance, and the kids weren't going to school, and it felt like the whole city was flashing its eyes as it danced its way to the bedroom.

We walked down blocks of crumbling old houses with overgrown lawns—like a suburb in Peru after twenty years of Burmese rule—and yellow and blue and tangerine homes, with beat-up Chevys on cinder blocks outside, and men hammering away at old motorbikes with sidecars, and open windows, and broken gates, and then we came to a bigger place, white, with grand porticoes and Spanish moss in the garden, and men in white suits gathered at its entranceway.

"Okay, I go in here," said José. "Maybe you take some pictures, you read this article, you come to my house at eight o'clock."

"No problem," I said, leaving him at the Writers' Union, and then I went back to the hotel to get ready for the night. I napped for a little, wrote some captions, then picked up the clipping José had given me. It looked like some transcript of a speech—I couldn't tell the date—and it was printed in the special type that *Granma* now used for speeches by Fidel. I opened up a beer and began to read.

"*Compañeros, compañeras,*" the piece began, and I pictured an audience in some airy lecture hall, "my topic today is José Martí. *Libertad y Amor.* Freedom and Love. *Amor y Libertad.* For Martí, they were the two words that rang through the world from its dawning. For Martí, they were the sun and the moon of his every day. They were the first words of his teenage love poems, and the last words of his obituary. They were the words for which he fought and yearned as poet and as martyr, as philosopher and as fighter. For Martí, there could be no love without freedom; and there could be no freedom without love."

Kind of flowery, I thought, but I might as well go on.

You know, all of you, the details of his life—less a life, I believe, than a fairy tale. The boyhood of the Apostle on Paula Street, here in Havana, near the sea. At 16, he writes for La Patria Libre; *at 17, already, he is in jail. He is an art critic, a poet, he lives in Venezuela, Guatemala, Mexico, Paris, and Spain. He is consul of Uruguay, teacher of Spanish at New York City High School, author of seventy books. And then, my friends, you all know how he died, charging at the Spaniards on a white stallion; and that he died, this man of bridges and crossroads, in a place they call Dos Ríos.*

But today, on this golden afternoon, on this enchanted island that Pepe loved as a sweetheart all his life, I want to tell you about another Martí, a private Martí, Martí the apostle of love. For him, every poem was a love song, and every act an attempt to rescue his beloved from imprisonment. For Martí, nothing was abstract or dead; as he wrote of Emerson, so of himself, he "made idealism human" and looked on the universe as a living, breathing creature. And like Emerson, he strode from mountaintop to mountaintop, imploring us to join him. The Five-Year Plan he discovered was a Ten-Thousand-Year Plan; he looked on millennia as the rest of us look on tomorrow. Truly, he was, all his days, an avid suitor of Eternity.

Many of you know that the father of our country spent many years among the North Americans; that he worshipped and befriended the Transcendentalists; that he found in their noble souls an echo of his own. Many of you know that he hailed the United States as a paragon of freedom, "a nation of men," he said, full of freshness and possibility. And why should he not: this daring young man, from a land of poetry and revolution, coming to another young land, born of Revolution and driven by ideals? One dreaming rebel drawn to another.

Yet deeper than any of this was his love of love. Read his glowing essays, and you can feel the paragraphs burn your fingers. And beneath the fire, you will see again and again that what draws him, and animates him, what lifts him up and shakes him, is always and only love. Of Ulysses Grant, he wrote, "He fell deeply in love, which is a sign of personality. He married young, which is a sign of nobility." Of Emerson, he said, "All Nature trembled before him like a new bride. His whole life was the dawn of a wedding night." And of Whitman, he declared, "He was loved by the land, the night, the ocean."

But in all of this, I say, in every word and line, he was writing only of himself, a man for whom everything was love and love was everything. Humanity and Justice and Freedom were not just cold ideas to him, but warm bodies that he could embrace and hold, take to his wedding bed, kiss and make weep. For Martí was a lover all his life, who wooed his dreams as a young man does his beloved, singing outside her balcony, pacing her streets at night turning phrases in his head, never resting or stopping till he has won her hand and made her his.

I sighed but went on to the end.

And who was this lovely creature he courted? None other, my friends, than this island on which we sit, with her beautiful curves and sensuous ways; her eyes reflecting the sun and her limbs extended into the sea. This beautiful young princess of the Caribbean, hounded by an ugly giant and imprisoned in a castle from which she can only gaze upon the world. And Pepe, all his life, wrote poems to her and made plans for her escape. He watched the giant like a spy; he stole into the giant's castle; he tiptoed up the giant's stairs; and he waited and watched patiently for the moment when he could unfasten the door.

José Martí had many sweethearts, compañeros, but the one he could not leave was the one who gave him life and for whom he gave his life. Like any poet and romantic, he could only truly give his heart once. "A dawn," he once said, "is more revealing than the best book." For us, my friends, José Martí is our dawn, our morning star, our light in a time of unreason and despair. Let us learn from what he wrote, then, and look on our lives as the dawn of a glorious wedding night.

Kind of over the top, I thought, and a typical piece of Cuban passion: grand phrases and high ideals, but what did it all come down to? Was Fidel meant to be the new Martí, who had come to rescue the island? Or was he the ugly giant from whom the island had to be rescued? Like everything in Cuba, it seemed to point in every direction all at once, and the only thing I knew for sure was that it sounded like a teenager in love. Sounded, in fact, like the kind of person I was trying to put behind me.

When I went out into the street, though, it was the magic hour, and, for a while, you really could believe that this might be a magic place, the golden light catching the leafy lanes and faded yellow houses, the kids coming laughing out of the university's columns and down, in smiling pairs, the famous hundred steps. A little farther along, near the Quixote on Calle 23, a group of soldiers had set up speakers, and two fat mamas were doing a tango, right there by the busy street, and an army woman was swinging round a pencil-shaped kid to the sound of a pulsing salsa. A wedding car drove by, and the couple in their fancy dress stood in the back of the blue jeep and waved to everyone they passed, like triumphant monarchs touring their city. There was a blast of horns, and they waved at the wriggling dancers, and the dancers waved at them, and then the car sped up and they raced off toward their honeymoon. Behind them was the ocean and America.

I snapped a few frames quickly, while the light was still sharp, and caught the statue of Martí next to the Colina, backlit by the sunset, and the Journalists' Union, with its "Humorists' Wall" and "Wall of Lamentations," and the grand monument on which schoolkids in love wrote out their promises, and when I got to José's, the party was still going strong—kids debating Madonna, and girls cooking up beans and coffee, and the rooster strutting around (they called him "Reagan," someone said, because he never shut his mouth). José put on his best guayabera, muttered something to a girl, and then we were off, out into the night, and there was a buzz all around us—that nonstop coffee-and-samba, rum-and-rumba buzz that made the island feel like an African village dancing to Spanish guitars. There was never any Latin sleepiness in Havana at night—that torpid silence of the sun-baked square, the heavy church, the narrow, sloping streets. And the buzz was something different from what you find in the seethe and bustle of Hong Kong. This was something saucier, sly—to do with a curling eyebrow or a flirty smile. *Sirenitas* in cocktail dresses showed themselves off like treasures in a jewel case; and bright sparks in white flared trousers leaned against the railings, ready to scale their walls.

Everyone was dressed up, it seemed, though no one was going anywhere; the whole island was just jiving in place, like an old man setting his memories to music. The girls sashayed around the trees like waitresses at a cocktail party, the couples chattered and gathered outside an old Costa-Gavras movie at the Yara; somewhere, in the distance, some music students who'd just graduated were setting up speakers and dancing in the dark.

At the Nacional, I took the ten dollars José gave me and went into the Diplostore, and when I gave her my passport for the chit, the girl gave me a shy smile, and the music above her suddenly speeded up so it sounded like Mickey Mouse on PCP, and she crumpled over her receipt in laughter. By the time I was at the door, the girls around the store were all beginning to laugh, and dancing like crazy to the speeding tape.

At the Capri, we waited for our dates outside the Salon Rojo, and thirty minutes later they arrived, laughing and sweating from the bus, and looking like what you'd expect to see hanging around the baccarat tables at Atlantic City. The guy at the door wasn't taking tips tonight—there were too many better prospects, and the chance of tastier bids from the women in frilly *blusitas*—so José just said, "Fuck this," and we went off to Maxim's.

"She likes you," he whispered under his breath as the smaller girl—the one who'd spoken English to me that afternoon—linked my arm and we walked toward the sea in the dark. The other one— Cari, I remembered she was called—went ahead of us with José, and I had time to figure out what I had in hand: a spangly suit, bare arms, hair tucked behind her ears. A white smile and a sense of quiet mischief. Most of all, a rum-husky laugh, and that gravelly cigarette-roughened kind of rasp the Cuban girls have that tells you of all the pleasures that you're missing.

We followed Paseo for a while, in the dark, and then turned and went down some stairs into an even darker space. It took my eyes a moment to adjust, and then I could see we were in a small room— barely bigger than the ten-seat bar at the hotel—and it was more or less empty. A couple of blond kids—backpackers from Munich, I figured—were in one corner. A heavy black woman sat at the bar.

A solitary man nursed a glass of rum. On the wooden shelves there were a few ancient bottles of Havana Club.

"What do you want, Richard? Some rum, perhaps?"

José went over and pushed a few coins into the jukebox, and it was so loud in this tiny space that I had to sit right up to Lourdes, and when she wanted to talk to me, I could feel her hot whisper in my ear, strands of her hair tickling my cheek. I nodded back—no way I could hear any of what she was saying—and sometimes I whispered something too, my hand on her bare back. I figured it was like the bars in Bangkok, or teenage discos everywhere: keep the volume high, and everyone has to get real close.

When the first song finished, and the next one came on—"I Want to Know What Love Is"—she turned over my hand in hers.

"You do not work?" I heard her whisper.

"Sure I do. You should see me sometimes. Nights in a hammock in El Salvador. Climbing the mountains near Peshawar. Riding the trucks in the Sudan. It's not the usual kind of work, but it counts."

"Never before," she said quietly, "have I been with a man who has not been in the army or in prison."

I liked her for that—even if it did sound like a line—and moved in closer. José and his girl had got up and begun to dance, and then Lourdes and I joined them, turning around on a dance floor the size of a paper clip and trying not to bump into each other as we moved. When we sat down, she gave me a smile, picked up her drink, turned over the coaster, and wrote, *"Lourdes y Richard. La Habana, Cuba. 29 Julio 1987."* Then, smiling again, kissed me on the cheek.

I liked her for all of that, and José passed over some more rum, and Lourdes tapped out the rhythm on my leg and offered me a cigarette. She was twenty-three—she told me in my ear—and she'd had a sweetheart once, in Santiago, but that had been when she was in her teens. There'd been other guys, but you knew what Cuba was like: one night of love and then fifty nights of war. Sure, she'd met foreigners—I wondered then about her army-and-prison line—but she never trusted them: foreigners in Cuba thought they could pick up girls as easily as cigars. Her father was dead; she lived with her mother and sister and Cari. Her grandfather—this explained the dark complexion—came from Palestine.

"You like it, Richard?" asked José, smiling over at me.

"Sure," I said, and thought that any kind of pretty companion was enough. Sometimes we danced again. Sometimes figures moved around us in the dark. Sometimes José held the woman by his side as if he were her brother, sometimes as if he were something else. She smiled at me across the table. "She is a good girl," she said, motioning to Lourdes. "She likes you."

"I'm sure she's a good girl. I'm a good boy."

Lourdes patted me on the shoulder and tapped out another cigarette.

"You know this song," said José, as "Guantanamera" came on. "It is by Martí. From his *Versos Sencillos*. 'Yo soy un hombre sincero . . . ,' " he began singing.

I got some more rum then—give these guys a good night on the town, I thought—and when I came back, I found that José had picked up my camera, and he caught me by surprise as I sat down in my place, and caught me again, with my arm around my new friend. Then he turned to his own friend, and began to look less and less like a brother, as he kissed her brown arms, and squeezed her shoulders, and plied her with more booze, and she was kissing him back with half her body, and looking over at us with the other half.

"I thought she was your sister."

"No sister. *Esposa*," he shouted back over the music. "We were married, before. Two, three years before. Now we are friends. Is better like this. In Cuba, it's not so easy to be married. Better to be separate, no? Then you are free to love who you like."

"You're divorced, then?"

"*Más o menos*. You know how it is here. *Comme ci, comme ça.* Anyway, is time to go. You pay, and we leave," he said, and I shelled out a few dollars, and then we were back out in the dark. "So you and Lourdes, you can go to Malecón. Cari and I, we will go back to my house and make love."

"No, I will go with them," said Cari, who seemed to have had plenty for one night.

"Why not with me?" said José, pursing his lips and trying to kiss her.

She turned away. "I go with them."

"No. We go alone," said Lourdes, and she took my hand, and we walked down toward the sea, leaving Cari to fight it out with José.

There weren't many cars by then—must have been two o'clock, two-thirty—and things were mostly quiet. It was a night without wind, as usual. Only the occasional splash of the waves against the rocks, and sometimes the distant music of the nightclubs, or maybe a guitar somewhere playing the outline of a love song. A few boys in shorts along the seawall; sometimes a slow old car. When God created the world, I always thought, he made the Malecón last thing on a Saturday night, so sensuous was its curve as it wove around the back of the city like a languorous arm in the night.

We sat together on the wall, and she looked out across the sea into the dark.

"What is it like in America?"

"Same as here, pretty much. Lots of problems. Lots of sadness. Only a different kind of problem from the ones here."

"But the people there have dreams, right? Money, houses, cars?"

"Sometimes."

"And they are free to say anything? Free to visit other countries? Free to eat drugs?"

"Drugs, no. But free, yes."

"It is not like this prison, then."

"It's a different kind of prison." She fell silent then, and I ran my hand along her arm. When she turned to me, her eyes were bright, and then her hair was in my mouth, and I could feel the salt on her back, and taste the rum on her lips.

"So tell me about America," I heard her say.

"It's nothing. It's crazy. There are some beautiful places, but there's none of this salsa energy. It's like the difference between a rich man who seems poor and a poor man who seems rich." I kissed her again. "Isn't there somewhere we can go?"

"There is never anywhere to go in Cuba."

"I mean somewhere where we can be alone."

"We *are* alone. It's not like your country here. I cannot come to your hotel. You cannot come to my house."

"And when you have a lover?"

"You kiss on the street." I leaned in toward her again, and she moved back. "You do not understand, Richard. This is not America. Here, everything is a crime. Everyone is a spy. Everywhere, they are listening. If they hear you speak Spanish, if they hear me speak English, if they see us kissing, they talk. If we are alone, if we are private, they talk more. It is safer in the street."

I kissed her again, more deeply, ran my hand around her side, felt hardness, heard a gasp, pressed closer.

"To the rocks?" I said.

"No, Richard. It is not right." I almost liked her for that too—almost. "You go to the airport tomorrow?"

"Yeah. At nine."

"Okay. I come to the Nacional at eight-thirty. We go together."

"Okay," I said, and leaned forward again, and somewhere I heard a guitar, and somewhere, on the rocks, a woman sobbing and sobbing and sobbing.

She never came to my hotel. When I got up, after a fitful sleep, it was already eight-forty. The phone rang, and I grabbed at it, but it was only José, telling me he'd come to the airport with me. To wait for him in the lobby. I waited and waited. Once, I thought I saw her, but it was only another girl, with an East German guy, in the same dollar-store dress she'd worn for my camera. Another time, I thought I heard her name, but then I remembered that Lourdeses here were almost as common as hopes. Finally, José arrived, and we hopped a local taxi toward José Martí.

"So how about last night?" he said.

"*Comme ci, comme ça.* We kissed, but nothing more."

"In Cuba, is not so easy. Next time you can stay my house. More economical."

"And Lourdes?"

"She's a good girl. She'll do anything for you."

That left almost everything open, and José pointed out places of interest—the new wedding hall, the huge bust of Martí in the plaza, the site where the Mambo used to serve up girls to Yale boys fresh off the plane. Then he started talking about "our friend" and "our cousin" and how Elvis was an informer for the FBI, and I noticed how the taxi driver was watching us through his rearview mirror.

At the airport, José got out first and, when the taxi had gone, handed me two letters—for his "brother," he said. "So we meet again soon, Richard," he went on, giving me an *abrazo*. "You find me an apartment in New York, okay? And a place where I can buy some books?" And then he was gone, off to another deal, and I was closing the door on Cuba, and getting ready for Tegucigalpa.

When I got back to New York, I had a few days free—to do my laundry and collect my mail—and so I sent off the packets I'd been given, and went through some of the letters I'd brought back with me. You never know where contacts will appear. José hadn't sealed the envelopes—that way, he said, the authorities would think there was nothing in them. Some of them were just messages, with lists of shirt sizes and brand names and children's ages. Some of them were just formula recitations of love and pain. And one of them, which José had said was for his brother, was a badly typed message, in broken English, with no name at the bottom, to one Kent Ferguson at the State Department (Latin America desk), offering his services for the CIA. I spent a few moments wondering how I would have explained that one to the Cubans, or the guys at JFK, and decided that next time down, José owed me one.

Then I went through the phone calls I'd promised I would make. First I called Caridad's father—at the 516 area code, in some place called Babylon, New York—and I got a woman with a roughened Brooklyn accent; I could almost see her, with thick dark hair and gray eyes, and makeup here and there across her face.

"It's so nice a you to call," she kept saying, and then, "Callie, will you turn that thing off! Now! I'm trying to talk!" and then, back again to me, "I'm sorry. You know what these kids are like. So anyway, it's nice a you to call. If I see Luis, I'll tell him. He'll be real happy to hear about his daughter. She's the older one, right, with the black hair?"

"No, the blonde."

"Right. The one with the blond hair. Not Mercedes."

"No. Caridad."

"Caridad, right."

"Okay," I said. "Maybe I'll try again some other time. When will he be back?"

"Jeez." She sounded worried. "I don't know. He kind of comes and goes."

"But he's okay?"

"Okay? Sure; he's okay. He'll be back in a while." I thought of the two cars and the mansion Caridad had told me about. "We don't see him too much anymore, but he comes round now and then, collects his social security, wants to see Callie. He's doin' fine. He'll be sorry he missed your call."

"Okay. Catch you later," I said, and dialed some journalist José had told me about—some young guy in Miami, at the *Herald*. But he was eager to talk, and hit me up for names, and when he got round to José's friends—"that girl called Lourdes"—I decided we'd talked enough. "Okay. Be seeing you."

The only other message I had left was for Lázara's mother. It was a number in the Bronx. A ring, a long ring, another ring. Then a click, and I prepared a message for the machine, but instead there was a thick, slurred voice, sounding like it was coming from the ocean floor.

"Dime!"

"Right. I was down in Havana last week—"

"Dime! Oye!" The connection was so bad, I might as well have been still in Havana.

"Buenos días, señora. Soy americano. Periodista."

"You Cuban?"

"No. You speak English?"

"Un momentico." She shouted out for some guy, and I heard some dance music in the background, and, after a while, a male voice on the other end.

"Jes."

"I just got back from Havana. I have some photos of Señora González's daughter. Also a letter for her. If she wants some news of her, she can come round here and collect it."

"*O-ka.*"

"She can come today?"

"Jes, jes. Sure."

"Okay. You know West Broadway?"

"Broadway? Sure I know Broadway."

"No—West Broadway. It's different." I gave him some instructions, and a few hours later there was a pounding on my door, and there was a huge black woman there. As soon as I opened up, she walked in and hugged me, and said, "Thank you, thank you, I'm sorry." I told her that Lázara was fine, and that she missed her, and that she was real pretty, and that she was doing well at school. I told her that she had a nice room on Concordia. Then I gave her the photos.

The woman didn't say anything at first—she just stared and stared and stared—and then her whole body started shaking, and she was sobbing and heaving, and sobbing and wailing. "*Mi nena, mi nena. Por qué no te puedo ver? Mi nena.*" And she was sobbing and wailing, and I didn't know what to do, so I held her.

"It's tough, I know," I said. "It's been a long time," but she was holding on to me so hard her nails were digging into my shoulders, and her whole body was leaning against mine, and she was muttering curses and phrases through her snuffles that I couldn't catch.

It was a crazy thing: occupational hazard, I guess. Like being in Beirut, and some woman was howling when she saw the body of her kid in the street, and you didn't know whether to drop it, or whether to tell her that he'd left a body of his own in another street, or whether just to get the shot before the TV crews came in. And half hoping she'd keep bawling till the light changed.

This time, though, my camera was on the other side of the room, and the woman was hugging me like a cousin, and sniffling. Finally, she stood back and turned to me. "Thank you, thank you," she said, drying her eyes with her fists, and when I mentioned the fifty dollars I'd loaned her daughter, she said, "Thank you, I'm sorry. I put it in your door tonight. Tomorrow. By Monday, for sure." That was the last I ever saw of her.

II

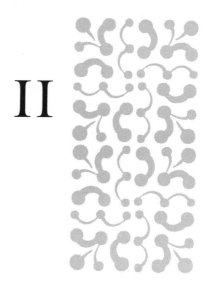

I didn't think about Cuba for a few weeks after that, what with the contra clashes in Honduras and the latest coup attempt in Manila. Sometimes, from Managua, I'd try to call the number Lourdes had given me, just to see what the story was, but usually the number just rang and rang and rang, and when somebody answered, it was the old woman downstairs, and she sounded frightened when she heard a foreign voice, and quickly put the phone down. Sometimes I read reports—in the *Herald*—about crackdowns and defections. Del Piño, the hero of the Bay of Pigs. Even Fidel's eldest brother, Ramón, the one you never heard about, had tried to make it out. But mostly, Cuba was on a different wavelength from the rest of the planet. The great thing about being there was that you could just screen out the rest of the world, forget everything you knew, and take a break from America. The hardest thing about being there was that when you left it, the whole place disappeared from view, and it was almost as if you'd dreamed it. Hundred-percent blackout.

I got a few calls from José on my machine in New York—hurried, usually, asking me to send a few thousand dollars to some guy in Jackson Heights, who would send him a Colombian passport—and occasionally I got a postcard from Lourdes or Caridad, saying, "I hope that all is very well for you, and for your parents too." Sometimes I got 3-D Russian postcards with those shiny surfaces that made all the words written impossible to read. I couldn't tell who they were from, and what they were saying, and whether they were offering me a favor or asking me for one.

And then, in mid-December, I got a card from England.

Dear Richard,
I do hope all is well with you. It was very good to have met you in
Havana last July. It really made my trip a good deal more interesting

than it would have been otherwise. Those nights at the bar seem almost surreal now, sitting in Winchester on these dark winter evenings. I was wondering, in fact, whether I might go again next year, at the same time, for a kind of sentimental return: Greece seems so tame by comparison. If you were planning to be there, perhaps we could enjoy a kind of impromptu reunion? I've half a mind to start a collection of Cuban jazz records.

In any case, I do wish you well with your photography: I imagine it takes you quite often to Havana. Perhaps we'll get a chance to toast the Queen again next July?

Wishing you all success,
Hugo Cartwright

P.S. I think I've persuaded the Headmaster to let me teach my Senior History Division something about the Spanish-American War. So Cuba is now my business too.

I pictured to myself the sweating red face and the spectacles, and remembered how I'd got Hugo to pose by the pool at the Capri for one of the shots I'd sent to German *Geo*: he was famous now. The Empire in the tropics. Hockney goes Latino. And nocturnal. But I'd pretty much forgotten about his card by the time I scheduled a trip to Havana that July. Things were quieting down in Central America, and I wasn't billing as many days as I would have liked. Cuba, I figured, was a cinch: the government was canny enough to schedule Carnival at the same time as the Anniversary of the Revolution, so I could get two stories in one: Fun in the Sun, and the Calypso Graybeard. I also had a long-running thing I was shooting on the worldwide trade of money for love.

I was staying in the St. John's this time—more gritty texture— and as soon as I got off the late flight from Toronto, I walked out into the streets to get a taste of the Cuban night. It got into you like a kind of pounding rhythm: no way you could sit still while the whole country seemed to be pulsing around you. Down on the Malecón, the street was one big mess of boys in rows in color-coordinated suits, and girls in sparkly bra things, trailing boas, and lit up faces in masks. Everyone always said that the Revolution had really cleaned the celebration up. Before—that was the magic word here, "before"—it had made Rio seem like a toddler's birthday party by comparison.

I bought a beer and walked among the dancers. *"Hola, Richard!"* came a cry. *"Te recuerdas de mí?"*

It was a face I didn't recognize: black, with silver eye shadow, under a silver kind of bathing cap.

"No me recuerdas? La amiga de José. Myra."

"Sure," I said, while figures slipped past me in the dark, like peacocks on the strut, and a few Chinese guys under a winding dragon, and the gays enjoying their big public outing of the year.

"So you've been to see Lula?"

"Lula?"

"Lourdes."

"No. I only just got here. Business."

"Bueno," said the girl. "She's waiting to see you. I think she's over there," and she pointed me over to the viewing stands. I weaved in and out of the trumpet players then, and saw sitting on the ground the same woman who'd invited me to her store the year before, and someone else greeted me by name, and there were boys bobbing around slowly, and Tropicana rejects, and women with staring eyes doing some kind of voodoo number. I looked for her eyes, her delicate features. All around me, the usual whispers and blown kisses. *"Oye." "Dime." "Pssst."*

And then I recognized her smile, a little shyer than most, in a body swathed in feathers: like an earthly angel among a team of twenty or so others, wriggling in formation.

"Richard," she cried, and her arms were around me.

"Qué tal?"

"Richard," was all she answered. *"Ven acá. Conmigo,"* and I watched her disentangle herself from the group, and blow a few kisses at her friends, and whisper something to a tall boy with a hip-hop haircut, and then she was with me, and linking me by the arm, and we were walking away from the music, away from the crowds, along the boulevard, toward the silence and the dark.

"You got my letters, Richard? And my posters?"

"I think so, but the government always takes a cut."

"Your government?"

"Your government, my government, it's all the same."

"Oh, Richard, I am so happy to see you. *Qué sorpresa!*" and she was holding me by the hand now, and it was cooler, and there were fewer people in evidence, and I was tucking my camera in my pocket. One thing I knew—I was back in Cuba, where you never knew how a night would end up, or who was leading whom. Where were we going now, I thought, and what was her plan? To fix me up with a cousin? To give me herself? To get me her mother's shopping list?

On Belascoaín we turned right, and walked past the huge, phantom bulk of the Central Hospital, and then down Concordia. She knocked three times on a decaying old door, and a black woman with a scarf opened up, and she led me up the broad stairs, and along a balcony where the washing flew in our faces, above a tiny courtyard, and then into a kitchen as small as a bathroom.

It was empty, and dark, and a side door led into her bedroom.

"Sit down, Richard. You want *café?* Beer? What can I get for you?"

"A beer sounds great."

She went out to get it, and I looked at her bedside table: an old Russian postcard of Jesus, a small picture of Martí.

"*Mira,*" she said when she came back, and she went across the room and showed me the altar where she kept her treasures: a wrinkled old black-and-white photograph of her mother, I figured, in her prime; a Gloria Estefan tape; and some books about Russian literature that she'd studied once. "*Mira!*" she exclaimed. "Look!" And there, right next to her heart-shaped mirror, was the picture that José had taken of us in Maxim's that night, our eyes red, the focus shaky, my arm around her shoulders, grinning in the dark. It was a weird feeling to see it there, in a homemade frame on her dresser: like when someone you didn't think you knew asks you to be his best man or the executor of his will, or invites you to read at his mother's memorial service, and suddenly you realize you mean more to him than you'd figured. She couldn't have planned it, I knew: she hadn't known I was coming till tonight.

"I just knew I'd see you, Richard." She smiled over at me.

"That's great," I said, and decided to let her airport nonappearance ride. "You mind if I take some pictures?"

"Of what? Of me? Señorita X, you can say. Of this?" She opened her closet, and I saw three outfits hanging there, and I didn't know whether that made her rich in Havana terms, or poor. She must have realized how soppy foreigners could get about Cuba and its shortages: she spoke English, after all. But then, when I waited for her to make her move—no, it wasn't prostitution, I was getting ready to tell anyone who asked, including myself: it was just an exchange of favors, what I had to give for what she had, just like in any love affair—she motioned me to get up, and led me back through the kitchen to the courtyard.

"You see, Richard?" She didn't seem frightened. "I was waiting for you. I knew you would come. I must go now, for my mother. But come back tomorrow. I will be waiting for you. You are staying where? Vedado? For how long? Okay, Richard, we have time."

And then she kissed me softly on the lips, and I was left to make my own way out into the night.

That night, though, when I got home, I had a weird dream. I was with Diane again, or it could have been Lourdes, and some other guy came in, and she put her head on his shoulder—it looked like the most intimate act in the world—and then he was whispering something in her ear, and I was going crazy—I couldn't take it anymore—and I ran out into the garden. And she came after, and she was crying, and through her tears she was calling out to me, "What's wrong? What's your problem? Don't you trust me? I was only kissing my brother goodbye!"

I got up kind of scratchy the next morning, but it was still early, so I went on down to the old city to catch it before the tourist buses came, while the schoolkids were still playing stickball on the ill-paved, slanting streets, and the old guys were gathering for coffee in the open-fronted bars, and the first light gilded the parks and plazas around all the aromatic sailors' world of streets: Obispo and O'Reilly and Empedrado.

Then, after breakfast, I went down to Lourdes's house, walking all the way down San Lázaro—along the big road where they held a torchlight parade for Martí every year on his birthday, and Pablo sang, and everyone waited to see if he got a bigger crowd than Fidel—and then threading my way into Centro Habana, and down to her cracked green door. It was locked now, and there was no way anyone could hear the knock, what with the music coming out of radios, so I sat on the stoop and waited.

Another bright Havana morning, and nothing much going down. A few kids playing hide-and-seek in vacant lots. A teenager cycling by, and a woman stopping to chat. Mothers with curlers dandling babies on their terraces; children crying from an upstairs window. Occasionally, a door would open, and some old woman—the last of the *Fidelistas*—would slouch out into the street and go off to do her errands. This street was like all the others: the paint all faded, the windows gutted, bare rooms visible through the bars—a pretty tropical afterthought where the cleaning lady hadn't come for almost thirty years. One time, a couple of grandmas of the Revolution picked me out as a foreigner: one hurried off, to tell the local CDR; the other came over and asked if I wanted to buy a turtle.

Then a woman came up and said, *"Richard, Richard! Qué tal?"* and she was kissing me on both cheeks, this woman I had never met, as if I were a son returned from Miami. *"La madre de Lourdes,"* she said, introducing herself, and I figured she must have recognized me from the picture on the dresser. *"Ven, entra, Richard. Lourdes vendrá pronto! Ven, ven!"* I followed her up to the tiny kitchen, and she called out something, and the neighbors came out to take a look at me: her daughter's prize specimen, a captive foreigner, with a camera. *"Quieres agua? Quieres café?"* she asked. "Sit down." I sat at a table in the weather-beaten room. There was a plastic bowl from China for cigarettes. A clock that didn't work. A framed set of pictures snapped from fashion magazines. A small Jesus, almost hidden. The centerpiece glass cabinet was empty except for a few dusty books.

"Y tu mamá, tu papá?"

"Very well," I said.

"*Y Señor Reagan?*"

"Fine. And your children?"

"*O-ka.* We survive. My son is in America. Here, *mira!*" She went into her bedroom and brought back a picture of a young kid, with Lourdes's Palestinian complexion, standing in front of a tenement in New Jersey. "He says it is like heaven." Then she looked over at me, her eyes aglow. This was her daughter's freedom sitting in her kitchen; this was her ticket out.

So she smiled at me, and offered me more *café*, and told me how she had a sister in Miami, and how for months her sister called her every week, and told her about her life. But after that, nothing. She'd got her son on the telephone once, she said, from the neighbor's house, but he'd sounded very far away, and couldn't understand anything she said. He'd promised to send her some spoons, but that was the last she'd heard from him. It was so good of me to remember her daughter, she said, it was so good of me to take her out.

A few cards, I thought, and now I'm like a son-in-law: even in the Philippines, it wasn't this quick.

Lourdes's sister came in—she looked about thirty-five, though I remembered José had told me she was still in her teens, despite her large thighs and bitter mouth—and sat down at the table and looked me over. "You have seen Lourdes?" she said. "She knows you are here? You will go to Varadero with her? What are your plans?"

"I'm busy," I said. "I'm only here for two weeks. I've got to work." When the conversation dropped off, I picked up the camera, and again, as soon as I did, the two of them were up, and off like giggling schoolgirls to change into their best clothes, and I sat and sat, taking pictures out the window, till they came out again, their lips reddened with some children's crayons, in fishnet stockings and CREO EN TÍ T-shirts. I snapped a few frames, and they gave off smiles that could have lit the room up without strobes. Then there were footsteps outside, and the door opened, and it was Lourdes, in shorts and a faded T-shirt that said WASHINGTON HUSKIES, and when she saw me, her face came to life: white teeth and olive skin.

I decided to give them some of the presents I'd brought for them as sweeteners, and Lourdes pulled the Charlie from the box and sprayed it on the warmer parts of herself, right there, in front of everyone: on the pulse of her neck, on her temples, on the back of her knees. Then her sister grabbed it from her and did the same, and the mother sat across from me, still glowing.

I pulled out some Marlboros I had brought too, and handed them over to her, and the mother opened up the box, and called in the neighbors, and within a few minutes, half the carton was empty.

"Look, I'm sorry," I said, Santa Claus busy on his rounds, "but I've got to go and work. Before it gets dark."

"I'll come with you, Richard."

"No, you stay here."

"What do you need? I can show you anything. The true Havana. The secret Havana. I can show you the old city."

"I've seen all that, Lourdes. I've already got all that tourist stuff."

"But I can show you what the people dream. What they say in private. I can show you all their hopes, next to the happy slogans."

She paused.

"A violent contrast," she continued, with her faint, white smile, and I remembered why I liked her: I never could tell how much she meant what she was saying.

Out on the street, we passed women dressed all in white turbans, with beads around their necks—*santero* priestesses, she said, or their disciples—and at one corner, a whole group of *numismáticos,* gathered in a kind of Masonic circle, trading strange terms and shouting numbers. We passed hand-painted pieces of cardboard advertising haircuts for dogs, and women with purple hair, and boys who called out *"Hola!"* to Lourdes, and *"Qué tal?"*

When we got to San Rafael, a small man came out from his store and put his arm around my shoulder, eyes pleading. "You have a card?" he said. "Here's mine. I too am a collector." I didn't know what he was collecting, but everyone was a collector here, ready to trade anything, hoarding coins or stamps or cigarettes in the hope that one day they'd be currency. José too, I thought, was a collector in his way, of foreign friends, of foreign addresses. Lourdes too.

"Look," said the man, and he pulled me into his house, where he had all the business cards he had ever received, arranged in albums, a gallery of foreign hopes. "Look," he said. "This is my passion." On all six surfaces, there were mementos of Carlos Gardel, tango posters, old records, tickets to concerts in Buenos Aires. "This is my life," he said. "My life, my love, my heart."

I signed his visitors' book and gave him a card—one a carpet salesman had given me on the plane coming down—and in exchange, I got some shots of him, smiling rheumy-eyed against the multicolored posters. He asked to take my picture too, in his house, and laboriously wrote out his address, so I could send him copies, and then we went on to the Sailors' Store, the only place in Cuba where you could get most Cuban goods.

"*Compañero,*" Lourdes said to the fat guard at the door. "This is a very important man from Italy."

"Very important," I said, and he let us in with a smile. "*Niña,*" he called after her, "remember me next time your brother has a chicken!"

In the aisles, they were selling telephones shaped like red high heels.

"In America, how much does this cost?"

"Too much."

"Nothing is too much in America," she said, and we went upstairs, to the eating area, where all the Africans were hanging out, sipping guava juice or dusty bottles of flat 7-Up while they traded stories. This was how they lived here, the students from abroad, using their dollars to buy goods they could resell to Cubans, or buying fans and juicers they could take back to the Isle of Youth to trade for human company.

"Now, Richard," she said, "I show you the true Revolution. The one the bearded one never talks about."

And then we went back out into the street, and she led me up to a small brown door. A woman with glasses opened up, brushing her hair back, and waved us hurriedly in, then led us through the darkness of a corridor. We passed a circle of chairs, set around some bottles of Jack Daniel's—a homemade, private bar. We passed two chihuahuas from Mexico and a Siamese cat she was raising in order to sell. Then we went through a door, and she flicked on a switch, and I was standing in a room full of spooky treasures: porcelain figures, elephant vases, the masks of African gods, crammed into every spare inch of glass cases that reached all the way to the ceiling. A whole cathedral of voodoo, with eerie dark faces on seven different levels, and different colors for every god. A sanctuary of darkness.

"The only one in Cuba!" said Lourdes proudly. "Nowhere is there anything like this." I wandered farther in, and took a few close-ups of the coconut faces and model cars on display. "This is Shango," she said, pointing to one deity. "The same god as *El Jefe*. And this is Obatalá," fingering another mask. "And this one is Oshún."

"And you believe in all this?"

"Sure. Why not? Even Fidel believes in this. Even Fidel went to Africa to learn from the gods." She stopped, and let her voice go down. "Usually, of course, I believe in Jesus Christo. But how long was Jesus Christo on the cross? Three days. And how long have we been on the cross? Twenty-eight years! How can I believe in him?"

While she spoke, two men came in, and as we moved into the shadows, the first of them threw himself flat out on the floor and started babbling something, muttering so fast I couldn't make it out, and shaking a maraca as he did so, and then stuffing some money into a jar. And then the next man came up and did the same, shaking the instrument wildly in his hand, and then the woman came in, and gave them both some pieces of cake and wine. There were bows, and whispered thanks, and smiles. It was like some ungodly inversion of a first communion.

"And over here," said Lourdes, motioning me toward a corner, after the men had gone out, "over here is *my* religion. My altar. Now you can see what I believe in." And she pulled open the lid on a huge Chinese vase. Inside, there was a mass of papers. There were scraps of faded newspaper clippings like the one I'd already seen, old pictures of the Prado when it must have been like Patpong, a few tattered copies of *Bohemia*. There were copies of ancient guidebooks telling New Yorkers where they could find whites-only clubs, and ads for nightclubs from the time of Prío and Batista. There were old articles from the *New York Herald Tribune*.

"You see, Richard? You understand? This is my bank account. This is my dream: one day, when he is gone, to make the true story of our country. The story the government never tells us about. This is my private Museum of the Revolution."

"I see," I said, though it seemed to me that the whole island was one dusty, glass-cased Museum of a Revolution that had faded long ago. "And so the Catholic churches are a cover for *santería*. And *santería* is a cover for this."

"Maybe," she said, and then, carefully, put the clippings back inside the jar, just the way she'd taken them out. "This is my secret treasure. This is why I learned English."

"And you keep it here because . . ."

"Because it is more secure. If they find it, they think it is from some traitor who went to Mariel."

I looked around again, at the grinning gods and the scraps of meat, at the broken axes and clunky pots, and then she led me back through the darkened corridor and out into the street. We passed rooms with their doors open, where old men were strumming guitars, and a man was selling copies of *The Godfather*. We passed North Koreans in white guayaberas, with pictures of Kim Il Sung pinned to their lapels. We passed boys selling ice creams from behind the bars of ground-floor windows, and kids from Chernobyl off to see their doctors.

"Hey, Lourdes," I said as we passed a poster of Che. " '*Ser Como Él.*' Be like him."

"That's easy," she replied. "He's dead."

It was getting dark by then, and when we walked past the old Cine Payret downtown, where *Falling in Love* was playing, Lourdes grabbed at my arm and asked me if we could see it. I ought to be shooting Carnival, I thought, I ought to be working the streets, but this was more intriguing and might lead to some more unexpected places. So I gave the guy a few pesos, and then we were back in the usual Cuban darkness. It was like high school again, all over again: that same sense of furtiveness and borrowed passion, and promises made in the shadows. Lourdes held my hand fiercely during the film, and she wasn't the only one sniffling as it went on; but all around us there were other kinds of noises: slow kisses and long secrets, and unfastening buttons, and rustlings and murmurs and gasps. It was weird in there, as if the darkness itself were whispering, and everything was charged: fingers on thighs, lips on flesh.

Lourdes's eyes were glazed when we came out, in the shadow of the old Capitol building—a perfect replica of the one in Washington—and I was heated up.

"Look," I said, "let's go to my hotel. It's not the Nacional, but it's got air-conditioning, and we can get some drinks, and it's private. No one watches the St. John's."

"I can't, Richard. I am not like the women in Coppelia."

"But where else can we go?"

"Anywhere. Not a hotel. It is not right."

"How about a club, then?"

"Okay. Not here. Here, everyone knows me. In Vedado."

So we took a taxi back up to Coppelia, but the Karachi was closed, and Scheherezada wouldn't let me in. The Tikoa wouldn't let her in—it felt like we were the first interracial couple in Jo'burg. At the Karabali, I went to the head of the line, and a black guy with a beard told me to go to El Coctél, across the street; at the Coctél, Lourdes went first, and they told her she was in, as long as she paid in dollars. We slithered in through the nine-inch crack in the door— these places could make Area seem democratic—and took two stools at the bar. The place was so dark you couldn't see the drinks; when the bartender gave the couple next to us the bill, they needed a flashlight, like in the cinema.

Around us, in the booths, couples were necking, and writhing, and who knows what else. Some Iglesias was on the system, and the guys behind the bar were slipping bottles of rum to their neighbors while telling customers they were out of rum. We sat on our stools, looking into the dark, and Lourdes was ready to slip five bucks to someone to kick some couple out of a booth, when I decided I'd had enough.

"Come on, for chrissake. I've had it with this darkness thing. I didn't come all this way just to be with a woman I can't see. You could be anyone, for all I know. Let's just go back to the hotel."

"No," she said. "Don't you understand? This is Cuba. What does a Cuban and a foreigner mean? What kind of couple is that? And what kind of woman do you find in a hotel?"

"Great. Why do married couples go there?"

"Only so they can get rum, and maybe hot water, and eat in the tourist restaurants. Their wedding is the only time in their lives when the government allows them to live like tourists, like outsiders in their own home. So they go there and sit in the bar, and then make love at home. To make love in a hotel—it is like giving your *novia* a card with a love poem already printed."

"So you would prefer the street?"

"I would prefer America."

"*Mi vida*, the street is the closest to America you're going to get."

"Thank you, Richard," she said, and slamming down her glass, she walked out, and I was left alone in the dark, in a room full of shudders and moans.

When I got back to my hotel, I couldn't get to sleep at first. I thought and thought about what was going on: I liked the girl, but I didn't want to get in too deep. I thought she was on the level, but that only made things harder. I could cut my losses right now, I figured, get out while the going was good, and just concentrate on the shoot with Fidel. I could go for it, and hope we wouldn't get too close. But something was still nagging at me, like when you're trying and trying to remember someone's name, and you can't settle on anything else till you've got it. There was something here I had to retrieve; it was like Lourdes was something on the tip of my tongue.

·   ·   ·

The next day, when I got up, I figured I'd take my mind off her by going to José: his apartment was kind of like the AP wire, I always thought, spitting out rumors around the clock, fresh gossip, the latest "facts" about the state. Plus, it was like a nerve center for the underground and for all the writers, good-for-nothings and members of the shadow economy who liked to hang out around the fringes of the world.

"Hey, Richard, *qué tal?*" he said, as soon as he opened the door, as if I'd been away two days. "Come into the kitchen, have some coffee: strong, and with sugar, right?"

"Right."

I looked around me: some students were stretched out on the floor, listening to Tracy Chapman on the record player and arguing about whether she was a woman or not, and a pretty girl was at the stove, cooking up some pork and beans, and a couple of others were sitting in the corner, waiting to see if the day was going to end up in the Tropicana or the Salón Rojo, and Ricky, the dog, was yapping, and backed away when I came toward him, a Cuban right down to his untended coat.

"So how you doing, Richard?"

"Great. And you?"

"Fine. Is always the same with me. Hey, you remember Luis?"

"Sure." The tall, handsome black boy came up to me with his smile.

"Look, Richard, my brother is living here. We make a room for him," and taking me out to the roof, he showed me where they had constructed a complete bedroom since the last time I was here, and erected an outside sink, and bought a coffeemaker. Their apartment was as full of remodelings as Trump Tower.

His "brother" was a frizzy-haired mulatto from Santiago who looked nothing like Luis, and compensated for his lack of English with a smile. "Don't worry," he said. "Be happy." I had long since stopped trying to figure out family relations here, and how Chinese-featured José from Camagüey had a black brother from Santiago, and was introducing me to a mother who was all white in Havana.

José's attempts to explain all this had only made things worse: he and Luis were brothers, he'd told me; they were raised by the same wet nurse; they were brothers in Combinado jail. Even the simplest things were complex here. Like when Lourdes told me *"Yo te quiero."* Did that mean "I like you" or "I love you"? Come closer or stay put?

His "brother" went back to playing dominoes with a friend on one corner of the roof.

"You see," said José, with his wry smile. "True Revolutionaries."

"How come?"

"They are following *El Jefe*. You know Fidel once played this game from five in the evening until ten in the morning?"

"Sure. And never stopped talking all the time," said one of the boys, looking up, smiling.

Then there was a knock on the front door, and Luis opened up, to a boy who looked like a Greek god, his frilly shirt open to the navel, a tangle of dark curls, soulful eyes: the kind of guy Helmut Newton would have cast as Pan.

"Richard, this is Carmelo. He was a dancer in Tropicana. But now he is an underground man. You know Mariel? Fidel sends all the *maricones*—the gays—to Mariel. But Carmelo doesn't want to leave. So he becomes an underground man—like Dostoyevsky, you know? He marries a dancer and they live in Vedado."

"Better than prison, I guess. Better than Florida."

"I think it is the same as prison."

Carmelo, understanding nothing, sat down and ran his fingers through his curls.

José led me to the edge of the roof, and we looked out at the whole city stretched out under the blazing Havana sun, still and warm in the silent morning. It was a strange feeling, being on top of Havana, in this blue vacuum, out of time, out of space. No way you could imagine the rest of the universe here; no way you could see beyond the moment. Just one big sensuous waiting room, where some people slept and some made out and others played dominoes, and a kid asked his mother if it would all be over soon.

"So, José, how come I never see you working?"

"Working?"

"You're always free."

"You call it free. I call it work. It's not easy to live like this. But I work. I walk up La Rampa sometimes, and if I see strangers, I give them my card. And maybe I give ten people my card, two come here. And with these two I make work."

"What about a job?"

"A job! Five pesos a day! Forget it! I can get some old guy—a *Fidelista*—to do my job for me. For him, five pesos makes him a millionaire. For me, it's nothing."

The coffee boiled on the stove.

"In Cuba, you understand, you don't need to get money; you need to get friends. *M'entiendes?* So it's better to work in the hospital, because then you can get food. It's better to work in a restaurant, because then you can get rum. In the United States, I know, it's different. Maybe you work hard, you get money. But here, you work and you work and you don't get nothing. I have many Cuban pesos—I am a millionaire in Cuban pesos—but with pesos I can only buy things I do not need; anything I need is only in the dollar stores. So maybe I'm a millionaire here, but still I'm living like a beggar."

"Sounds like friends are a kind of currency."

"Sometimes. Sometimes, no. With you, Richard, is no need. I like you." He clapped me on the shoulder and smiled. *"Compañeros, no?* I don't need your money."

Just then there came another knock on the door. José motioned me with his eyes to the bedroom, just in case, and I went in and checked the place out for light. At first, I couldn't hear anything. Then José's broadest chuckle, and two softer voices, and he was speaking English. I came out and saw two girls, one pale and freckled, in a red T-shirt and baggy pants, the other cool, blond, in some kind of Nepali harem trousers.

"Richard, this is Anna, right? And Ilse? From Germany."

"Hi," they said, all smiles. I knew a lot about them already, I figured: vegetarians, disciples of Petra Kelly, semi-Buddhists, studying despair in the Third World.

"You want some coffee?"

"*Ja.* This is great."

We sat down, the three of us, around a little table on the rooftop.

"You're tourists here?"

"*Ja.* You can say this. We are here to see the Revolution. We were trying to go to Nicaragua. But maybe this is better."

"I think it is. I live in Managua now and then. Most of the people you'll meet there are from Berkeley or Düsseldorf."

The girls laughed. They would have looked pretty if they hadn't been so serious.

"Here." José put three cups down before us.

The girls looked around them in the sun-baked morning. No noise in the air, no factories, no planes. No sense of purpose, no hurry, no direction. Every day a day off here, a day for daydreams and reminiscences.

"This place is like heaven," said the freckled one. "I would like to stay here. I know, you do not have everything here. But you do not need to have everything. You have history. You have spirit. Human warmth. This place is real. No plastic, no videos. You know, in Buddhism they say that life is suffering. You taste life only when you taste suffering."

"Sure," said Jose dryly. "This is Paradise."

"If we were truly free, we could come here, and live and help you."

"And if we were truly free, we could go to Germany to help you."

Then there was another knock on the door—this place was like Grand Central Station—and there was no point in all three of us running for cover, so we sat there, while José opened up, and a kid in a clean white shirt came in, looking like he was on his way to meet his future father-in-law: the latest model in Communist Yuppie.

"Ignacio. This is Richard. Anna. Ilse."

"Swell," the kid said in fluent English. "How's it going?"

"Great. We are here to see your history."

"Then you must know about our friend?"

We looked at José. "Sure. I am a piece of history. Richard, I told you before, no? I am a grandson of Martí."

"Grandson! Martí died in 1895."

"Sure," he replied smoothly. "Son of the grandson."

"José Martí's children are known."

"You think he never slept with another woman? He was a true Cuban—the father of the nation right down to his *pinga!*" José and Ignacio laughed, and I thought that José was a true Cuban too, right down to his chutzpah: a self-styled great-grandson of the Revolution, who played his cards both ways.

"If Martí were here now . . ."

"*Ja*," said Ilse. "He was a man who did everything, no? Like Ho Chi Minh. And he was in prison, no? All the great ones are in prison: Gandhi, Mandela, Fidel too."

"Me too," said José. "I was in Combinado four years. Sometimes there was no light. Sometimes I was alone. Three times I tried to kill myself."

There was a difficult silence.

"And you know what Martí said about America," José went on. " 'At last I live in a country where each man seems to be his own master.' "

"*Ja*, but he also says, 'I have lived inside the monster, and—' "

"Sure," said José. "But look at Fidel! Even Fidel loves America! You know he took his honeymoon in New York? You know when he was a student, he sent a letter to Roosevelt and asked him for a ten-dollar bill? You know he ate hot dogs in Yankee Stadium?"

"You do not know this," said Anna. "You have never been outside. You do not know how lucky you are. You do not know what the world is. You have hopes here, ideals."

"Hopes for what? For it to end?"

"No. You have this faith. This sharing: every person helping every other person. Like members of the same collective. Like a kibbutz."

"Sure. Like a family. For thirty years, we are Children of the Revolution, children of a father who says that children must be quiet and must sleep without food and must be told what to do every minute of our lives. For thirty years, he's telling us not to pray before our meals, and not to go to other countries, and how we must never forget our obligation to our parents, and how we must give our lives for our family. For thirty years, we hear him say, 'You are too young to think for yourself. You must wait. You must wait.' If this is a family, Combinado is a family."

"You cannot believe that?"

"I can believe it. I do believe it. In Cuba, you have to believe everything." José was calming down now, he was getting quiet. "In Cuba, you believe everything or you believe nothing. Because everything is crazy. More divorces than weddings. More deaths than births. This guy's in prison, but that guy's in Miami. Nothing makes sense in Cuba."

"So you don't believe Fidel?"

"Sure I do. Sometimes I think Fidel is the most intelligent man in the world."

"No!"

"Sure. Who else could make such propaganda for the *yanquis?* Who else could make all this country want to go to Miami and buy a Cadillac and listen to Madonna?"

"Yes," I said, unable to hold back. "But who else could help him the way the U.S. government has? They're his best ally—trying to put bombs in his cigars, invading Girón and Grenada, so he can always tell the people that all the problems are because of the embargo and he's standing up against Goliath. The two are a perfect league of thieves. Partners in crime."

José chuckled.

"They deserve one another, like a snake and its poison. Fidel can't live without an important enemy. The U.S. can't live without a military threat. It's a marriage made in heaven."

The girls were looking uncomfortable now. "So what do you do if you hate everything here?" Anna asked.

"Get drunk," said José. "Make love. Make music. We are like animals here. Sex and rum and sleep are the only things that are not in the ration book."

"So you want to live like Americans? Gangs. Drugs. People on the street. Bodies everywhere. A police state."

"I want to live like humans."

"Okay," said Anna. "Thank you for the coffee. We must go."

"Thank you," said Ilse, smiling all around, and the two of them let themselves out.

"Too bad," I said.

"Is okay. Some are like that. They want to live here for two years. But after two weeks, they want to leave."

"But if you feel that way about the situation, why don't you act on it?"

"I do. Eleven years now, I am trying to leave."

"Why not do something more? About Fidel?"

"And what then? Look at his friends—Ochoa, Raúl, the rest: first-class bastards. They are worse than him—they have only beards, no brains. Only guns, no ideas. And the imperialists in Miami? Forget it!"

"So better the devil you know than the devil you don't know?"

"Sure. Better we wait. Better we do nothing. Most people here, they know only the Revolution. Maybe the other ways are worse. So we wait. Keep quiet. Find a girl. Make business."

He cleaned up the coffee cups.

"I give her a seven," said Ignacio.

"Anna?"

"No. Ilse!"

"And Anna?"

"Four."

"You know what they say?" José said. "When you turn out the light, a blonde looks like the sheet: you can't see her in the dark. A black girl looks like the darkness: you can't see her too. But a mulatta—ah, a mulatta shines and shines in the dark, like a jewel."

"Okay, Carlos," said Ignacio, laughing. "I go now."

"Okay. *Luego.*"

" 'Carlos'?" I said when Ignacio had left.

"Sure," said José. "Is better. More secure. I have many different names. So if someone is saying, 'What is this José doing?' I can say, 'José? I don't know him. Who is he?' And if someone is looking for Carlos, I can say, 'Who is Carlos?' Is better like this. In Cuba, you must be many people. But these stranger girls, they don't know. I tell you about the library woman?"

"No."

"Last year, I met a woman from a library in England. Not so beautiful, but friendly, intelligent. We go to Tropicana, we drink some rum, and then I feel her hand on my leg. 'What does this mean?' I say, and she smiles a little, and we dance. But it is late, and her plane leaves at ten o'clock next day.

"The next day, at twelve o'clock in the night, there is a noise at my door. I think it is the police: they see me speaking English to her. They see me in the dollar store. But no, it is her. 'Why do you not leave?' I say. 'I love you,' she says.

"So she stays with me one week, and I teach her some Spanish, and she teaches me to speak English like an Englishman, not like a gangster from Miami. Is good. Okay. But then, when she goes home, she sends me a letter saying she loves me too much, she can never write to me again. And I want to say, 'So I am just your Caribbean souvenir, no? Like a postcard? Like a sunglass you pick up and carry and then leave behind? So you can always have romantic memories of your vacation in Caribbean. So you can always tell your friends about your boyfriend in Havana.' "

It was the first time I had seen José lose his cool, something cracking way inside him.

"But Cubans use foreigners too."

"Sure," he said, recovering himself. "We find some girls, we go to Tropicana on Sunday. Okay?"

We met the next day at the old Johnson Drugstore at the bottom of Obispo, Lourdes and I, to do some shopping for her aunt: I guess the news that a foreigner was around had spread. Lourdes said she wanted to show me more of the city, and though I figured I knew it well enough by now, had seen plenty of easy ironies and smiling faces in empty rooms, I knew that seeing her city would be a way of seeing her. What was important to her, what she valued. After all this time, I still couldn't figure the girl out: I liked it that she was coming on so slow, but I was getting edgy too, and restless. When love is a commodity, you wonder why anyone's giving it away for free. Or what the hidden costs might be.

She was waiting for me this time under a poster, put up by the local CDR, imploring her to GIVE BLOOD.

"Richard," she said as soon as I came up to her, "I want to buy a present for your mother."

"Great. That's like taking from the poor to give to the rich."

"I know. But I want to do something for you."

"Okay."

So we stopped in at a house and she bought me a black voodoo doll that I knew was going to be hell to pack, and then we went into the old Casa de las Infusiones and ordered some medicinal drinks. In the distance, I could hear trumpets and percussion, crazily jaunty even at this hour. Everywhere, people sitting or drinking or playing music in the trees.

"You have a map?" she said.

"Of Havana?"

"Not Havana. I know Havana. Of America."

"Only this." I got out my Pocket Flight Schedule, and she took it from me and went through the United Airlines routings as if she were tracing the lines on the palm of a man she loved, saying the names out loud to herself, asking me questions sometimes— "These are Indian places: Oshkosh, Kalamazoo?"—reciting the Spanish names as if they were a kind of incantation. It must have been fifteen minutes before she gave it back.

Then we went out into the nearest dollar store, where the ancient Chinese fans were going for two hundred dollars, and the refrigerators for two thousand. Young girls sat and grinned around movie-star glossies of Fidel thirty years before, and key chains with Che's face on them; Romanians picked up black dolls in bikinis that looked like wild-eyed spirits.

"Lula!" a bearded boy shouted then, and he came over and kissed her on both cheeks. So then there were three of us, going down to the magic ceiba tree marking the Founding of Havana, where Lourdes scavenged for coins and came up with two nickels. "For you," she said, bringing them back to me. "For us."

"*Come mierda,*" said a policeman nearby, hearing her speak to me in English. Eat shit.

The bearded boy spat in his direction. "*Aquí estamos muertos,*" he hissed as we went. "If Martí were here, things would be different. If Martí were here, he'd be a freedom fighter."

"You mean a *Fidelista*—or one of Fidel's enemies?"

"Martí loved his country."

"Sure. So does Fidel. So do Fidel's enemies."

"If Martí were here," the boy went on, obstinate, "if Martí and Che and Camilo were in power, there would be no problem. No Communism; only equality."

We turned down old, half-paved streets, where lonely boys stood in doorways and women looked out from the railings of their terraces. "You know Fidel killed Camilo? Because all the people loved him. When he went into the street, everyone shouted, 'Camilo! Camilo!' When Fidel went out, they had to hide him in a dark car. Why do you think Camilo died?"

"It's true," said Lourdes. "Why did Frank País die too? And Che? And all the rest? Do you not think it is strange that all the Heroes of the Revolution are dead? Why is it all the ones the people loved are gone? Is Fidel so hungry for the blood of martyrs? Why does he find his friends only among the dead?"

"Soon you'll be blaming him for the death of Christ."

"I am saying the truth, Richard. Why don't you listen? Where are the Heroes of the Revolution now? Where are they? Dead. No threat to Fidel; no threat to the system. When Camilo came to Havana, in 1959, the people sat on his car and put their arms around him. You know what his name means? One hundred flames! And what do we have now? Only a few ashes."

That was the great thing about dictators, I thought: they always gave the people someone to blame. There was always a prime suspect for every crime, even the ones that hadn't been committed yet. It wasn't worth reminding her that streets and schools in Cuba could be named by law only after the dead; it wasn't worth saying that dead men always seemed heroes because there was nothing they could do wrong now. Whatever happened, the people would always say that the guy at the top was guilty and everyone else was innocent. And there was never a shortage of rumors here. The Americans were going to invade tomorrow. Che was coming back from Bolivia to rescue the Revolution. Reagan was a secret Communist.

We stopped in at the car museum where they kept Camilo's Oldsmobile and Che's Chevy and even Vilma Espin's jeep ("This is where she made love to women," Lourdes whispered). There was a pair of jet skis too, given to Fidel by Japan. "Why does Fidel not jet-ski to Miami?" Lourdes whispered fiercely. "He doesn't care anything for us. He only has thoughts for his mistress."

"His mistress?" I led her on.

"Socialism," she spat.

"And what about his private life?"

"What private life? You know what he said once? 'If Carlo Marx were a woman, I would not love her.' He has no time for women; he only wants to use them. You know Tina?"

"Che's lover?"

"Sure. She gave everything to the Revolution. She married a Bolivian, she sent Che to Europe, she gave them secret messages on the radio. And what did she get for it? Nothing! These men are married only to their lives."

"Like Martí."

"No. Martí was bigger than Fidel. He had room for Revolution and for Love."

As we walked, a woman called out, *"Compañera,* can you tie my baby's laces?" Lourdes went over, and did them up so softly that the baby never cried. I think I fell in love with her right then, just the way her bitterness passed, and she went over without hesitation, and she summoned a tenderness for the baby that she usually kept in hiding. It made me wonder how she would be if she were away from all this craziness.

Then some black boys strolled past, calling out for matches, and then the bearded boy disappeared into a doorway, and then, as we walked down Perseverancia, we came upon Caridad, in a thin white shirt, looking—as usual—like she was going to cry.

"Eh, niña, dónde vas?" Lourdes called out to her.

"Nowhere," she said, and so she joined us as we slipped into the Hotel Lincoln for a drink. I ordered a Cuba Libre, and Cari got a Habana Libre, and Lourdes, waving her glass in the air, said, "To a Lula Libre! Let's drink to an independent Lourdes!"

Around us, Herb Alpert was blasting away, and then he was followed by Silvio, singing *'Adónde va la sorpresa?'* while the bartender went off to the bathroom to change some money. Everyone in the hotel seemed to be coming or going to the bathroom, counting money or looking around nervously, except for one couple in the corner—newlyweds, I guessed—who sat over two tiny glasses of Coke, saying nothing. On the wall there was a huge wooden statue of the Three Monkeys. See no evil, hear no evil, speak no evil.

Silvio struck up the refrain again, in that tremulous, heartbreaking way of his—a kid cracking into first love—*'Adónde va la sorpresa?'*—and the high notes blotted out the whispers and murmurs in the bar. This place was safe, Lula said, we could talk about anything here, and she started telling me things about Fidel in my ear, and it felt so good, her hot breath on my lobe, that I wanted her to talk and talk about the slow death of her country.

Soon it was getting dark, though, and Cari had someplace else to go, and I figured that now was the time with Lula. If she was leading me on, I didn't know where it was going; I only knew that I wasn't getting any pictures out of it.

"Look, let's go somewhere," I said as we went out into the darkening street. "How much longer do we have to wait?"

"It's not safe."

"It's never safe round here. This is the goddamn land of unsafe sex."

"Why can't you be patient?"

"I am patient. But I can't wait forever."

"In Cuba, we can wait forever."

"Great. That's what makes you a Cuban. I'm a foreigner. I can't wait. Nor can my editors in New York."

"Why do you have to be like this?"

"Because I don't have time. I have to go to Artemisa tomorrow, to shoot Fidel. Then to Cayo Largo. Then I leave. I can't wait."

"You go to Artemisa? Great. I will come with you," she said, eyes bright. "I have an aunt in Artemisa."

"That's wonderful. But it doesn't help us right now."

"Okay, Richard. Let me show you something. I will show you where we can go. Tell me what you think."

Beside us, the buildings round the Parque Central looked like headless ghosts gathered about the street. Teenage boys circling the striding statue of Martí. The streets of the old city like slatted bars on a window. Godforsaken apartments lit up only by the flicker of black-and-white TVs, and old women in old dresses sitting under crumbling ceilings, trying to catch some monster movie from the States.

Once, as we walked, she suddenly whispered, *"Silencio!"* and we passed a couple of Minint men, in their uniforms. Now and then, we saw figures moving in an unlit room, or shadows stirring on a terrace. Sometimes we heard whispers from the dark places—*"Ay, mi cielita! Ven acá!"*—sometimes a white eye rolling, as if in some voodoo trance. The moon was high above the Malecón, and everywhere were shadows.

Finally, we were standing before a shabby, dingy entrance, unlit, with a sign that said HOTEL SAN JOSÉ, on the corner of San Martín. Next to the sign was a picture of a couple, with a pair of soft drinks. Inside, on the wall, a poster of a girl at a Varadero beach. An old man sat in the *Carpeta* area, and another, even older, a black tie loose around his king-sized neck, sat wheezing on a stool beside the entrance. It looked like any whorehouse.

A couple in army fatigues came out, holding hands, and the old man told Lula we could have a room in forty-five minutes or so. He motioned us to another room, and she called out for *"El último,"* and we joined the line. There was an ad for Miller beer on the wall, and some pictures from a Swedish porno mag. A few couples sat on chairs, looking as if they were trying to ignore the smell. "He says it is five dollars," Lula whispered.

"Enough," I snapped. "I didn't come here to visit a five-dollar love hotel. I want this, I can go back to Manila. Let's just go to the St. John's. I've paid for it; the people there are cool. What's your problem?"

"One night in the St. John's, and then two years in Combinado. My dream."

"I can make it right for them. Slip the chambermaid a few bucks."

"Richard. You know the girls in these hotels? How do you think they stay there? How do you think they pay the police? What do you think the government does with them? This is at least a hotel for people in love."

I'd had enough of it then, and I walked off toward the sea. Lula came running after, catching up with me as we crossed the wide boulevard. The girls were sitting along the seawall, occasional wind blowing the hair around their eyes. The boys were sitting eyeing the girls, or watching the foreigners watching the girls. Everyone was waiting, waiting, for something, anything, to happen. Sometimes, on the rocks below, a couple gasped. Sometimes a boy gave a wild whoop and jumped over the wall, down to the rocks, to retrieve a hat carried there by the wind. The night was all expectation: the boys pushing themselves against their *novias,* the old women whispering prayers to the dark, the girls hiking their skirts and listening for a foreign accent.

Everyone waiting, waiting, and somewhere, in some near-empty room, somewhere in the city, *El Líder* pacing up and down, memorizing the tables of international debt statistics, or coining a new slogan: like one of the gods in the old Greek myths, playing dice games for the souls below.

What happened the next day I remember as a dream almost. As if it never happened, or can only be figured out from what came later. It seems strange, after all the trips, and all the nights in distant hotels, that it had never happened to me like that before. I guess you know it's something like love when you run out of comparisons.

And later, it's as if you've crossed some threshold you didn't know was there. And you notice the way she frowns when she's putting on her makeup. Or how she holds her fork. Or which earring she takes off first.

I remember meeting her at the Parque Central at ten o'clock, and I remember she was dressed in a sky-blue pantsuit, her hair loose below a sky-blue headband. I remember her arms were bare, and there was a thin gold bracelet around her wrist. I remember she greeted me with a smile, and a quiet kiss, and then said, *"Vamos. We go to Artemisa,"* and we walked toward the *colectivos.*

"My mother saw you with a girl," she said.

"That was you, Lula."

"No. Before. Last year."

"Last year, maybe. Someone for my work. Like a model."

"At night—in Centro Habana?"

"Sure. Night is when I make my best pictures."

"And who was this girl?"

"I don't know. I don't remember."

"Okay." She looked at me again. "This time I am your guide, your model. You want to see Cuba, I show you."

We got into an old car then—I think it was a Plymouth, with no dials and no lights and no handles on the doors—and soon we were driving south, out of the city, past Cojímar and the Playas del Este, the lonely palms and the blue on our left. Then, as we came near Santa María del Mar, suddenly she told the driver to turn right, up a dirt road, and we bumped and banged toward some huts. *"Aquí,"* she said, and we got out, and walked past a few shacks, her finger to her mouth.

"You will not tell José?" she whispered.

"No."

"Come on. I give you a surprise."

At the last of the shacks, we passed through a doorway, into a little room, with a kitchen next door. A woman—her name was Nelida—was in the kitchen, cooking plantains and beans and rice, in a blouse and denim cutoffs, two children playing around her legs.

"You want to use the room?" she asked. "Is okay. But tell the foreigner not to talk."

I wondered how often this had happened before; I wondered whether this was part of Lourdes's guided tour.

We closed the door to the kitchen, and she put on the TV, with the volume real high. "If they hear you," she said, pointing to the next house, and then she drew a finger across her throat. We sat on the bed, the only place to sit in the room, with a hundred images of Paulina Porizkova looking down on us.

"You can take off your shirt. So you will look like a Cuban."

I took it off, and lay back against the headboard. On the walls were pictures clipped from foreign magazines—wall-to-wall photos of Rossellini and Elle McPherson, full-page posters of Travolta, ads for Calvin Klein. On TV there was an old John Wayne movie. I reached for my camera, and she put her hand on my arm.

"*Ven acá,*" she murmured, and I rolled toward her on the bed.

She sat me up, and got out a hairbrush from her purse, and she started brushing my hair, as fiercely as a mother. I saw the opening in her dress where her skin began, I smelled the echo of her Charlie.

She brushed, brushed, brushed my hair, and I closed my eyes.

"*Mamá!*" It was one of Nelida's kids, crawling in through the door, bare-chested, golden-haired.

"In the kitchen," she said. "Leave us alone."

He pushed past us, and into the hiss and crackle of the kitchen. The door closed behind him.

I sensed her heart beating, heard her say something to herself in Spanish, saw the golden cross around her throat.

"You will not tell José?"

"No. Why should I?"

"I have to be careful."

She slipped off her shoes, and began kissing my back.

Tingled, I rolled over, and found myself next to her face. John Wayne was shooting Indians on TV. Slowly, I tucked her hair behind her ear, and ran my finger down her cheek and along her chin. She took it into her mouth, eyes closed, as if it were a candy. I followed with my own mouth, and ran my hand down her back. It felt salty and warm, flecked with sand.

Her lips were glistening now, and her top came off. I ran my finger up her inside thighs and heard her shiver, moan.

"Now, Lula?"

"Now," she said, and I put a finger to her wetness.

She shrugged off all her clothes then, and, slowly, she straddled me. I looked up to see her face, clenched, looking away, as she moved faster and faster and faster, her body circling around and around, my hands on her breasts, her face looking away, urging herself on, and riding me with increasing fury until she stopped for a second, and her hair fell over her face.

Outside, there was a sudden thunderstorm. "No words, Richard," she said, putting a finger to my mouth. And then, on the wet sheets, I could feel a cold hand on my side: Nelida's son, in from the sudden rain.

W e went all together, the two of us and Nelida, after the rain had subsided, to Artemisa, the old car jouncing along the open sea, the driver singing *canciones de amor,* my arm around her shoulder, she leaning against me and whispering a line I couldn't follow: " '*Luego, Después del rayo, y del fuego, Tendré tiempo de sufrir.*' " We drove past processions of small towns, and it felt as if we were going to a wedding: every province had dressed itself up in its prettiest skirts, with new pictures of Che, and SOCIALISM OR DEATH posted up on every pillar and restaurant and doorway, and little red-and-black flags with "26" on them pasted on every inch of space. WE FOLLOW YOU, said the signs on every wall, on every house. WE WILL NOT FAIL. Take note of our Revolutionary fervor, they were saying; pass by us, Angel of Death.

It reminded me of what José had said once, about Pascal's wager: the Revolution was the same, he'd said. No one knew what it was going to do next, whether it was benign, whether it was god or devil; but the safest thing was always to say that it was good. Believe in it, and at least you had a chance of coming out on the winning side; doubt it, and you were doomed from the beginning.

When we got to Artemisa, the streets were strung with party lights, and on every door, on every wall, there was a slogan. SIEMPRE ES 26. ESTAMOS CONTIGO. VIVA FIDEL! There was a fiesta feeling everywhere, and the bars were open round the clock: like a permanent Saturday night when school is let out, a white night of the soul. Every night was prom night in Cuba in those days, but this was something special.

"You know the Moncada?" she asked, as we wended our way through the crowds, toward the main plaza and its stores. "You know every fighter in the Moncada was an *artimiseño?* Ramiro Valdés, Julio Díaz, Ismael Ricondo? *Todo, todo,* from Artemisa!"

I'd never heard her so caught up in the Revolutionary spirit, and I couldn't tell whether it was the day or the place that had brought it out in her, but I decided to can my Moncada spiel, and not ask her what it said about the Revolution that its great heroic moment was a fiasco in which the rebels were slaughtered, and their leader himself, Fidel, had left his glasses at home. This was not the moment for that: every year, the anniversary of the Revolution was celebrated in some "model town," and this year Artemisa was the chosen one, the place where the old man would shout hoarse promises to his bride.

Everywhere around us, people were moving. Little girls dressed up as for church, and electric bulbs running on wires above the parks, and somewhere there was a rumor that Los Van Van was going to be playing in the park. We went to Lourdes's aunt's house, and when she saw us, she kissed us all, and took us in, and there were shouts and cries and kisses. A few minutes later, we were out again—some ancient family feud, and some cousin asking Lourdes why she'd been to jail.

"Okay, Richard, tonight we sleep in the street," she said. "You learn the Cuban way."

We made our way back to the plaza then, and it was more packed than ever, and I didn't know if it was a rock-concert gig or a town-hall meeting. In a bare patch of grass next to a school, someone had set up speakers, and the word was that Grupo Sierra Maestra was going to be here any minute. For now, there was some local group, pounding out salsa dance tunes, and one whole field of young Cubans wriggling in place with the moves their mothers had taught them.

I bought a couple of beers for the girls, and we found some seats, and they began dancing, Nelida wiggling with a cabaret dancer's frenzy, Lula moving more slowly in place, like a rich girl in a Kuwaiti disco.

"Hey, compañero, qué pasa?" said the black man who suddenly appeared beside us, a trim, muscular guy with a close-fitting shirt: he could have passed for Pelé.

"Hola!"

Lula pinched my palm, and I knew what that meant: stay quiet, say nothing, this guy was trouble.

"My name is Fredo," he was saying, in English, and I pretended I didn't hear him, and jived closer over to Lula. If he wanted to hit on Nelida, this was his cue.

But he didn't take the hint, and came moving over to us, dancing all the while, arms moving back and forth, in a leisurely, controlled way that had more power to it than sex. "Is good, no?" he said, not leaving the English. "You like this country?"

"I dislike this guy," Lula whispered, with her back turned. "He's making my skin move."

"Hey, *compañero?*" he said again, smiling to the beat. "What part of Havana do you live in?"

I kept on dancing.

"Ah, maybe you are an *extranjero*. You come from Canada, maybe? *Estados Unidos?*"

"South Africa," I finally answered.

"South Africa? What part?"

We were dancing all the while, Lourdes in a kind of distracted way, her mind not moving with her body, Nelida in some drum-beating trance of her own, the guy in short, compact motions, like a piston.

"You will hear Fidel tomorrow?"

"Come on," said Lourdes. "Let's move." We tried to sidle away then, and he kept following us: to run was like setting off a burglar alarm, to stay was like admitting our guilt. "Come on," she said more urgently, and then we were snaking through the dancers, and he was beginning to follow us, and then at last Nelida came out of her spell, and grabbed his arm, and said, *"Baila conmigo, niño,"* and she was rubbing herself against him and puckering her lips, and we figured that that was the last we'd see of her tonight.

That left the rest of the night before us, and nowhere to go. We couldn't stay at her aunt's house, and we'd let the taxi go, so there was nothing for it but waiting at the bus station for a bus to Havana they said might never come. Outside the bars and restaurants, people were sitting on steps or standing against walls, looking into the distance: the usual three-hour *cola*. Every house looked like a party or a Christmas cake, but there was a man watching in every entrance, and when you turned off the main drag, you stumbled into dirty puddles.

For a while, we made a kind of makeshift home in front of a closed door, and I bought us some beers, and we cuddled and got close. But then things started getting heavy, and she got nervous, and every time I kissed her, she looked around for the security man. So we headed back to the bus station and got into the line. There was nothing to do there, as usual, but hold one another, and gossip, and wait.

"You know, Richard, once there was a long *cola,* a *super cola,* a *tremendo cola,* the longest *cola* in the history of Cuba. And a guy came up, with a beard, wearing army clothes, and said, '*El último?*' and they led him to the back of the line. And as soon as everyone else saw him there, they all found ways to leave the line or go back home, until the guy was alone at the front. 'Hey,' he said to the last guy to leave, 'what is this line for?' 'Oh, it's for leaving the island,' the man told him."

I wondered why she was telling me this kind of story in a crowded place like this—on the eve of Fidel's visit, no less—but I figured she knew what she was doing, and decided to go with it.

"Here," she said, as we were pushed closer together by the line. "Let me show you this." She pulled out from her pocket her pink wallet, and, searching through it, drew out an old sad black-and-white mug shot, not much bigger than her nail.

"Your *esposo?*"

"No. My father. I never told you his story?" She stopped for a moment. "He was a *Fidelista* before; he loved Fidel. He used to say that Cuba was the only country that was free. That had no bosses. He went to Russia to study for him, he gave everything to the Party. And then he fell in love with a woman, and her husband found out, and this husband was in the police, and my father was sent to jail, and that was it. The one true friend of Fidel, and they let him die.

"I believed in Fidel too, before. He had so many dreams; he was so strong; he gave himself only to his country. I was a good *Pionera* in school; I wrote essays about Che. But then they killed my father. And after, I told you, there was one time I was engaged. He was a good boy. Very good. Kind. Patient. Not like the others. It was my first love. And then, one day, it was like this: there was a fiesta, and there was a *cola*, and I was young, and I could not control myself, and the police were trying to command us, and telling women they could go first if they would go behind the wall with them for five minutes, and I got mad, and I kicked a policeman there, and they took me to prison. My *esposo*, he was there, and he shouted at them, and told them to go to hell, and they called him a traitor, an imperialist, and he was in jail for six months. When he came out—it was different. It was never the same again."

I looked at her then, and saw that it was about something more than bread and plane tickets, and as tangled as any family history. "That is why I learned English," she went on. "That is why I love Martí. Because he wanted to do something with his life. Not only to wait, to sit, to visit a foreign country and hope that things will change. He tried to change things himself, to make things better." She smiled up at me then, and said, "Better we kiss. You must enjoy this Cuban evening," and she relaxed her body into mine.

The minutes passed, the hours passed, it seemed, and the line got longer, and there was never a bus in sight. At one point—it must have been three a.m. or later—someone got out a guitar, and a few drunken boys began beating out a rhythm on the walls, and a girl started singing, and Lula joined in from where she was standing, and, in a faint, high voice, she sang boleros and then Cuban songs, and then Yoruba songs and Beatles songs and even Russian songs. The time moved more quickly then, and the *cola* itself became a party, with frantic strumming and the beating of walls, and voices, two or three, taking melodies for a walk. Then the bus came, and suddenly the line, so patient, broke into ranks, and there was a scuffle, and someone shouted *Hijo e' puta,* and a big white guy took a swing at a black, and someone kicked at Lourdes, and hit her in the leg, and we climbed up amid the mob, and grabbed some seats, and she fell asleep in my lap as we lurched back toward

Havana. It must have been five-thirty then, and the sun was just beginning to rise, but I was too wired to crash out—I had too much to think about—so I just sat there, with her head resting in my lap, stroking her hair and watching her face, and seeing the sun come up over the sugarcane, another morning-after in the glorious Revolution.

The next day, I went back to Artemisa to shoot Fidel. I knew I could get him easily this time—the crowds weren't as big as ten years before, and the backdrops, with all the dignitaries seated on the stage, framed by huge billboards of Lenin and Marx, would be perfect. I went early, by bus, almost as soon as I'd taken Lula home, and I took with me my Olympus OM2, the kind they don't make anymore: small enough for me to shoot from the hip. It was a good move. There was some other guy nearby—a freelancer, from Tacoma or somewhere—who'd set up a tripod in front of the stage. He'd waited six hours to get this place, I heard him saying. But before Fidel even came out, the security guards moved over, and started hauling him away. He didn't speak English, he said, in good Spanish, but they knew that trick, and they handed him over to a bystander who spoke English, and who explained to him, "They want to know why you are taking so many pictures." "This is a great day for me," he said, deciding that he did speak English, and I almost felt like cheering him on. "Fidel is my hero. All my life I have waited for this moment." "That's fine," said a guard, speaking through the bystander. "Please enjoy this moment," and he opened the back of the camera, and tore out the film.

I got a few good shots early on—with negative space above, and room for a banner in case someone wanted to use it as a cover— and Fidel kept talking, talking, in a rolling, slow Spanish so clear even I could follow: that was his gift, I thought again, to make a declaration simple enough for even a child to understand. But pretty soon the rain began to come down, really hard, and people started filing away, or just gathered closer in circles on the muddy ground, huddled over their picnics of bread and beer. The light was going fast now, and Fidel was still standing there, gesturing, roaring, shaking his fist as he recited the year's harvest statistics, and I decided that I'd had my moment, and began to pick my way around the puddles, and over the people sitting under plastic bags and the kids reveling in the muck.

At the back of the open field, a few boys were practicing dance moves, and the rest were heading home in streams, like a crowd in the fourth quarter of a football game when the home team's down by 27. I saw a car circling for customers, and I flashed a few dollar bills at him, and he quickly came over to me, and as he did, I saw a couple of kids speaking English—Canadians, I figured—and asked them if they wanted to share, to bring down the costs.

"Great. That's really kind of you," said the girl, shaking her head dry, and looking as if she'd just won the lottery.

They crowded into the back, and as we began to thread our way through the crowd, the old Revolutionary battles started up again.

"That was just magic back there," she said. "I could feel it. Something special."

"Sure. Because you were with the Rent-a-Crowd guys, the ones who are paid to go and clap."

"Okay, Greg. That's fine. You be cynical. That's great. Fine for you. But I could feel something. Not always, for sure, but sometimes, just for a moment, I could feel what this whole thing was all about. Like being caught up in something bigger than yourself. Caught up in a wave, a current. Like giving yourself for something."

"Caught up in the rain, more like."

"Okay. You want to listen to Reagan or Thatcher, that's fine. That's your prerogative. It's just that these people have something else. Five eggs a day, three eggs, two eggs, it doesn't matter. Because they are happy."

"Easy for you to say. You have all the eggs you want. And a ticket to Toronto next week."

"You know I don't mean it like that. These people have dignity. They take themselves seriously. They're trying to achieve something. They know it isn't going to be easy."

"What dignity is there in waiting in line and bartering? In dressing yourself up so you can get a foreigner to buy you a tube of lipstick? In selling yourself by soft-selling your country?"

"So you think it's dignified to live in suburbia with Geraldo on TV and the kids shooting up in the sixth-grade classrooms and the murder rate in Washington higher than in Lebanon?"

"I'm not saying North America's perfect. But just because our home's fucked doesn't mean that this place is any better."

"At least it's pledged to something. At least it still has ideals. At least it's trying to be itself."

A heavy silence fell. The car grumbled through the rain.

"Okay," she finally said. "We agree to disagree. Okay?"

"That's exactly what you can't do over here. You've got to agree in Cuba."

"Okay, Greg. Will you let it go?"

He was silent for a moment. "It's just that six hours in a bus to see an old guy speaking in the rain while everyone else is filing out isn't my idea of a historical moment."

"Did you see them dancing in the back?"

"Sure. They dance like that at Grateful Dead concerts. Does that mean Jerry Garcia is the savior of the world?"

"He is for me," I said, figuring I couldn't take two more hours of dialectical materialism in action. "You should see the kids in Managua."

"I told you we should go there," the girl told her friend.

"You go to the Café Lennon, and you see all these students reading the works of the great Roberto Weir. Deadheads of the world unite: you've got nothing to lose but your brains!"

That shut them up. And when we got to Havana, I decided just to expense-account the whole thing; this couple had enough problems without being bankrupted by a taxi ride.

When I got back to my room, I lay down to map out the evening. I could shoot nightclubs, I thought, or the old guys with their arms around nubile teenagers. I could try José's house, or the love hotel. But pretty soon I realized I wasn't thinking of anything but Lourdes. It was a strange thing; I wasn't prepared for it: it felt like I was betraying my job. There's only one thing in photography, and it's focus. The only thing that matters is keeping your mind sharp and clear. No distractions. No second thoughts. Keep your mind as polished as your lens. I remember once, in Seoul, I'd been working the same time as Jim Nachtwey, and just the way he stood there, in the middle of all the tear gas and the pellets, completely erect, as motionless as a Zen priest, catching moments in his lens, it was like watching a master at work.

But with Lourdes, it was like something else was coming into the picture. I couldn't get her image out of my head. She was everywhere: at the edge of every picture I saw, there was her face, or the way her hair fell down, or her eyes in the dark of the bar. I hadn't even taken a picture of her alone, and yet she was in every picture that I took.

I couldn't figure it out, this spell: it wasn't just her face—pretty girls are a dime a dozen. It wasn't just the way she'd shown me her world, or fallen asleep in my lap. It wasn't even her mischief. Maybe it was just the fact that I couldn't figure her out: when I saw her in my mind, I always saw rings of smoke curling around her head, and I could hardly make out her slow smile, her musky eyes. Sometimes, when I was tired, I played our whole time together through, like slides on a carousel, and saw it all as a story about her getting dollars, and some presents for her mother, and a way to join her aunt in America. Sometimes, when I'd just made some picture and was all fired up, I'd think of something she said, or the way she'd broken away from me that first night, and it felt as though the streets were singing. It was like the whole crazy country: look at it one day, and you'd see this grotesque, sharp-featured hag. Then click your eyes into a different kind of focus, and the image resolved itself into a beautiful girl. The kind of optical illusion they teach you in high school.

Now, though, I knew there was no way I could work. I lay on my bed, and the more I thought of the last bed I'd lain in, and the last night I'd spent—without any bed at all—the more I felt so full up that I couldn't stop moving.

But there was no way of getting in touch around here—no faxes or answering machines—so it had to be the old-fashioned way, like in the old movies: the long nighttime walk to her house, the pounding on the door, the whispered thanks to anyone who'd open up, the run up the stairs, the quick survey of her kitchen. This time she was there, thank God, and I told her I had to talk, and I almost pulled her with me out into the street.

"We can go to the Central Hospital," she said. "It is safe there."

"No," I said. "It has to be now. I can't wait. I've got to be with you. Something has changed."

"You mean Santa María?"

"No. I mean Artemisa. The *cola,* the songs, the bus. If I want sex, I can have it with any girl in Havana."

"So you don't want me." Her smile was wicked.

"I want you now."

"Okay, Richard, come." She led me down to a local bus station, and there were a few old cars parked outside in the dark. "Dollars," she said to an old guy, and he opened up his Packard, and we got into the back. "Where are we going?" I whispered. "Nowhere," she said, and sat close to me. I felt the down on the back of her neck, kissed the soft spot behind her ear. She said something to the driver, and he took us toward the beaches to the east. In the dark, on the seat, she ran her hand under my shirt, and I felt her tongue on the tip of my ear. Soon my hands were under her shirt too, while the driver paused to look around, and we passed through the long, ghostly streets of Havana. "Here," she said at last, when we were on the Via Blanca. "Maybe you take a walk for fifty minutes, an hour, *compañero,* and then we will give you dollars." The man got out, taking the key with him for security, and then I was saying, "Come here, *angelita,*" and she was flashing her anarchist smile. "So, Richard, you believe in angels, but you do not believe in God?"

The next time it was the same almost: the long drive through Havana streets, some *compañero* at the wheel, dreaming of all the things he could buy with his dollars, and she guiding him through the dark, and I guiding her, and our stolen whispers, and our urgent sighs. Then a long slow hour by the sea, in the back of some creaking De Soto, and the feeling of being a kid again, breaking every rule.

Or sometimes the slow walk through the crumbling streets, and the clamber up the darkened staircase, and the fumbling for the light. "No talking," she'd whisper. "No words. Here. In the kitchen." The sound of belts unfastening, the rustle of jeans falling at our feet. The picture of Che above us, the statue of Jesus in the corner. The sound of gasps, and her fist in her mouth as she tried not to scream.

Then the flight from the darkened apartment, down the unlit staircase, and out into the night.

Dear Stephen,

I fear this may turn out to be an unreasonably long letter, but the thing is, so much happens when one's here, and later, when one's back in the dining hall or going up to books, one can hardly believe that any of it happened at all. I suppose writing to you is a way of reminding myself that it really did happen, and that the Hugo who will later read this is the same one who was in the thick of all these tropical adventures. It's hard to believe sometimes.

As perhaps I told you before, in Cuba even the most unexceptional episodes have a way of coming back to haunt one, and they tend to reverberate as few excitements do. You may recall that I told you about the old cathedral in Havana, and how eager I was to attend a service there. It seems such a melancholy place, I wanted to see how it might be different as a place of worship. So I went to attend a mass there a few days ago. I don't know if you remember, but I used to be a very keen campanologist as a boy; even now I find some kind of solace in the bells.

In any case, it was a rather sorry gathering, as you might expect: there were only a few bare pews of worshippers, all in their Sunday best, yet still shifty somehow, and not very full-throated, as if they were all keeping an eye out lest a group of Fidelistas break in at any moment, and couldn't remember that Castro himself was once a Jesuit boy. So their mumbled singing hardly began to fill the place, and by the end, as you can imagine, I was more than ready to take my leave.

Before I could quite exit, however, I heard a voice address me in English: I suppose he'd seen the map inside my pocket.

"Excuse me, señor. You are from Germany? Or Canada?"

"England, actually."

"Ay, England! The land of kings!"

"Well, yes, in a manner of speaking, I suppose so."

"You live near the Queen?"

"Not terribly near. But in the same general direction, yes."

"You come here as a tourist?"

"Yes. I love it here. This is my second time."

"Ah, for you, señor, it is so beautiful here. I love your country too. But I cannot visit."

"No. It's a shame." There was a pause. "You have relatives abroad?"

"My mother only. And my brother, he went to Mexico three years ago. And my father, he is dead."

"I'm sorry."

"Señor. Can you take this to my mother?" He handed me a faded envelope, with a picture of the British Museum on the stamp.

"I suppose so. The trouble is, though, I don't live in the U.S."

"Is okay. You live outside. That is enough."

"Fine. Well, in that case, perhaps I'll be on my way," I said, with a heartiness I didn't really feel. "Very pleasant to have met you. I do hope we'll meet again."

"I hope this too," he said. "In England. At the home of the King."

Something about the conversation rather took the spring out of my step, and I wasn't quite in the mood to make the tour I'd promised myself of the colonial patios. So I popped instead into the Bodeguita del Medio, this very famous old place where Ernest Hemingway and Allende and everyone seemed to drink, and I bought a mojito, the lethal rum concoction that is the spécialité de la maison. Because I had nothing to do, I suppose, I opened the envelope.

"My dearest, unforgettable Margarita," it began—I could translate it quite easily. "I hope this finds you well, and your parents too.

I think of you every day. I dream of you every night. Here it is always the same. We cannot get rum. We cannot get chicken. Your brother is no longer with Martita. Even in the cathedral, it is not so easy to do business. The money you sent me for the passport is all gone. I gave the money to the man from Peru, but then I heard nothing. Now I think I cannot wait any longer. I cannot live any longer. If you read this letter, please send me more money. Or a ticket. Or a visa. If you do not, I think I will die. I ask God many times why he must make me suffer, when he will come back. But always I hear no answer. No answer from God, no answer from you. And every day, there is a new restriction. My darling Margarita, sometimes at night I think we are together again, and you are in my arms. But then I wake up, and there is no one. I think very soon I will die. With all my love, Ricardo."

I don't know why, but my heart was pounding as I read the letter. The right thing to do, I suppose, was to send it on as if I'd never opened it. But still, somehow, I felt as if I'd trespassed, as if I'd walked into a room at a time when two people were being intimate. Somewhat on an impulse, I decided to go back to the cathedral, and give it back to the man, but by the time I got there, the door was locked, and the whole square was empty, save for a young boy who suddenly materialized at my side, and—absurdly—two pigs. So I went back to my room, with the letter in my pocket, and I felt as if I were a spy somehow, or a traitor, and I half believed that even the woman at the desk was looking at me differently. I know that the Cubans are a passionate people, but still it was hard to know what exactly the letter portended. It all made me feel a very long way from home.

In any case, I look forward to seeing you soon.

With all warmest wishes,

Hugo

Just two days after that [I found myself continuing in my diary—knowing, I suppose, that I'd never send the letter, but wanting, somehow, to catch the strangeness and the drama of the place before I forgot it], *I took myself off to Cayo Largo, one of* those pristine honeymoon resorts they have over here, which are reserved exclusively for tourists, and which one can visit on a day trip from Havana. The whole thing was something of a travesty, as usual: the entire planeload arriving at eight o'clock, to be greeted by dancing bands and rum cocktails for breakfast, and offers of a tour to inspect the local turtles.

I felt a little out of place, not surprisingly: I'm not a great one for water sports at the best of times, and I felt a little self-conscious sitting on the beach, reading On the Road while groups of bronzed Teutons disported themselves as if in some Aryan holiday camp. Nonetheless, it was certainly the most beautiful beach I'd ever seen, and it seemed as good a way as any to pass a morning in the tropics.

They treated us all to a very hearty lunch (one of the waiters asking if I knew Pete Townshend, and some of the Germans cracking jokes about the advert for the beach—"Alone, virgin and yours"), and at five o'clock we gathered round to be bused back to the plane. Needless to say, as soon as I turned up, I was told that there was no bus at all, and there was no plane: I would be obliged to spend the night on the island. Not a bad way, I suppose, of their getting me to pay for two hotel rooms in a single evening. It was quite an inconvenience—I hadn't brought my things with me, after all—but I realized that there was no sense in arguing, and that I might as well chalk it up to experience: treat it as one of those adventures one so seldom has at home.

In due time, a minivan did arrive, and took us all to a hotel, and when we arrived at the place—a rather rickety kind of post-Stalinist extravaganza, well suited to North Korean ophthalmologists' conventions—they handed me a key, and sent me up to the second floor. No lift, of course, and not a great deal of lighting on the stairs. Cuba is a place that can make Winchester seem luxurious by comparison.

When I opened the door to my room, I found there was someone standing there already. Even more astonishing, it was the American photographer I'd met here a year ago, Richard. He was standing by the window, fiddling with some lenses, and when I came in through the door, he looked at me as if I were a spy. And then, recovering rather, came over and said, "Dr. Cartwright, I presume."

An extraordinary coincidence, I suppose—but then, coincidences *seem to occur with such regularity here that one's inclined to believe they may not be coincidences at all. For example, the nice man at the hotel suddenly appears at the table next to yours in the nightclub that evening, and you realize that he may not be just a nice man from the hotel. Or the man on the bus turns out to be the neighbor of the friend you've just been to see. Things have a way here of circling round. Besides, having written to Richard, I suppose I shouldn't have been so taken aback to see him.*

Nonetheless, it was a great surprise, in its way—we hadn't planned it—and I was glad of the company. At the very least, he was rescuing me from three hours of Kerouac.

We went down to a bar which they have out by the swimming pool—the Medusa, as it's called—and ordered some drinks.

"So what brings you here?" I asked.

"Oh, the usual. A story I'm shooting for Rolling Stone.*"*

I couldn't help but be impressed. "On Cuba?"

"Naw. Something global. 'Love in a Cold War Climate,' they're going to call it. About the love trade around the world. You know: girls at the Jinjiang Hotel in Chengdu getting cozy with overseas Chinese businessmen. Poland becoming the largest center of mail-order brides outside the Philippines. The French agency that sets up guys with girls from Transylvania. Even the Americans who want to get English brides—and vice versa. The usual game."

"Now you mention it, I do remember hearing about something like that in Russia."

"Sure. I've seen more 'Russian marriages' than you've seen beers. Some kid learns Russian at school, goes for a six-week course in Leningrad, meets some Natasha who comes on strong to him. Late-night talks about poetry and politics. Late-night wedding at some deserted office. He returns home, takes care of the papers, and she comes over, and then heads off. End of affair, end of innocence. Kid's left wondering what's hit him, and the West has a new entrepreneur on its hands."

"And that happens here too?"

"What do you think brings all these three-hundred-pound Mexican truckdrivers down here? The art museums?"

"But I mean, it's not always like that. You can't deny that the

Cubans are among the most openhearted and generous people around."

"Sure. And they know how to turn that to advantage. If they're going to have a good time anyway, they might as well have one with a foreigner, and see where that will lead. Prostitution feeds off foreignness as much as love does."

It was funny, but the more he went on like this, the more I felt he was putting on a show, for himself perhaps as much as for me. Pretending somehow, or not letting on that he was vulnerable. He reminded me sometimes of those Sixth Formers we have whose very anxiety to prove their worldly wisdom makes one rather doubt it.

"So you think it's political?"

"Everything's political down here, my friend."

"Even falling in love?"

"Especially falling in love." He took another sip of beer.

"So what do you say to something to eat?" I said, rather to dispel the mood, and then we made our way over to the glass-fronted restaurant a little further along the beach. I must say that the only good thing about Cuban food is that there usually isn't much of it: another of those austerities for which school is rather a good training. So we reconciled ourselves to the inevitable moros y cristianos, and a bottle of Spanish plonk, and I asked him about his past. I could see that he wanted to talk tonight, and that he wouldn't let me rest till he'd had his say.

"However did you get into this business in the first place? Did you train at a vocational college?"

"God, no, just the opposite. Got into it the usual way, with the usual story. You know: drugs, parental divorce, boarding school, all that, and then, in '68 or '69, I just decided to bag the whole thing and hit the road. Everywhere was wide open then, you could go anywhere you wanted, so I took the trail down through Iran, Kabul, and Kathmandu, and ended up in Goa. It was crazy in those days: you'd see all these people crashed out on the beach, living there for six months, nine months at a time, partying every night. Plus, there were all these guys going out to Indochina from there. It was an easy way to make a living: every few months, you could go over to Saigon, hook up with one of the big agencies—AP, AFP, one of those—and *then make enough money to go back to Goa and hang out some more. None of us had any training, but none of us cared. It was the ultimate teenager's wet dream: there we were, seventeen, eighteen, out in this exotic world of temples and jungles and bar girls, with all the dope we could want, and hammocks on the beach, and guys with AK-47s partying next door.*

"Plus, we could tell ourselves we were heroes. Risking our lives to bring back the truth. Braving the front lines to educate the masses. We were the latest Cartier-Bressons and Bischofs. And all the time we were having the party of our lives, the one that the guys back in California would have killed for. We never wanted it to end.

"Did, though; had to. So I went and shot South Africa for a while, Beirut, Belfast, El Salvador: all the garden spots. Couldn't get out of Southeast Asia, though: just kept on going back there. Used to stay at the Tropicana, down in Bangkok—the Troc of Shit, we'd call it—down in the old part of the city, where the glitz suddenly ends, and you're in the middle of Indians in prayer caps and klong artists and Muslim guys with calculators working out how much a three-some costs. Where every girl looks like an Annamese princess. So there you were, with these wild trips going down every night. You'd go out with some sexy, drop-dead teenager, and the next day you'd find out she was an ax murderer—or a post-ops falsie. Then you'd go out to Site 3, and these Khmer Rouge heavies—real murderers—would come out and bow and wai and invite you into their huts for dinner. You didn't know if you were coming or going; no knowing the lay of the land, we'd say, when you're in the Land of the Lay."

"Not ideal, though, for long-term relationships."

"Not ideal at all. Not ideal for anything except war-zone love. You'd see all these guys who were completely hooked on the rush. Couldn't get it up unless there were grenades popping around them. Wouldn't go for a girl unless she was a killer. But still, you know"—he looked pensive—"I wouldn't trade that life for the world. I'll never forget the first time I went into the jungle. It was wild. I was completely green: open as a barn door. This guy just came up to me in Bangkok, on the street, and said, 'How about going to Cambodia?' And the next thing I knew, I was, like, thirty-five, forty clicks over the border, in this country full of crazies. And the forests

were full of these spirits—you could really feel it—like something that had been uncorked after all these years. It was spooky; real spooky. And sometimes you'd see these weird images at night—just the way a woman smiled at you, or a temple suddenly appeared where you didn't expect it—and you'd be in this whole other world, like a kind of druggy dream where everything made sense, even your Zen and your pot. And it could put you into some really weird places in yourself. And then you'd come out, and the next day you'd be watching videos with the relief workers in Aranya. Almost like it'd never happened."

We heard a group of guitarists practicing in a garden.

"And through all this you never got involved?"

"Never stopped getting involved. Involved up to the knees. Involved in every way. But if you mean married, sure, I got hitched. Like I told you before. To an Englishwoman, in Singapore. Diane. Met her in Jakarta. I was there on my way back from East Timor, she was working in Surabaya for Juliana's. It was kind of like tonight, I guess: two foreigners far from home in a distant place, couldn't fail but end up together."

"Juliana's was a shop?"

"No, you know, the disco company out of London that supplies half the world's hotels with deejays? Diane had worked for them all over—Beijing, Bangkok, Damascus—even some of the men-only postings, and now she was just starting out in Indonesia. I guess there weren't too many other romantic prospects over there."

"So what happened?"

"The usual. She was a deejay, I was a photographer: the only thing we had in common was that we were never there. I'd go out usually at, like, six-fifteen in the morning, and she'd come home from work at four, four-thirty. Most of the time, we weren't even in the same time zone. But anyway, by then, I was too far gone for anything domestic. I mean, after seeing half the people in the world living in huts with no food, you kind of lose your appetite for Dutchess County. Plus, you get spoiled."

"In every sense of the word, I should think."

"Right. You get into this thing where you know you can go anywhere in the world, first class, and wherever you go, there's a

Mercedes waiting for you, and a squash court, and girls who will look at you as if you're some kind of war hero. And you get to know all the shortcuts: how to stay in the hotel in Manila where you can charge the girls to your room; how to change money in the street in Lima and then bill the company at official rates; how to find some kid in Africa who'll do all your hard work for you while you just sit around the Intercon counting the bikinis."

"And Diane?"

"Well, Diane and I were great as long as there were about five thousand miles between us. It's like you guys say: 'Asia to bed, Surrey to wed.' "

"And you lived in New York?"

"We lived all over. I'd got married before once, when I was a kid: to a girl in Saigon I met in a bar. That one lasted about as long as the flight back to L.A. But Diane and I did have something, some kind of connection. It was like telepathy sometimes. I remember this one time when I fell asleep, and she was right next to me, and I dreamed I met a woman in a restaurant. She invited me to dinner, this cute and friendly Korean girl, and we didn't know what was going to happen. And when I woke up, Diane was looking at me, real intense, like she was haunted. 'I've just had the strangest dream about you,' she said. 'About losing you to a Korean girl, who'd invited you to her house for dinner.' So it was like, sometimes, on one level, I couldn't get close to her at all; and on another level, we were so close I felt suffocated."

It may sound strange, but for all his worldly wisdom, I really did feel that in some way he was an innocent. Not in the way that one usually understands it; God knows, he'd seen plenty of wars, and enough corpses to stock a brigade. But there was still something undeveloped in him. Like one of those boys who's been so much the class leader that he's never really had the chance to be something less.

"You know, it was always truly weird with Diane," he went on, "but there was always something between us, and I could never get a handle on it. It was like sometimes I felt I was in a souk, in Cairo or Damascus, and the night was falling, and I was getting deeper and deeper into this maze, and there were people calling me from their stalls, all these men in hoods, with leering faces, and the last few words of English were disappearing, and the night was falling, and I was lost in some crazy swirl of patterns and colors and smells. And somewhere there was a muezzin calling. And this wild Arabic music in the dark. And men—only men—lined up along the outside of their stalls in hoods, their faces lit by candles, calling out to me, and all these swirling letters like sand on every side, and I could hear them calling, saying, 'Here, my friend. My friend, over here. I have something for you, friend. America, over here!' "

"And in the end you find . . ."

"You find you're lost. Completely wiped out. There is no you. Only a few candles, and some hooded faces, and the dark, and no idea at all how to get back to where you started."

He said nothing for a minute, and we let the silence rest. Then he held up the bottle to the waiter, and motioned for another.

"How about you, Hugo? Here I am, spilling out my guts, and you haven't said a thing. Just taking it all in, like a goddamn tape recorder. How about your love life?"

"Not much to talk about, really."

"But you've had some adventures."

"In a manner of speaking."

"That seems to be your favorite manner. You were to that manner born. When was the first?"

"First?"

"Romance."

"Well, there was a girl at Oxford, she used to sit behind me at all of Thomas Phipps's lectures. She'd been at school with my sister. I took her punting once, but neither of us was very experienced at that kind of thing, so it rather fell flat." He was silent now, expecting more. "I suppose the first time I was involved, in a more concrete sense, was in Seville."

"A girl with a rose beneath her teeth and a scarlet smile?"

"Not exactly. She was English, actually. Staying in the same pensión as I. We met over breakfast one morning in a café."

"And . . ."

"And . . . well, we spent the day together. Looking at the Moorish

*buildings. She was an art student, on holiday from Florence. And . . .
well, you know Seville; it's hard not to think of poems and guitars
when you're walking underneath all those balconies."*

"So you had her?"

"Well, not in so many words." *It struck me that he was patron-
izing me in much the same way the boys do sometimes: as if they
can't imagine that their teachers ever have hopes, or friends, or love
affairs—or any lives out of school.*

"And—let me guess—her name was Carmen."

"Imogen, actually."

"So you and Imogen got cozy in the cobbled alleyways of Seville?"

" 'Cozy'? Yes, that's rather a good way of putting it."

"Okay," *he said.* "End of interview. Let's crash."

*We got up then, a little the worse for wear, and returned to our
room. I must admit that I was warming to him in a way: he didn't
seem ill-intentioned, and I was beginning to suspect there might be a
kindness in him that he wouldn't acknowledge. Rather a Henry
Miller type in his way. Just as we were getting ready for bed, I asked
him—I don't know what made me do it, but it seemed the right question at the time—*"Do you have a girlfriend here in Cuba?"

"Do I, don't I, do I, don't I," *he said, stopping what he was
doing. And then I understood what he'd been wanting to talk about
all night. That was the first time I heard mention of a girl called
Lourdes.*

"I tell you, Hugo, it's like I was saying before." *I could hear his voice
in the dark, from the next bed, as if his mind was ebbing back and
forth.* "This place really turns you around. It leaves you feeling like
a pig at a barbecue. Like a stuffed pig at a bargirl's barbecue. I mean,
you know all these people have a native warmth and sexiness. And
you know they want to get everything they can from it. And you
know that in part they just want to have contact with the world."

"Exactly. Don't you think they're just happy to see us because
they live in such isolation? They just want to talk to us."

"Yes, I know. But there's more to it than that. The first time we
went out together, she knew I was a foreigner, right? And she started

coming on to me so strong, I just told myself, 'Whoa! This girl is ticketing herself faster than a travel agent!' But then, I don't know. I wrote her some cards, and she wrote me some, and she never asked for anything, and things got kind of blurred. And then, when I came back here, I got to thinking that maybe she liked me in spite of the fact that she had a reason to like me: that something more was going on."

"I can quite believe she did."

"So anyway, now I'm in kind of a state. I don't even know whether to call her mi novia or mi amiga."

"Compañera, I would have thought, is the usual locution."

"Thank you, Hugo; I appreciate it." I felt a little ashamed of myself. "You know, with the other girls, it was always real straight. Check in, sign the bill, check out again. No wasted motion, no hidden taxes. But with her, it's different. Even when she's not around, she's all around me. Usually, it's kind of like a light switch, and I can turn it on and off whenever I choose. But with her, it's more like a night-light or something. And even when I want to go to sleep, even when I need complete darkness, even when I'm ready to close up shop, there she is, still shining, still switched on in some part of me."

"Why don't you take her to America?"

"Easy for you to say. I'm married, for one thing. And anyway, what kind of life is she going to have over there? Where are her friends going to come from? And what if she is working for Fidel?"

"It's easy, I should think, to find reasons for not taking her. But reasons aren't really the point, are they?"

"Then what is the point?"

"Why don't you marry her? That sounds like the usual thing. Get a divorce and marry her."

"Sure. If I married her, I'd probably have to bill twice as many days as I do right now—two twenty, two thirty a year. I'd see even less of her than I do now."

"Sounds like an excuse to me."

"Great, Hugo; if you're so hot on this idea, why don't you marry her?"

"Thank you," I said, and felt again as if I were back in school.

"I'm sorry," he said, and I remembered how Americans are so

eager not to give offense. "I guess I'm just all tangled up. I'm sorry to have laid all this on you." And then he turned round, and I left him to his sleep.

It had been an exceptionally full evening, and I slept in late the following morning. When I awoke, it was already light, and he had gone out. Off to take more pictures, I suppose; I had to admit, his devotion to his job was quite exemplary. It was a curious thing, being alone in the room with his things, especially after our conversation of the night before: it was like the kind of intimacy you have at school sometimes, when you've been through so much with someone that, whether you like it or not, at some level you realize that you're bound together for life. And it was odd, too, to be surrounded by his things, the things he carried round with him. His press card was lying on the desk, and the wallet in which he kept his first wife's picture—he'd shown it to me over dinner, though now I think of it, it was his second wife, the Englishwoman—and a whole folder full of clippings about Revolutionary movements, and a handy Spanish phrasebook in which you could ask how much a duck à l'orange cost.

There was something oddly touching, actually, about all these things—all that they said about his various hopes and aspirations—and I suppose it was that which prompted me to do what I did next. It's not something I'm proud of, but it's also something I'm not terribly happy about keeping to myself—and it's easier to relate on paper (maybe that's why I'm writing this all down in the first place)—but I went across to the door, and pulled up the bolt, and then I slipped back and looked through his things. I have no excuse whatsoever for this—my only excuse, really, is that it's a habit I developed when I was an assistant housemaster. And in this instance, it reminded me of how one would find teddy bears hidden away amongst the boys' posters of rockets and soccer stars. Because the main thing I found in the pile was a diary. It was written in a rather childish hand, very large, with only a few sentences on every page. But the sentences were of a kind that rather shamed me. They were all about the secret book he hoped to put out that would, in his words, "educate the world." He had already decided he would give the profits to some organization called Direct Relief International, and take some of the money to give to some woman in the Philippines: he'd written down her daughter's date of birth on the front page. On the frontispiece, he'd even copied down—and this is so American, I couldn't help but think—"Changing the world is the only way of changing ourselves."

I did feel somewhat uneasy, intruding on his private self like that, but I'd already told myself that it would make me more sensitive to his interests, and more apt to see beneath the tough guy who kept banging on about his adventures. At breakfast, in fact, when he came up to my table by the beach, I found I was looking at him a little differently.

"Taking pictures of suffering and misery?" I said, and he looked a little taken aback.

"No way. Not on Cayo Largo." He looked at me strangely. "This is Bacardi country. Anyway, I'm going for a run, and then I'll see you in the lobby at, like, eleven o'clock. They said there's going to be a bus to the airport at eleven-fifteen."

There was, as it transpired, but it wasn't much of an airport, and there was certainly no plane.

"What's the story, compañero?" he asked one of the staff, who was sitting under a fern.

"No problem, señor. Please wait. Be patient. A plane will come."

So there we were, in this odd thatched hut, on an island full of turtles, engaged in the two most frequent activities in Cuba: sitting and waiting. I hadn't brought my backgammon set with me— hadn't brought anything other than the Kerouac and a Tom Robbins, though Richard had everything, for his work—and there wasn't much to do, what with the salsa music blasting out of the bar, but talk.

I don't recall every one of the details, but he gave me the kind of accounts that would have had the boys simply spellbound: actually, I had half a mind to invite him to the school sometime. He'd been to Afghanistan once, and had traveled sixty days—forty of them with diarrhea—to meet some guerrilla chieftain, whom no one had seen for four years. He'd spent a week with Lord Moynihan—the now *famous degenerate peer, from Eton I think, who used to run brothels in the Philippines, and married a new prostitute every year. He'd lived for a spell in Paraguay, with a local woman "to clean his house" and a collection of photographs of the president with his teenage girlfriends. And he was full of wisdom—if you can call it that—about how the best way to learn about a country was to cross-question the "Guest Relations" girls at all the best hotels, who apparently take their relations with guests very seriously indeed.*

All very impressive at one level, of course, but I couldn't help feeling that there was something sad about it too. Which feeling I articulated.

"Sure, it isn't the "Father Knows Best" dream. But someone's got to do it. Someone's got to go out there, and give up the easy chair and the two cars in the garage, and actually bring back reports from the world. Otherwise, there'd be no artists, no newspapers, no explorers. Some people are made to stay at home; some are made to wander."

"And you're one of the ones who are made to wander?"

"Yeah, I think so. And now I'm on this course, it's harder to get out than to just keep going."

"But don't you think there's something dangerous in all this? It seems to me that all this moving is partly a way of not asking any questions of yourself. And even the photography is a way of giving answers—concrete images—to questions no one's asked."

"Sure, you could look at it like that. But the way I see it, you've got to keep moving. You've got to keep your eyes open and fresh. You can't afford to fall into a routine. It's like this place. The first time, the second time you're here, it's just terrific: adventures every day. Come here for a week or two, and there's never a dull moment. But just imagine living here. It'd be a nightmare."

"But yours is hardly the kind of life on which to base a future. Always moving; always on the surface of things."

"I'm not thinking of the future: my job involves catching the moment. Right now, the here and now, the truth of this instant."

"And that's what you tell your girlfriends too?"

"Look, Hugo. I'm not saying this is the best life. And I'm not against commitment. But how many different commitments can you

make if you're going to give yourself fully to anything? And don't try coming off all high-and-mighty with me. Girls like it too. Maybe that's something they don't teach you in those schools of yours, but they get a kick out of romancing just like we do. It doesn't always have to be to have and to hold. And if they're asking for it, I'm not going to deny it to them."

I said nothing.

"And don't just say it's me. Go out East sometimes, and you'll find half your schoolmates screwing their way across the Orient. Swire's, Jardine's, W. I. Carr—all those Hong Kong firms are made for British schoolboys who need to prove their virility to the world. The Empire never died; it just got privatized."

There was silence.

"And they don't even get pictures out of it."

At that point—none too soon, on every count—the plane at last arrived, and we crowded into it and took a couple of seats in the back and ordered two Bucaneros. It wasn't exactly the Concorde: the toilet was a hole in the floor, with black knobs on the door like in all those old Tintin books set in Central Europe. One tiny hole in the wall said, "For Clothes," another said, "For Choes." It must have been the only door in the world where the Open and Closed signs were visible only from inside.

Richard, however, was in no mood for diversion. As soon as I returned from the loo, he started up again, and I felt again as if I was merely an audience to the conversation he was holding with himself.

"I don't know. I just don't know where one thing ends and the other begins. Like with Lourdes. My heart tells me one thing, my conscience another. Look at it one way, and it's selfish of me to focus on her, when there are ten million others suffering on this island, whose only crime is being less attractive to me. Look at it another way, and it's selfish of me to concentrate on their stories, when Lourdes is crying on my shoulder. You can't win."

"Or lose, either." And then I thought I was being too hard. "But yes, I do see what you mean. It's the same with the teaching, really.

It's not the most exciting job in the world, but one does feel as if one's having some good influence, perhaps. Or as if one can do a little bit to help them in later life."

"Sure. If you want to spend your whole life in a school."

"Quite so." Though, I'll confess, it seemed to me that he'd been doing the same thing.

"I'm sorry, Hugo. I'm boring you."

"No, not at all. It's fascinating."

" 'Fascinating'!" he said, and I felt the sting.

When we arrived at the airport, he shouted out for a taxi—he was always in a terrible hurry, so it seemed—and we drove back into Havana.

"Are you in the Nacional again?"

"No, the St. John's."

"Rather roughing it, isn't it—by your standards?"

"Yeah. But it works better this way. More privacy. More mobility. Also, I can engage in a little redistribution of income. Charge the magazine for the per diem, and then give all the extra money to the Cubans. Kind of like Communism in reverse: take from the system, give to the people." Another quixotic touch, I thought.

"So anyway, you want to get a beer before we call it a day?"

"Wouldn't say no."

"Maybe the Capri again?"

"Certainly."

Behind us, I heard a couple of men hissing for our attention.

"Hey, Canada?"

"No."

"Russos?"

"No."

"Inglés?"

He must have decided that it was too late for tricks; he pulled out a card that said "Periodista."

"My friend, hello!" The larger of the two boys came up and extended a hand. "How are jou?"

"Great. Just great."

"Jou like music? Jou come with me and John. We go to Malecón. We drink some rum, we find some girls, we go dancing with his sister."

"Great. I'd do anything to meet with any member of his extended family. It's what I came here for. To meet John's great-aunt, his great-aunt's cousin, his son-in-law. To get down with his neighbor." The boys looked confused, and then started smiling: I suppose from their point of view it was better to be in on the joke than outside it. *"O-ka. We go now, buy some ron, find some chicas. Jou come to Cuba, jou got to meet chicas."*

"Met plenty already, my friend. It's your grandmother's cousin I'm interested in." And then—rather effectively, I thought—he turned his back on them and walked on.

"You see that?" he said, as we went into the Capri. *"Now imagine they were girls. Wouldn't be easy to say no to them, right? And pretty soon, you're spinning like a top again. I mean, they're nice girls, but they want to get something out of you. And they don't know a thing about you, don't know you from Adam. So what's the basis of their love? They give you all these forget-me-nots, but you're no different from the next Hugo who comes along. The next guy with a credit card. I don't blame them; it's a matter of survival. But it makes you think love is just war conducted by other means."*

"Funny, though, that they took us for Russians."

"Every foreigner's a Russian here. Unless he's an American."

"Though, actually, I was rather thinking that you don't seem very American at all."

"Maybe because I've spent most of my life abroad. And half the time, in any case, I'm trying to pass myself off as a Canadian or a Brit."

"But even the way you talk isn't entirely American."

"Comes from being on the move, I guess. Having an English wife. Spending time in Hong Kong and Singapore. Working for the Sun-day Times, *perhaps. And with Diane—when we were together— I was locked into that whole English expat scene. The memsahib looking after the house and the amah looking after the blond kids,*

while Daddy looks after the business interests, most of them con-
cerned with his mistress in Manila and the Chinese secretary he
needs to take along to interpret for him."

   "It sounds to me sometimes as if you've almost seen too much of
the world."

   "And it sounds to me, Hugo, like you've seen too little."

And then I was back in the city of whis-
pers, of rumors and muffled kisses, of hints and solicitations. *"Eh,*
Richard, qué tal?" said Lázara, coming up to me suddenly on the
street and kissing me on both cheeks, her fourteen-year-old sorcerer's
eyes flashing. "Where have you been?" "Oh, everywhere." *"Dime.* I
knew you were here. My mother says she saw you in the street last
week. With a girl in blue, she said, a young girl, like a *novia."* "Must
have been José," I said, and thought of her mother in the empty
room, with its refrigerator and blinking TV, overlooked by Carlo
Marx. At the window all day, watching and waiting. "No, she says
it was you. She remembers your bag. From America, right?"

   Later, outside the Hotel Sevilla, a bus passed, and I was sure I
saw her, sitting talking to a boy with frizzy dark hair. "Lourdes," I
shouted, and then she turned, and for an instant I was sure I saw her
smile, but it was too difficult to catch, and the bus was turning, and
it was like a glimpse into another life, a secret self, all the sides of
her I hadn't seen. She didn't work, she had no place to go, why was
she riding the buses? And looking so different, with her hair up, and
her makeup different, like an actress taking the part of Lourdes?
Who was that guy I saw you with? That was no guy; that was my
life.

I was back in the spell again: I had to see
her. I headed toward Concordia, and as I got closer to her house, I
saw her in the street, arm in arm with the bearded guy we'd met,
laughing as they walked, and she whispering something to him.

   "Lourdes," I said, going up to her and grabbing her by the arm and pulling her toward the sea. "We've got to talk. I'm going crazy."

"You're hurting me, Richard."

"And you me. Who is this guy? What's going on here?"

"No one. I want to be with you."

"As long as I take you to dollar stores and nightclubs."

"No, Richard. That's not it."

"As long as I tell you stories of America and send you postcards of the world."

"No, Richard. It's you."

"So what do you want?"

"I want to see your pictures."

Of all the things in the world, that was the one I hadn't expected.

"You're saying that. You want to get on the right side of me."

"Okay! It's better I don't want?"

"Why do you want to see them?"

"I showed you the picture of my papá: I told you my life. You said you understand. Why can I not understand your life, your hopes?"

"You really mean it?"

"Of course I mean it."

"Okay. I have some pictures in my room. Not many: only the ones I always carry round with me. Like your crucifix, you know? To keep me from all evil, and remind me what I believe in."

"Any, Richard. I know nothing about your life. Your house, your mother and father, your job, your dreams. All I see is your camera."

"So we go back to my room?"

"No. That is no good. We cannot do it in the street. You come to my house tonight, we go to my sister's room."

"In the dark, right?"

"Why not? Always in the dark."

It must have been nine o'clock when we met, and her mother was already at the table, and Cari had been sent out to a nightclub, and it felt like we had the whole place to ourselves. But as soon as she saw me, she put a finger to her lips. "Don't talk, Richard," she said. "Everyone here is a spy of love."

"*Entonces Español?*"

"No. They will know you are no *cubano*. Please, Richard, for me: my sister's room is next to the neighbor's home. They will hear everything."

So we made all the preparations in silence, brought in a lamp from her room, and collected all the lights we could, and still it was like looking at prints in a darkroom almost: no way you could see the light and shade, and the colors lost their brightness. But it was either that or nothing, I figured, and even a little light was better than none at all. I was glad to give her this; it felt like I was handing her a candle and she was stepping across another threshold inside me, like the first time someone comes to your apartment, and starts rearranging your furniture. Or the first time she says your name aloud, while naked.

I began with Managua: pathos was there for the taking in those days, a civil war in a country full of poets that had been wiped out by an earthquake, and all the bright hopefulness and sadness of the rosy-cheeked *brigadistas* from Amsterdam and Boulder, and the weeping mothers, and the little girls in their Sunday dresses, and the fresh-faced junior-high-school boys saying goodbye to their sweethearts as they went off to die. Managua was a sermon waiting to be delivered. This is what Washington's money does. This is what Moscow's ideas achieve. Fools on the left and rogues on the right; and the people, unsuspecting, always in the middle.

And this is what happens to people without defenses: in front of a church, the streets run red with blood. Kids practice curveballs next to ditches piled high with corpses.

I showed her the other pictures I'd brought for her, most of them of kids: the eleven-year-olds on the streets of Angeles, the smiling boys, with young monks' faces, who join the Karen fighters in the Shan States, the orphan centers along the Cambodian border. I showed her some pretty stuff too—laughing dancers in Ubud, and lantern festivals in Hiroshima, and the strange stone faces you find if you ride horses through the valleys of Colombia. And I finished with the picture of her and the girls on the balcony.

I couldn't tell what she made of it, but when she was through, she looked at me, again without words, and motioned me to go through the pages again, and then, when we were done, she said, simply, "Thank you, Richard."

Then we undressed quickly, in silence, and when I wanted to say, *"Mi amor"* or "I want you," she put a finger to my mouth, or kissed me into silence.

And so, in the half-light, I took her in silence. I ran my hand along her body, and her eyelids fluttered, but she never murmured. And I pulled her to the bed, and lay on her back, kissing her up and down, on the pulse of her neck, on the underside of her ear, under her damp, tousled hair. And we went through the whole strange ceremony without words, like a married couple—no involuntary gasps, no statements of love, no shivers or gasps or moans. No promises, too, and no lies.

"If we were in Varadero," she whispered, afterward, and I said, "If we were in Varadero, what? You could be yourself? You could make up a part to please me? You could say all the things you think I want to hear?"

"Why so difficult, Richard? You know my situation."

"I know you're scared. But what's more important, your fear or your love?"

"This is Havana: how can I tell them apart?"

I stroked her hair, then, in silence, and she rested her head on my shoulder, and we both thought back, I knew, to the pictures we had seen. And every time, I thought, it was the same choice between talking and love: either we could talk freely in English, along the Malecón, or in Maxim's, or in the Central Hospital, or we could make love, and leave our speaking selves outside. Either we shared our minds, or we shared our bodies.

Afterward, there was the silent promise, and the sudden departure, and the walk through the darkened streets, and the long night, in our beds, alone.

Those were the days of midsummer heat: scorching afternoons and sultry nights. Clothes were getting looser, straps were falling off shoulders, shorts were getting shorter. Sometimes there were kisses when we met, but when I kissed her sometimes, I sensed her looking over her shoulder, or speaking under her breath. "Come," she said one day, "it is safer in the hospital." When we got there, they checked my camera bag at the entrance, and the woman got out my Olympus and looked at Lourdes through the lens. "*Qué bonito,*" she said, and handed it back to me with a smile. "Here it is always safe," Lourdes said to me quietly, "no problem," and sometimes I wondered whether she was turned on by all this cloak-and-dagger stuff, and sometimes I wondered whether she wanted to turn me on with it. Or maybe it was just that whispering was a habit here, the way bowing might be in Japan.

"Look, Richard," she said as we sat down amid the emergency patients. "For me, is better if we go out with some others. Already there are people watching us. They see us talking. They talk. They think, this *cubana* is with this stranger every day. They tell their friends, their friends tell their friends—in the Party. We need to change our color. Perhaps you can find a friend? I bring Rosita, and then we are like a different group."

"Who? José?"

"Not José. He doesn't like me."

"Then who?"

"You have other friends in Havana?"

"Sure, some guys at the embassy, a woman who takes pictures for the *New York Times,* a kid I hang out with in Miramar. No one I can trust."

"There is no one in your hotel?"

"Maybe one guy; I'll see what I can swing." And then, in a flash, I thought: *perfecto!*

It *was* perfect; here was a deal where everyone could gain. I never felt entirely sure of Hugo, always felt that even when I took his picture, something was missing. I could catch the face, the glasses, the mild-mannered schoolteacher: but there was still something hidden, which I couldn't see. I still couldn't figure out if he was here to make mulattas on the sly, or on some kind of super-undercover gig like his uncle, or whether, as with many of those upper-class Brits, still waters just ran shallow. What you saw was what you got.

But I knew he'd be grateful for company. And I knew he'd be the perfect partner: better than a Cuban, who'd be a walking security risk, way better than an American, who'd have friends behind him in the bushes—or anyone else who had strong opinions about the Revolution. Hugo would fit in like the invisible man.

So the next morning I went down to the Libre, and I found him in the dining room—he always got up at eight, he'd told me, and went promptly for breakfast at eight-thirty—and then I told him to meet me outside the Yara at eight that evening, for a surprise. When I got there, I didn't know what to think: he'd gotten himself up in this kind of white tropical suit, with a handkerchief in his breast pocket and a striped shirt. Like Humpty Dumpty playing Noël Coward.

When the girls arrived, forty minutes later, he looked kind of shocked: they were decked out in the usual style, in their spangles, Lula in her backless shirt and jeans, and Rosita in some short, frilly afterthought that ended at the thigh. Whatever else was going to happen, this was going to be worth the price of admission.

Hugo extended a hand toward them, but Lula, after what I'd told her, came up and kissed him on both cheeks, and long cool ebony Rosita, with her Ethiopian queen's neck, and legs that never stopped, just grabbed him by the hand and smiled. I've got to say, the poor guy took it well: *"Encantado,"* he said in his best colonel's accent, and she responded, sweetly, *"Encantada."*

The girls were hot for action—this was their night on the town with dollars—and so we went to the Capri. The hostesses were lined up like sweetcakes, and muttered when they saw us, while the teenage girls winked and giggled, and a few boys shuffled pesos from palm to palm. Lula whispered something to the guy at the door, kissed someone on the cheek, slipped a few notes in the right direction, and then the doors opened, and we were in like Flynn.

Inside, María Christina was singing some love song, and boys were flashing silver smiles and running their hands up and down bare backs. A few girls in the corner were trading kisses for pesos, and I recognized Nelida, from Santa María, at a little table covered with bottles of rum. Hugo looked as if he'd landed on a different planet. "Quite extraordinary," he said. "Unchanged in thirty years."

"You should see the joints in Vietnam. Midget hostesses in Dior dresses, sixty-five-year-old dudes playing clarinet and saxophone like Sihanouk himself, all the vodka you can drink." But Hugo had stopped listening to me. Rosita was standing by his side, with her arm around his waist, while the headwaiter winked and promised us a good table, a good deal. Hugo, I could see, had his hands full.

As usual, the main show, farther in, started at eleven, and the music was just a lot of Perry Como / Tony Bennett schmaltz to get the kids into a romantic mood, and soon the girls were singing along, closing their eyes, and the guys at the other tables were getting all smoochy, and I was just waiting for the fun to start.

Until it did, we made sure Hugo wouldn't get away, and we dragged him onto the dance floor, and soon all four of us were shaking it, though with Hugo it wasn't so much dancing as a kind of shuffling in place, his face getting redder and redder, while he pulled at the rim of his glasses every now and then, and looked as if he were practicing one of those insane medieval exercises they teach them in those schools.

"Get down, Hugo," I shouted over to him. "Shake it like you mean it."

"Thank you," he huffed back, "I'm trying," and I guess I kind of warmed to him right then. Lula had found her rhythm, and was swaying in place, very slow, very easy, none of that merengue madness but a more controlled kind of sensual shaking, beads of sweat forming at her temples, her straps sometimes slipping off her shoulders, her eyes telling me the same things they told me at home. Rosita was doing a sort of African thing, more tribal, with the spirits of the Yorubas dancing through her. Around us, on the floor, there were wet kisses and whispers, and the promise of more dollars.

"Hugo," I said as we went back to our seats, "I think she likes you."

"She can't really help it, poor girl," he said back.

"Get out there and wow 'em, Hugo."

"Indeed I will," he said, and I felt kind of soft on the guy again. In the craziness of Havana, he was like a long, cool glass of water sometimes; his very lack of color was what made him refreshing.

When we got back to the table, Lourdes was looking loosened up, and getting kind of amorous, and Rosita, well prepared, kept filling up Hugo's glass. The drink was getting to me too—I felt light and reckless—and I began touching my friend under the table, and trailing my finger along her secret parts, and down the cool cleft of her spine, and she, kind of excited and kind of drunk, was flicking my ear with her tongue.

Pretty soon, we were getting carried away, and I figured we might as well be making tracks.

"We'll see you guys later," I said, pulling her up and slipping the cash to Rosita, who was telling some mad, passionate story about her mamá—hands flying all over the place—and Hugo, looking kind of ruffled and red-faced, was taking it all in with polite nods. "Take good care of him, Rosie," I called as we left.

Then we were out, past the crowds, and out into the warm, still air. I led her by the hand down La Rampa, and off into one of the side streets. It was dark. It was silent. It was ours.

We found a little space in front of a boarded-up house, and we sat down in the dark. There were faint circles around Lourdes's eyes, and the beginning of lines: twenty-four, and already a creature of darkness.

I leaned forward to give her a kiss, and she laughed, and dug her nails into my neck.

"Slowly," I said. "Be patient. Like a Cuban," and I slipped the straps off her shoulders, and rolled them down her arms, and kissed her skin down to her breasts. There were murmurs above me, and I turned her, and moved further, feeling the unfastening cloth with my mouth, up, up, up, to the base of her neck, and then the back of her hair, where her skin was damp, and then the side of her cheek. She squirmed and shivered. I turned her over again, and slowly, slowly, pulled down her zipper.

"Not here," she said. "Too dark."

"Here," I said, and I brought down the whole rough fabric of her jeans, and pushed into her.

"Someone will see us," she said.

"Not here," I said, urgent in the dark, and her words gave way to cries.

The next day, when I went down to Centro, Rosita was with Lourdes at the breakfast table. The girls looked terrible: no makeup, old shirts, ugly shorts. That was the way it always was here: bright threads for the evening, and rags for everything else. The young girls looked at their mothers—even their sisters—and saw that the glamour was not going to last much past tomorrow night.

"Your friend is very sexy," Rosita said.

"I'll bet he is. Like a cold shower—or a plate of boiled vegetables."

"No, it's true." She looked hurt. "He was telling me about his life. A woman he once loved, and how he lost her, and how he comes to Havana because he doesn't want to get old." It didn't sound much like the guy I knew.

"When did he impart all this?"

"Last night. At the Capri, and then we went to the Malecón, and sat on the wall. Just talking. Looking at the sea. He's so romantic, so gentle. Not like a Cuban guy—they only want to get into your pants."

"Or an American," said Lourdes, looking up at me slyly.

"You know, he never even kissed me."

"Probably gay."

"Gay?" Rosita said. "No way. I can tell he's not gay. I know."

"He's just jealous," said Lula. "Wishes he could be more like that."

"Yeah, right. Wish I could say, 'Oh, sorry. Do you think it would be possible for me to come?' "

"Be quiet, Richard," said Lourdes. "Can you find Hugo again? So we can go out tonight?"

. . .

And we did end up going out a few times after that, till it felt like quite a team. He really did seem to go well with them—I guess shyness or inexperience or whatever can seem like a turn-on in a place where everything's always hanging out— and he warmed to their attention. He still seemed kind of a soggy chair to me, washed out in some way—always sitting for some Snowdon photograph—but he was easy company, and when the heat was around, which it always was, I felt better with him there. Lula was right. In Russia and China, they only get uptight if a foreigner's with some woman who *isn't* a professional.

Sometimes, though, the whole setup made me kind of queasy. Usually, I could just tune Hugo out—it was like, when they've got dance music in one corner of the room, you never notice Debussy in the other. But I remember there was one night at the new bar in Marianao, one of those open-air places that had begun to open up, not far from the Tropicana, for Cubans to dance in—a kind of counterrevolutionary Tropicana. We'd been there for a while, and I was feeling pretty juiced, and Lula was in the mood, and I kind of forgot Hugo was around.

It was the usual scene: teenagers mooning into each other's eyes, the *colas* an excuse for everyone to stand closer to one another, the boys holding the girls, with their arms around them in all the right places. The boys from Habana Vieja wriggling on the floor—their homemade kind of break dance—and their sisters waving their asses around. We went off for drinks, and on the way, I took Lourdes's hand and led her to a corner of the garden and told her what I'd like to do with her, and she gave me her soft, thoughtful kind of smile, and I leaned forward and kissed her through her T-shirt.

When we got back, Hugo was just sitting there, alone at the table, watching us in that schoolteacher way of his.

"Where's Rosita?"

"Believe she went to the loo," he said. And then, pointing to my pants: "I believe your slip is showing, as they say."

I looked down, and saw that Lourdes's bra was hanging out of my pocket, where I'd stuffed it. It made me feel kind of funny, to tell the truth, him telling me that, and her sitting there too, and the wet round circles on her T-shirt.

The very next day, Lourdes had to go to the dollar store. For a pot her mother needed.

"Okay," I said. *"Vamos."*

"No, Richard." She pulled at my arm. "It's too dangerous. If we go again, they will begin to see us. They look for these things. They make notes. The guards at the counter. The taxi drivers. They know us too well."

"Then what do you propose? I give you my passport, you go alone?"

"No, no."

"I go alone?"

"No. You don't even have a pot—you tell me you do not have a kitchen. How will you know what to look for? I remember you told me that in your refrigerator you keep only film."

"So what do you want me to do?"

"Find a friend to come. Maybe Hugo."

"Hugo, Hugo, always Hugo."

"What's wrong? Are you jealous of Hugo?"

"Sure. I'm really jealous of an out-of-shape teacher whose idea of a good time is reading a new translation of *The Peloponnesian War.*"

"You sound jealous. You do not marry me, but you want to own me."

"I'm just tired of Hugo, that's all. Hugo's become like our dog or something. He's cute, we take him everywhere, we always want to cuddle him. We've become hostage to him. Dangling like puppets on a string. I don't know why you have any time for him."

"He sees me. Rosita too. He listens to us. With him, I never feel like a *jinetera,* or a Tropicana dancer. It's as if I have a true life. He's not a *bailando suave* kind of guy; not a playboy. He treats me like a woman."

"Maybe that's because he's scared shitless. He doesn't know what to do or say with a woman—he's probably never been with one before."

"So what? How does that change anything? Maybe it makes it better. Anyway, I think he is sweet, and anything you say is not going to change it. He is the first man I've met who is not always thinking of his *machismo*. For him, the *pinga* is not everything."

"I'll say. For him, it's nothing."

"Okay. You laugh. But you are the same. Before, I thought it was only Cuban men who were like this. But now I see the strangers— I mean, the foreigners—are all the same: Mexicans, Argentinians, Spanish, Italians. Why do they come here? Why do you come here? When you meet a woman here, do you think of what her life is like? No, you only think of how long it will take."

"Fine. If that's how you feel, you can go out with him. The only straight man in Havana who won't attack you. I don't have to take care of you, and help your mother."

"Richard, don't be crazy." She leaned across the bed then, and, in the dark, she took my hand, and slowly, very slowly, she guided it here and there. I felt the static of her hair, the cold skin at the back of her neck. I felt the warmth coming up from various places, I felt hard places and soft. She slipped my hand under her shirt, and she collected one finger and took it in her mouth. Another night of darkness. Darkness and silence and wetness all around.

There was nothing much going down the next night. I'd told Lula we'd take a break—allow the plainclothesmen to spend at least a night at home with their wives—and I'd taken all the pictures I needed already. There wasn't much I could work with at night anymore, because everything was undercover now, like a samizdat whisper just beneath the sound barrier. The sound of deals being made, and love, plots being hatched and leaked, friends being made and exchanged, the whole gray surface of the day peeled back like a sticker on a package. In the Colina and the Presidente, around the side streets of Centro and the corners of the Parque Central, from one end of the city to the other, the steady rustle of questions. "Change money?" "*Qué quieres?*" "*Por qué no, mi amor, por qué no?*"

I figured I might as well drum up some action of my own this time, so I went to Coppelia, and checked out the kids along the circumference, then got in line for an ice cream. A tall black kid appeared at my side. "Hey, how you doing?" he said in slick English. "You remember me? Walter. From Habana Vieja. Before, we talked about the *nueva trova*. You like the Cuban music, right?" I remembered him, and the smooth lines he'd picked up from his Jamaican father. "We're having a party tonight. Right now, in Miramar. Come along," he said, and I figured it was as good as anything—a trip into the unknown—and so we hopped a bus and drove along the wide deserted avenues, past rows of decaying mansions.

Inside the house—two large, empty rooms—a Danish professor was sitting on the couch, politely sifting through some Cuban records. A boy with golden hair was showing off the Laura Branigan records he'd bought in Africa. The party, I guessed, would be the four of us and the empty room.

"Great to meet you," said the kid, in the easy deejay patter he'd picked up in Angola, and when I heard he'd been in Africa, I decided to become a Canadian again.

"How you like our country? It's great, isn't it? Greatest country in the world."

"I think so. But not everyone in Cuba seems to think so."

"What do they know? They haven't seen the world. I tell them, 'You go to Africa, you come back a patriot.'"

"Sure. I can see that." He smelled of aftershave, and gave off the kind of sheen you didn't usually see around here. "You picked up a lot over there."

"Sure. I learned English. I got records, stereo system, everything."

"And the war?"

"It's nothing. It's something we've got to do, right? Help our friends in need. Like the *yanquis* in Grenada. Like the Russians in

Afghanistan. Before, we had help from the Germans in our Revolution. Now it is our turn to help others."

"You think you are helping the Angolans? I was down in Kinshasa one time . . ."

"Sure. We're helping the world. Teaching them things. Showing them they can make it. A small country does not have to be a weak country. The *yanquis* don't understand this. They just say, 'Communist menace,' 'Red under the bed,' all that shit. They have these guys—like Springsteen—say, 'Born in the U.S.A.' Just imperialist propaganda."

"You think Springsteen's an imperialist?"

"Of course. Why does he sing that song?"

The Dane was studiously reading liner notes, Walter was sitting on his hands against the wall. I knew this was a conversation that was going to get a lot worse before it got better. "Look, I've got to cruise now. It's been great meeting you."

"Sure," said the kid. "Great to meet you." He had no rancor: I half expected him to ask me if I could get Springsteen's autograph for him.

"I'll show you the way," said Walter. We walked along a deserted street that looked like some set from a Capra movie, so quiet and suburban, a leafy calm from another time, and then a guy suddenly came at us from the shadows.

"Your papers?" he said to us in English.

Walter got out his *carnet;* I decided my passport would be better than the press card.

"Italian, huh?" he said. "Maybe I talk to you." And he turned to Walter. The kid looked up at him politely, and motioned me with his hand to take myself off to the bus.

I left him there, then, paying the price of a dialogue in English.

The next afternoon, after I'd mopped up some of the side streets, I went to pay my dues with the Interests Section, listening to some guy who'd been in Moscow, Prague, all the places guaranteed to make you a Revolutionary, tell me how he'd wept when he'd seen Fidel take the country on TV, how the guerrillas had been his heroes as a kid, but "now, it's like being betrayed by the only woman you love." Standard State Department stuff: we hate to do this, and we respect and honor our enemy's interests, but . . .

As I walked down Concordia, toward Lourdes, I heard the tinkling of a piano from a broken house; saw a bust of Martí, on the left, through falling buildings; caught flashes of a pure blue sea. As usual, there was everywhere the smell of rotting food, as much a part of Centro as the stink of spilled strawberry ice cream was the perfume of Coppelia.

Her mother was there when I arrived, sitting drably at the table, waiting for something, anything—some gossip, a new saucepan, a letter from her son in New Jersey. Around her there was a whole chattering circle of girls, like tropical birds in the treetops: Caridad, in her tight turquoise top, thick, as usual, with circles of perspiration; Lula's cousin Marielita, dressed for a party in a sheer, braless halter, her huge brown eyes ringed in black; and Lula, in some sleeveless white thing, her gold cross delicate against olive skin. A few other girls too, whom I didn't know, called Concepción and Aurelia and América. And there, in the middle of them all, Hugo, looking kind of embarrassed, in one of those green army-issue British sweaters, grinning at everything they said and looking a little nervous, sweating furiously around the temples and tapping his fingers on his legs.

"Hello," he said. "Didn't expect to see you here."

"Nor I you. Are you gathering intelligence?"

"In a manner of speaking," he said. "Researching the potency of beer." I tried to size up how they were pairing off.

"So, Richard," said the mother. "Where do you go?"

"New York."

"New York." She looked appreciative. "So you know Ramón Fonseca?"

"Don't think so."

She looked surprised. "New York is a big town?"

"Like Havana."

"Bigger, actually," said Hugo. "As big as all Cuba, in fact, in terms of population."

She ignored him. "But here in Havana, I know everyone. You're sure you've never met him?"

"Sure."

"You go back when?"

"Two days from now."

Slowly, she got up and trudged off to her room. While she did, another girl sauntered in, and there was kissing all around. *"Me voy,"* said Marielita, and she stayed where she was. The new girl gave her news, and the other girls hissed and chattered, and Hugo gave an embarrassed grin, and Marielita said, *"Vamos,"* and went to the fridge to get some water.

The mother came back, and gave me a folded letter, addressed to someone in St. Pete.

"You can take this for me?"

"No problem." I knew that that was the deal here: they were your eyes and ears in Cuba, you were their link to the world. A cameraman and a carrier pigeon. When I got back to the hotel, I'd check the letter out. After what had happened before, I figured that Cubans with letters were like Palestinians with bombs—willing to plant them even on their pregnant girlfriends.

Lula and Cari went into their bedroom, and the rest of us sat and talked, but no one had anything to say. *"Me voy,"* said Marielita, and she showed no sign of moving.

"Richard, can you tell me one thing?" someone asked. "Why does my father never write? When he went to Mariel, I was a child. I talked to him for an hour by the boat. He told me that he loved me, that he would never forget me, he told me that he'd send me money and a ticket to join him." Her eyes were almost watering. "Every month I send him a letter. I am always waiting for him. Why does he never write?"

"My *abuela* the same," said América.

"Many times, the letters never arrive," I said, though that sounded hollow even to me. "Many times, the government takes them."

"What government?"

"Yours, mine; it makes no difference."

"*Me voy al Malecón*," said Marielita, and she disappeared into the bathroom. We heard her relieving herself—nothing was private here—and when she came out, she'd changed out of her Flintstones T-shirt into a kind of loose white vest, and her tiny denim shorts were a ball in her hand, leaving her with nothing below the waist but some flimsy white underthing and the outline of her pants. "*Me voy*," she said, and Lourdes's mother sighed as if another body was being lost to the Revolution.

"Rather a *Delenda est Carthago* scene, don't you think?" said Hugo, and the girls, following nothing, looked at him in wonder.

"Sure," I said, and there was silence again. A little later, Lula and Cari came out, ready to party, in happy colors, with skimpy T-shirts down to their brown thighs, and some lipstick they'd cadged from a neighbor who'd married a Mexican.

"*Vamos*," said Lourdes, and I got up, looking to see what Hugo would do.

"Richard," she said, "before we go, you can show my mamá your American Express?"

The whole group leaned in even closer, around the table, as I pulled out my credit card.

"And how much you can buy with this?"

"Anything. I can buy a TV. A CD player. A plane ticket. But it's dangerous. You have to pay it all back next month."

They looked at it in silence, and relayed questions to Lourdes. "And when does it stop? When you die?"

"More or less."

They handed it around, and pronounced my name on it, and tried not to smudge it with their fingers, and Lourdes explained how it was run through a machine that read the code.

"You have others? Visa, MasterCard?"

"Sure," I said, trying to show her this wasn't my favorite line of questioning.

"Then show Mamá. Show them all." I shook out the whole batch, including my frequent flier cards, and my library card, and a few strangers' business cards I kept handy for giving out at road-blocks.

There was silence at first, then excited conversation.

"And you have cards you can put in a machine and get money?" "Yes." "In any place?" "Anyplace in the U.S., sure." "And you have computer cards for the rooms in hotels?" "Sometimes." "Here in Cuba we do not even have keys."

"I think we should be going now, don't you?" I said to Hugo.

"Actually, I think I'll stay here for a while," he said.

"Okay. I'll catch you later."

"Goodbye, Richard," said the mother, coming up to me as I rose. "Take good care of Lula. Be good to her." She stood still for a moment, her hand resting on my shoulder. "She is a good girl. Take care of her." I didn't know whether it was a blessing or a warning.

That night, like most nights, we got no farther than the stoop. The taxis weren't running, and the bars downtown were shuttered, and the girls didn't want to walk. So Lula just went into some neighbor's house, and came back with a bottle of rum, and Cari went off in search of a party somewhere, and then the two of us were sitting against the wooden door, and I was letting her tell me about the glories of America.

"Look," she said, taking a long swig from the bottle. "In America, you can have everything you want. Everything. You want a car, a video, a washing machine, you can have it."

I'd heard this conversation before, and more than once. "And you don't work, you get nothing."

"Yes. But you have choices. Look at my brother. In Cuba, he got nothing. Intelligent. Handsome. Hardworking. But he can do nothing here. Only the same as a deaf old man. So he goes to America in March, and already he is making business. In New York; New York, New Jersey. You know this place?"

It was easier to say I did.

"And he has color TV. Swimming pool. Lincoln Continental. He is like a Party official there."

"But I'll bet he misses Cuba."

"Of course he says he misses Cuba. But he never comes here. Who misses poverty?"

Some boys ambled down the street and stopped to ask the time, and one of them, noting I had a watch, asked me why Michael Jackson had a white face. Then they borrowed the bottle from Lula, took a swig each, and went on their merry way.

"You see, Richard? You see what the young people in Cuba do? Nothing. They can talk or they can drink. They can sleep or they can make love. That's it. In your country, you can do anything at night."

"Like sleep."

"But you have freedom."

"Sure. Freedom to suffer, to sit out all night, to do drugs or psychotherapy. I know it's no party here, Lourdes. I know you can't live. But it's not so great in other places too. You saw my pictures."

"That is your job. You make money out of misery. You need to find suffering. That is your mission too, I think. If you are in New York, you look only for photos of people starving in the streets, dirty people, dying people. Of course the world looks terrible to you."

"That means it is terrible. I don't make the news; I just record it."

"But what I would record is different. What you see is not the truth; it is Richard's truth."

"Maybe."

"And I have different eyes."

I could see this was going nowhere, so I walked her across to the seawall, our home away from home. I was getting impatient now—I'd drunk too much—and she was getting antsy too.

"Lourdes," I said. "We can't keep doing it like this. Always meeting in the alleyways, always making love in silence, always keeping everything a secret. It isn't real."

"Then you have two choices. You can marry me, or you can take me to Varadero."

"What's so special about Varadero? How's it going to make anything different between us?"

"Varadero is not Cuba. I can be there with you. For that time only, I am not a Cuban. We can kiss, we can talk, we can make love there; we are not from different countries there. Here, if they find you making love to me, they put me in prison, like a *puta*. You understand? When you showed me the pictures, you told me how families and villages in every country are proud of their daughters, whatever they do. But here, where is there room for pride? Only if you escape."

"And you want the freedom to find out that the places you dream of are not like your dreams?"

"*Claro.* I want only this freedom. If I do not have that, I am always thinking of Florida or Bolivia or Barcelona."

We fell silent then, and I looked out at the sea. Sometimes the place was so beautiful it made you want to cry almost. It was like seeing some young, lovely woman on the arm of a short, sleazy general. The soft breeze off the sea; the intermittent lights of cars, winking along the Malecón; the Nacional above us, like a giant beached galleon: it was like a romantic's Eden. And here I was with the brightest Eve in Havana, and she was asking me to rescue her from Paradise.

Then she was touching me on the leg, and her eyes were blazing as she talked. "Do you know what it is like, Richard, to live in a shadow? Everywhere I walk, there is the shadow of *El Líder*. He is everywhere I turn. His face is in the next room, and his eyes are watching through the window, and his voice is on the television in the neighbor's house, and his words are on the radio, and in *Granma*. He is everywhere: there is no room left for me. Except in the shadows.

"You come here, and for you everything is beautiful: the blue skies and the quiet beaches and the colored houses and the pretty girls. But the ocean is closed to us. The beaches are for tourists only. Even the skies are forbidden. I cannot get on a plane and visit you. I cannot do anything unless I am with a foreigner. I cannot buy a sandwich, I cannot help my mother, I cannot give my friend a birthday present, unless I am with a foreigner."

"But you don't know what it was like before. You never saw it under Batista. You think it was better when there were three hundred whorehouses in the city, and five families in every six lived in *bohíos,* and the Americans just came down and gave you ten cents to do them under the roulette table?"

"Because it was bad then does not mean it is good now. Because I was sick when I was a young girl does not mean I cannot be sick now. You keep asking me why I can only live in the dark. But what else is left for me? It is the only place where I do not have to see his face, and I do not need to look at the old posters, and I can be myself. I can only be myself here if no one is looking at me."

"Okay," I said. "That's enough talking," because I knew where this would lead, and I knew we'd been there before. It made me think of a tide, and when it rolled out, it revealed all these glittering things along the beach, and then it came in again, and all of them disappeared.

I took her by the hand, and we left the sea, and walked down toward Habana Vieja. Along San Rafael, thumping with music beneath us, and past the red-lit nightclub in the basement of the National Theater; past the Cine Rex and the Hotel Bristol and the Cinecito. Past the América Libre electronics store, all boarded up now; past the kids circling the park. Sometimes a Chevy shuddering past, or whispers round a *colectivo.*

We walked across the darkness of the Parque Central, where the money changers hissed *"Qué hora es?"* at me, and down to a dark, small plaza. She turned toward me, and I felt her nipples through her T-shirt, and she bent down, and kissed me through my jeans, her tongue making circles on the fabric. I pulled her down, and traced her outline with my mouth. Then I stood her up again, and backed her against a tree, and we were hardnesses soldered together. For a moment, we were outside everything, far from Cuba, far from darkness, outside time, caught in a flashbulb light. Then we were alone again, in a dark plaza in Habana Vieja, with our different lives, and the eyes of the Leader watching us through the slatted windows.

We'd arranged to meet again the next morning, in Vedado, and I'd figured we'd need to do some last-minute shopping, and then maybe I could get her to come to the hotel with me for a last-night celebration. I wanted to give her something to remember me by—I realized then she still didn't have any photos of me except the one that José had taken—so I put on the white shirt that I knew she liked, and I washed my hair at eight-thirty exactly, so it would look just right when we met at ten, and I didn't shave the day before, so I could get an extra-close shave today. I wanted her to see I cared.

It was a bright and quiet morning, with billowing clouds, by the time I reached the ocean, and the sea looked like a pair of blue eyes, guarded but ready to sparkle: the usual Cuban mix of surrender and suspicion. I leaned against the wall and watched the buses make the turn and labor toward downtown; followed the chambermaids up above, searching the bushes of the Nacional for stray bottles to take home; saw the kids just looking out to sea. I began to get restless after a while, and looked at my watch. Ten-fifteen. Then ten-twenty-five. Then ten-thirty. I was beginning to sweat in the heat, and the lines I'd prepared for her were slipping from my mind, or souring.

"Hey, Lula," I said as I saw her approaching, and then I realized it was just another dark girl in a spangled T-shirt, and my smile had been wasted. It was ten forty-five now, and I had lost forty-five minutes. Forty-five minutes with no photographs. Forty-five minutes with no Lula. Was she getting cold feet? I thought. Had I got the wrong place? Was the whole thing a setup?

And then I saw her running toward me from the bus, breathless, but with a smile.

"What happened?"

"Oh, you know how it is here."

"No, how is it?"

"Different, Richard. You have been waiting?"

"Yes. I have been waiting."

"I'm sorry. *Pero ahorita,* I want to do something special for you. Show you someplace you have never seen."

"The dollar store at the Hotel Vedado?"

"No." She looked hurt. "I want to go to the cemetery. Cementerio Colón. You know this place?"

"I don't think so."

"Come. I will show you. It is something I promised myself: like a prayer. Richard must see this before he goes. Then he will know how it is for me. This is the only place in Havana where I can go to be calm. I want to share it with you. So it is not my place, but ours."

We crossed the street, and waited for the *guagua*. They were still running then, in the daytime, and we jumped on one, and she gave me two of the five-centavo coins that felt like play money, and we followed Calle 23 up, up, up, toward the Hemingway farm, past the Avenida de los Presidentes, past the Banco de Sangre, past the Cine Charlie Chaplin.

"You know why they like Charlie Chaplin here?" she whispered in my ear. "Because he is like the government. A fool. Small, cute, full of tricks. And always the ending is sad."

I put my arm around her waist, and thought how everything was like the government here: the government was so ubiquitous that everything seemed to reflect on it. When we came to the baseball cafeteria José had told me about, we got out, and in front of us stood the huge ceremonial archway of the cemetery gate, the robed Virgin resplendent at its top.

We passed through the grand entrance and walked into the city of the dead. There were giant sepulchers everywhere, ornate, sculpted, with weeping angels and robed saints and family histories, and huge domed monuments and marble plaques; there were walled tombs and minichurches, and thirty-foot statues of Jesus with his arms extended for forgiveness. On Calle 1 and C, she pointed out a statue of Innocence, eyes blindfolded. At the Milagrosa—a statue of an upright figure, clutching a small cross with her right hand, and cradling a baby with her left—women were placing roses in her fingers, and touching the lid of the brass casket beneath, and walking around the statue counterclockwise, some touching the feet on the baby, others resting their flowers in tree-trunk vases at the base. There was no noise here, and no commotion. Only the silent, touching ceremony of the women and, now and then, a long, slow procession of white station-wagon hearses and mourners all in black.

"You see what I mean?" said Lourdes softly. "You see why I

come here? Something here is pure, is clean. Like in the days before. It is like we are no longer in Havana."

"I see," I said, and my anger of an hour before was forgotten.

"Here I can come and feel empty," she said, walking away from me. "There are no posters of El Señor here. No slogans. No offices. Nothing can go wrong here, nothing reminds me of our world. When I am tired sometimes, when I am worried, I come here, and my mind is calm."

"Only here?"

"Only here. Because no one is making a deal here, no one whispers from the corner, no one tries to hear what we are saying. I could say anything to you here—about Fidel, about my hopes, about Martí, anything. But I do not want to. I want to forget all that. It is like a church for me."

"A sanctuary, kind of?"

"Sanctuary?"

"Tranquilo?"

"Tranquilo, yes. When I am here, I am free to think." A small family walked past, carrying roses to a marble statue. They walked slowly, and with dignity, together. "You see the people?" she said to me. "They are different here, pure. They are not thinking about money or food or sex. They are not worrying about la situación. They are thinking about human things; about their mothers and their grandfathers. They are innocent again. I think this is like Havana a hundred years ago. In the time of Martí."

"And when I come here," she went on, standing still, and looking at the grieving angels and the sad madonnas and the Milagrosa's eyes, protective above the roses, "I feel I can talk to the old people. And ask them about their hopes and memories. Because maybe some of them never wanted to die, or had plans and feelings they never spoke. Or maybe some died who chose to die. Or someone lost his girlfriend, and had no life again. Or maybe they fought in wars, or maybe they are watching us now. All their thoughts, all their feelings, come to me here, and when I leave, I am like a different person."

"Purer?"

"Purer, yes, and calm. Like those angels they keep in taxis? So when I leave, I have new plans, new energy. Maybe a new me. This place is like a new birth for me."

We walked around some more, not talking, both in our own separate silence, and in silence I followed her around sepulchers, and down avenues of graves. There was no sound anywhere, except for the occasional snifflings of old women, and the sound of footsteps on gravel, and a cock crowing in the distance.

Before we left, I asked if I could make a picture of her, next to the Milagrosa. She went up to the figure and held her fingers in a ball, knocked three times on the brass lid, then walked around the marble forms, resting her joined hands on her chin and closing her eyes. Then she stood with one arm around this patron saint of miracles, a rich woman who had asked to be buried among the poor, and only later, when I got back to the city, and developed the image in my darkroom—a dark-eyed girl in the city of answered prayers— did I realize that that was the first time I ever caught a picture of her alone.

That evening, Lourdes was waiting for me when I got to her home, and she told me that she wanted to make the circuit of her neighbors' houses.

"But this is our last night together."

"Yes. And everyone wants you to help them."

So we made the rounds of her neighbors, and her neighbors' friends, and the cousins of her neighbors' friends, and all of them, as she had warned me, had letters they needed taken to New York. "Include a photo for them," they said. "Send it to my uncle, my aunt, my cousin." "I have a message," they said, "for *mi padre* in New York." "I want you to send this letter for me to Ronald Reagan. You have good connections: will you do that for me?" The addresses were smudged, or to towns not listed in any book, or to places without street names or people no longer alive. Dead letters to dead souls, saying, *Querido / Inolvidado Hermano / Padre / Abuelo,* saying, "I have not written before. I hope you are well, and your family too. Here things are not so good. I need food, I need clothes,

I need money. I do not want to ask you for your help, but you are the only person I know in North America. Please reply quickly. Please send me something. Not through the mail—the government will take it. But give it to someone who is coming to Cuba, give them the money to give me. Here things are not easy. I am waiting for your answer. Please remember me. I never forget you."

Inside, there were sometimes prescriptions—this was the country with the best doctors in the hemisphere, and no medicines—or ill-spelled scraps listing sizes of jeans, or names of offices they'd heard from friends, or friends' cousins. Some of the letters were left unsealed, some of them were scrawled in writing no one could read. I was used to it now: I packed light when I came to Cuba—just my equipment and my diary and things to give away—and when I went back, it was always with a full suitcase.

We went into Marielita's mother's house. It could have been anyone's—it was everyone's—and friends were shuffling in and out of all the rooms, while an old man lay outstretched on the floor next to the balcony: the extended family seemed to reach all the way through Centro Habana, as if everyone was in it together, even if brother could not trust brother, nor *novio novia*.

On the table in the living room, under glass, there were pictures of the family in Florida: their new Datsun 280Z, their condo in Coral Gables, their wet bar. *"Mis primas,"* said a fat woman in curlers, and there were three pretty girls, discernibly Cuban, with diploma hats over their big hair, and juicy red smiles and bright eyes, three Cubans who'd never heard of Camilo.

There was a large framed picture on the wall, of some pouting, curly-haired toddler; and a Marlboro packet; and a collection of ads for Heineken. There was a tiny antenna on the TV, on which, the woman said, you could get eight stations. There was no bathroom anywhere, though: one room served the entire building.

"Tell them about your house," said Lourdes, showing me off. "How many rooms it has, how much it costs. Tell them."

But before I could do so, the woman was pulling me by the arm. *"Mira,* Richard. Take a picture for my mother!" And she got a comb and dragged it through her hair.

"Now the two of us with the dog."

"Now Cari, and then one of me and *mi novio.*"

Photos went off, smiles went on, neighbors came and grinned from the doorway. *"Oye,"* said a neighbor, bursting in. "Can you take a picture of my baby? For my sister. She is in New York." She copied out an address in Queens. I moved closer to the baby, and it screamed and screamed and bawled. Everyone broke up. "She's scared of you. She sees the camera, she thinks you are a spy!"

Lourdes took the camera from me and, coochy-cooing, snuck up to the baby, and took a picture of its smiling face.

Then someone grabbed the camera and looked at it the wrong way round. Someone else wrote down, "Olympidu." Some kid began playing with the lens cap, back and forth, back and forth. I pulled it away, and took one more. "So you will make two copies, Richard? Two copies? One for her, and one for my *abuela?*"

It was Cari, at my shoulder, grabbing my arm, and her face was creased, almost desperate, and I thought this time the tears might really come. "The nice size, okay? Not small. Nice. You will not forget?"

"No."

"One for her, and one for my *abuela* in New York." She was talking as if the last ship was leaving the port.

"Is not too expensive?"

"No, it's fine," and I thought of where these snapshots would go—to drug dealers in prison, to women who couldn't speak Spanish, to P.O. boxes that were long since reassigned, to others who wanted to forget everything that had anything to do with Cuba. To cousins who could not remember the little girl of twenty years before.

I'd had enough by now, I figured; I needed time with Lourdes; if I didn't stop them soon, I'd end up shooting eleven rolls full of people whose faces I couldn't recognize, and sending their pictures to all the wrong people. This never happened to Capa, I thought. So I took a few more pictures, for myself, of their pleading faces and excited smiles and knockabout hopes in these dismal, empty, forty-watt rooms, and then I told them I was out of film, and we took off.

As we sat along the sea, old men waving bottles came up to us, and jabbered crazily, and then reeled off into the night, like Old Testament prophets shouting warnings to the dark. Girls in torn stockings primped their hair and put on smiles. Dollar changers sat along the wall, muttering numbers under their breath.

Lourdes was quiet that night, and I guess the sea made her think of the distance between us. I was quiet too, after seeing her in the cemetery. Again, it was when she was farthest from me that I felt closest to her, or could see most easily what I loved. I thought that maybe this would be the moment.

She sat with her hands around her ankles, and I tried to make it easier for her by following her eyes out to sea. I didn't touch her; I left her to her thoughts. I was an expert at departures.

"*Misterioso*," she said quietly.

"Right."

No oil rigs in the distance; no winking lights of cruise ships. No lights at all tonight: only the two different shades of dark. You could almost imagine how it must have looked to the strangers from some distant party, walking down the long lawns of the Nacional to look out toward Miami. But the party was long over now, and the streetlights were hardly lit, and when she needed to take a pee, she had to go across the street to the space behind the gas station that never had any gas.

"Lourdes," I said when she came back, and, in the dark, her name sounded very intense.

She nodded.

I touched her cheek, brushed her hair, tried not to check on the light.

"What are you thinking?"

"Nothing," she said.

"You won't tell me?"

"If I tell you, you will be angry," and I told myself, She's waiting for me to ask her, and she doesn't know, can't know, that I will.

"I won't, I promise."

"I was thinking about the jeans," she said, "and hoping you wouldn't forget my size."

Something broke in me then, and I left her to her silence, and a little later, I walked her home. The street outside was empty and dark. She held me, I kissed her, she held me so close it was as if she wanted to impress herself on me, to brand my body with her name. She pulled back to look me in the eyes.

"You will not let me down?" she said. "You will not forget?" Her eyes were large and silver in the dark.

"I won't let you down. *Yo soy un hombre sincero.*"

"Like Martí," she said warmly, ruffling my hair.

"Cómo no?"

"You do not have room for me in your case?"

"I wish I did."

"I am small. Duty-free. No tax."

"I wish I could, Lula."

"You will write to me often, every week, Richard? And come back soon? Please don't forget me. Don't forget me." It was like seeing a photo fade before your eyes—a Polaroid in reverse. I could almost see her fading out of view, and the images getting blurry, and then just a big black space, exposed.

"Please remember," she said, and the last thing I saw of her, as I walked away, she was behind a big car at the far end of a long and unlit street.

III

The next time I went down there, it was to shoot a piece for *S.I.* Linares, *El Niño,* was coming out of his teens then; Victor Mesa, *El Loco,* was still running the bases like a madman, wiggling his hips every time he jumped on home plate; Ajete was coming in from the bull pen to throw smoke. No one knew how old these guys were—some of them had been on the team for twenty years—but still they played like the Revolution in cleats: sharp, cocky, full of bravado. They played baseball the way Capablanca played chess: in the high Cuban style, all glitter and flamboyance. And I knew they'd be a story for years to come—the Pan Am Games in Havana, the Olympics in Barcelona, the increasing pressure to defect. Fidel's last PR weapon, storming the world and exporting the Revolution. I'm going to shoot the latest incarnation of the Havana Sugar Kings, I told the editor, the team whose last game was canceled in 1959 because Fidel had just taken the capital; the truth was, I was going to shoot Lula.

It was never hard to find anyone in those days in Havana: you just had to walk down the street, and you'd meet eyes in the darkness, or find friends leaning out of windows, or see schoolboys coming toward you with a smile. The whole city was a circle of informers. And for someone like me, if I had a camera around my neck, a city of friends too, friends who invited you to come with them to the Diplostore where their cousin worked, friends who could tell you where José was, because his cousin's sister used to be their *esposa,* friends who told you to forget José in any case because they had friends too. This time, when I got to her door, it was locked, and I didn't have the patience to sit and wait all night. My first night in Havana, I was always on flame, and ready for adventure. I went up to a ginger-haired kid who was coming out of the house next door, and asked him if he knew where she might be.

"She likes the movies, right?" he said.

"Right," I said, though that was news to me.

"There is a new Brooke Shields movie here. Near the Capitol. I think she is there."

I went down the street to the old place where we'd gone before, and shoved a few notes under the till to the girl, and went in, the ghost of the opera house behind me. Inside, it was still pitch black, darker even than the porno cinemas in Asunción. I stood by the door to let my eyes adjust, and then I fumbled down an aisle, bumping into outstretched legs, putting my hands on shoulders, hearing cries of surprise, feeling strange hands on my thighs.

Even after a few minutes, I couldn't see a thing. I found an empty seat and sat down. But soon I felt a hand tugging at my shirt, heard someone eerily close to me. Onscreen, Brooke Shields was immaculate as ever. Offscreen, I began to make out necks, and arms, and masses of dark curls, and sometimes I could hear sniffles too—or were they gasps? There were couples all around, the usual sea of murmurs. A flash of skin, hands on legs, a shiver of pleasure here and there. The cinema was a true democracy: everyone was equal in the dark. No way you could tell brown from black, friend from sister, rebel from spy. No way you could tell here from there. Around me, the sound of boys unbuttoning shirts and blouses, girls turning for long kisses; urgent whispers, tiny moans.

And then, just at the moment when the father sees David and Jade going for it on the living room floor, I saw her, or what looked like her: a small face, dark hair, a thin white shirt, two or three rows ahead of me to the right. I couldn't be sure it was her, but it looked like her, the way she turned, when she smiled at the person beside her, and sometimes the smiles became open-mouth kisses. I saw the way her jaw moved, wondered if that was how she moved when we were together. I thought I saw her tuck her hair behind her ear, with the quick, impatient flip that was hers and hers alone.

I tried to get closer, thought of moving down the aisle, but the place was packed, and the audience was preoccupied, and all I could do was sit there, amid the whispers and gasps, looking at Brooke Shields, looking at her, looking at her looking at Brooke Shields. Looking at her not looking at Brooke Shields.

When the lights came on, there was a final chorus of snuffles, and a sudden rush of black and brown and golden limbs. I tried to follow her, but I lost her in the crowd, distracted by some other black hair, another white shirt, and when I pressed out into the street, she was nowhere to be seen: just hugs, kisses, tears, and then someone calling "Ricardo": José, at my side, eyes red. "So what you think, Richard?" he asked, as if I lived down the street. "I think is too sad. I see this movie three times, and every time I cry."

"Sure; me too. Look, José, I'm sorry: I've got to split. I'll look in on you soon."

"Sure, no problem," he said, and then I was running back the way I'd come, hardly caring why José had seemed so calm to see me, and what he was doing, crying over Brooke Shields and then materializing by my side.

When I got to her door, it was open, and I took the stairs two at a time.

"Lourdes," I said, knocking on the kitchen door. "Are you here?"

"*Claro,*" she said, opening the door, and hugging me.

"Where were you before?"

"Only here. Same as usual. Doing nothing. With Mamá and Marielita." She looked so happy to see me, I thought she couldn't be faking it. Her shirt, I noticed, was blue.

"You were here all night?"

"Where else? I've been waiting for you, Richard: you said you were coming tomorrow."

"I got an early flight."

"Good, is good for me." She looked me all over. "Oh, Richard, I am so happy to see you," and it was true, I could tell, she was glowing all over. "Marielita was in Varadero last month. At the Siboney. Before, in Cayo Largo."

"*Cómo no?*" said the saucy teenager with the jet-black curls.

"She met a man, a Spanish man. Very kind. He's old—sixty, maybe seventy—but he takes good care of her. He has come here three times already. Every time, they have to hide her from the wife. But he takes her to Varadero, Cayo Largo, everywhere."

"Sure," said Marielita, blasé. "There is a store in Cayo Largo where you can buy everything: shirts, jeans, perfumes, *todo.*"

"And Varadero too, right?"

"Varadero is like Miami Beach," said newly wise Marielita. "They have cable TV, and glasses wrapped up, and every day at breakfast you can eat as much as you want."

"That's great," I said. "But I'm here on assignment. I've got to shoot some baseball."

"Sure," said Lourdes, and I remembered why I loved her. "We have baseball on this island."

I was staying in the Lincoln that time, so I could be close to her, and collecting receipts from a girl I knew in the Libre, and paying the difference to Lula. In any case, good hotels were not so different from bad hotels by then: most of them were serving up deprivation in equal measure. The biggest shortage of all, I always thought, was of a future; the government mass-producing images of the past, while people kept their eyes firmly focused on the present.

Things, in fact, were not going well for *El Máximo,* especially now that there was a guy in the Kremlin even younger than he was. Already, the students were beginning to talk about Tiananmen Square and asking why Russian magazines were banned, and the streets were buzzing with news of Hungary and Poland. In response, the government was doing nothing but filling *Granma* with more and more articles about Oliver Stone, and stocking the TV channels with more and more movies about race riots and drug dealers and *mafiosi* in America. Sometimes, in Cuba, it was like when you repeat the same word over and over till it stops making any sense, or when you stare so hard at a spot that your eyesight blurs.

But Fidel wasn't hassled by any of it. You could still see his touch in every street, and newspaper article, and slogan, but he kept his person completely out of view. Living in Havana in those days was like living with some medieval depiction of God: the guy was everywhere present and nowhere visible. He was in every conversation, in every room and corner, but no one knew a thing about him. He'd created a personality cult without a personality. And the less people saw of him, the more they talked. What was he planning? When did he sleep? Who did he love? What—in Fidel's name—was going on?

The believers used to say that Fidel was God. But God at least rested on the seventh day. With Fidel, that was never so certain. Here was a guy who would micromanage pebbles; who would not only count how many angels could dance on the head of a pin but would tell them how they should be dancing, and what kind of pin they should be using. Here was the only guy working in a place where nothing—and no one—ever worked. And the only guy on the job in a place where everyone else was permanently on hold.

Thirty-one years without changing his clothes; thirty-one years without refining his hairstyle. The other one-name icons—Madonna and Prince and Cher—had at least to keep changing their acts to keep themselves in the public's eye: not Fidel. He just fixed the public's eye to keep it on himself.

I was shooting black and white this time down, because the whole island seemed to be turning black and white. Fewer and fewer cars now, less and less light, a whole country emptied out: instead of cars, they'd gone to bicycles, and instead of bicycles, horse-drawn carts, and soon the horse-drawn carts were being drawn by goats: the whole crazy island was slipping backward through history, moving back and back into the pre–Industrial Revolution. It reminded me of the time with Diane once, when we'd gathered to watch a video of our wedding, and someone had pressed the rewind button by mistake, so you could see us walking away from the altar, out of the church, back into our separate cars—all at top speed. A perfect augury of things to come.

"But what about the sea?" the guy at the agency had asked. "The royal palms. The reds and greens of the old cars. That whole tropical rainbow, Cape-Cod-in-a-G-string kind of thing: Meyerowitz Goes Mambo."

"But what about the dark?" I'd said. "The streets without shadows. The stores without goods. The pots without rice. Everywhere, across the island, in bars and hotels and parks, just darkness." It made me think of the line José had told me once: I have two homes, Cuba and the night.

The thing to do, I figured, was get the baseball out of the way as soon as possible, and then get out the heavy artillery for the real stuff. So I took in a couple of night games at Estadio Latino Americano, joined the guys in the bleachers with their paper cups of beer and their single slices of cheese pizza on paper plates, under signs that read: USE YOUR FREE TIME! PRACTICE! That was as close to the Revolution as I ever got, I think, shooting the breeze with these cheerful, toothless old guys, out to enjoy the night air, and to forget all the other contests going on around them. It could have been a ballpark anywhere, except that tickets were free, and there was nothing to eat except pizza and beer, and the boards on the left-field wall said: READY TO CONQUER!

One time, I hitched onto some official delegation of "North American Sports Journalists," dragged down here to witness the miracle of Cuban training, and we were taken to special seats behind home plate, where a Minint guy told us about Gooden and the Mets, and how Keith Hernandez had been a complex man, and Strawberry needed to get traded. He had his cousin send him tapes from New York, he told us: belonging to the government meant his boxes could get through.

After that, I went out to one of the sports compounds they'd just built—the only modern, glittery palaces on the island—and watched the national team in training. They were something: it was like watching a carnival of gods barnstorming the heavens. The Harlem Globetrotters, taking on the world. The game was so easy for them, they had to find ways of making it interesting: stretching doubles into triples; throwing a guy out at the plate from deepest center field; stealing bases with no outs and a nine-run lead. Their only competition was themselves: in that way, too, I guess, they were like the Revolution.

And the pictures were so easy, all I had to do was click: every guy on the team, it seemed, had a kind of smooth panther's body, like I'd seen before only on Carl Lewis. If Linares were in America, everyone said, he'd be on every Wheaties box in the country. Mesa was flashing his golden bat. Kindelán, Gurriel, Pacheco, looked like they could close their eyes and hit it over the fence.

And in the dugout, the manager, Fuentes, elegant, silver-haired, hunched over his notebook, like he was penning sonnets in his spare time. A poet in the company of kings.

I finished the baseball story in a couple of days—taking pictures in the stands, in between innings, using fish-eyes for the bleachers—and then I went back to Havana to pick up Lourdes.

"Today," I said to her as soon as I came into her sister's bed-room, "I have a surprise for you. A birthday present; only six months early. Put on your red dress; we're going to Varadero."

She was ready within fifteen minutes, and then there were thirty minutes of asking everyone which dresses she should take as extras, and then there were forty minutes of taking requests. But her eyes were sparkling so brightly that they could have lit the room in a blackout. We went down to the park and I unpeeled a few green-backs, and soon I felt like a hooker at a bar mitzvah. The guys were swarming around me, and some women were spitting at Lula, and soon we were in the back of an Eisenhower-era Plymouth and the sea was on our left.

We followed the blue for two hours or more, down empty roads, past Camilo Cienfuegos, Santa Cruz, Matanzas, and when we arrived at the Internacional, the bellhops hissed kisses at her and looked her up and down. We got a room on the third floor, over-looking the sea, and as soon as I closed the door, she came toward me and put her arms around my neck. I leaned in closer, and felt her untether the camera from my neck, and put the lens cap on it, and take it to the far corner of the room, and set it up against the wall.

"No rivals this time. Only me."

"Only you," I said, and I kissed her where we stood, and kissed her again, feeling the place where her hair was damp, and I unbuck-led the belt on her jeans, and let her slither out of them, against me, and when she fell on top of the bed, I fell on top of her, turning her over, and whispering kisses on the back of her neck and her ear. Long, snaking kisses that made her writhe. My fingers along her sides, my mouth at the cusp of her lobe. "No, no," she murmured, and turned over, and I was on top of her, and running my finger down.

Later, after it was dark, I pulled back the door to the terrace so we could hear the sea hiss and curl while we made love, I slipping into her from behind, she looking out to sea, in the distance some samba coming from an empty restaurant.

And even later, at the silent hour of the night, when it felt like we had the whole world to ourselves—the disco had closed, and the final sandy consummations were over—she leaned up on her elbow, and looked down at me. There was moisture at the corners of her eyes.

"Do you ever get lonely, Richard?"

"I have my work."

"I asked if you get lonely."

"I move too fast for that. I'm never in one place long enough to notice I'm alone."

"So you're running away from your loneliness."

"I didn't say that."

"I did. I know how you're feeling, Richard. But it's okay; I'm here. You need never feel lonely again," and she opened her arms to me, and I rested against her chest. Coming back to her was like coming home.

Sometimes we spent all day like that, just tracing our bodies with our lips and fingers, or tracing the history of our times together—you mean you knew even then? Even at Maxim's that night? I never knew you noticed. You felt my hand upon your shoulder? When was the time you knew?—and sometimes we just lay in one another's arms, safe behind our FAVOR NO MOLESTAR sign, for twelve, sixteen, eighteen hours a day, scarcely stirring, closing the world out, and replacing it with our own world, our own words, our own history. Sometimes, when I'd wake up, I'd see her looking at me from above, with a smile on her face, as rapt as if she were looking at the surface of the moon.

One day she told me she would teach me Spanish—true Spanish, she said, a poet's Spanish—by getting me to learn by heart some verses of Martí. "It's very easy, Richard. *Versos Sencillos.* 'Simple Verses,' you would say. All you must do is say them after me."

"Okay."

"I say the words, you say them after, right?"

I nodded.

" 'Yo sé . . .' "

" 'Yo sé . . .' "

" 'Los nombres extranos / De las yerbas y las flores . . .' "

I know, I know, the alien names of the flowers and the grasses.

" 'Y de mortales engaños,' "

And of deadly deceits,

" 'Y de sublimes dolores.' "

And of sublime sorrows.

Sometimes she'd drop a line of Martí into my mouth like a Life Saver. " 'Sólo el amor engendra melodías,' " she said, after we'd made love. Only love makes melodies. And another time, from an essay of his, "A married man commands our respect. Woman is the nobility of man."

"And that line you told me in the car to Artemisa?"

"Later, after the fire and the lights, there will be time for me to ache."

One day, we got up early and I asked her if I could take some pictures of her—for the memories—and she said nothing, and I shot her at dawn, along the sea, and on the terrace, into the light; in the magic hour, wrapped in green curtains; on the pink balcony in the dusk. I shot her at night in her slinkiest outfit, with the chintzy pink lamps behind her; I shot her against an old T-bird in the dark; I shot her alone, in our room, under covers. Sometimes I tried a trick a Chilean guy had shown me once, and I went over to her, and gave her a deep, long kiss, along her neck, her cheeks, her ear, and then, just as she was unwinding, and her eyes were losing focus, I stepped back, off to one side, and clicked the release, and there she'd be, in the lens, the Lula that no one knew but me, spent and tousled, with a kind of blurry sexiness.

"Lula," I said when we were through. "I'd like to say a prayer for you."

"I thought you didn't have a God."

"I don't. But that's okay. I just want to pray to something above us that we can always be together."

"You're a romantic, Richard," she said, trying to keep the smile from her eyes.

"Don't say that. I'm a reporter."

"I don't think so."

And then I closed my eyes, and thought about her happiness, and hoped that everything would come out right for us.

When I opened my eyes, the room was black.

"You can turn the light on again."

"I never turned it off. It's a blackout."

"Goddammit," I said. "Doesn't anything in this stupid island work?"

"Don't worry about it, Richard," she said to me.

"Easy for you to say. You don't have an editor waiting for your shipment to New York."

"You are making pictures for an editor?"

"No. I don't mean that," though I could tell from her voice that something was gone.

"Then what do you mean?"

"Only that it's impossible to get anything done round here." I fumbled for a flashlight, and I heard her move across the room.

"You are in Cuba now," I heard her saying. "Learn to do things the Cuban way. Be patient. Be calm."

I saw her at the window. "You like the sun, the bright light, the beaches; that is the easy part to like. Like a girl at her fifteenth birthday. Where's the skill in that? Why can you not love the mystery too? The night?"

I felt her coming across the room, smelled her perfume drawing closer.

"Why can you not learn to love the dark?" she said, and her lips were on mine. "In the dark we can feel closer." Her breath on my cheek. "In the dark we can hear things more." Her sigh in my ear. "In the dark we can sense more." She was unbuttoning my shirt, and her lips were on my chest. "In the dark we can smell more. Things are warmer in the dark." Her hair along my chest, her hands warm along my back. "Learn to love the dark, Richard. Learn to make love like a blind man."

"Don't shout," I heard her saying. "Why shout when you can make a dark new world?"

After that, the blackouts happened every night almost—I felt I could set my watch by them—and sometimes we just lay there in the dark, and listened to the clatter of *"Dime"*s and keys and crackly music in the corridor. One time, she picked up a candle from the table, and when she lit it in front of her, I saw the hollows in her face, strange ridges and indentations, and circles around her eyes, as if we were ghosts now, in our own shadow kingdom.

"Lula," I said softly. "I'd do anything for you."

"Then marry me."

"Is that the only thing that will make you happy?"

"The only thing. What are you afraid of, Richard?"

"Of losing you."

She lay beside me now, and I felt my lie between us like a block of ice.

That was how it was in our Varadero life: my hand on her moist neck, her hair draped around my wrist. I wetting a finger and running it along her lips till they glistened, she taking me in her mouth and brushing my sides with her hair.

"This is our own Revolution," I whispered to her in the dark. "Our own new Cuba. See no evil," and I kissed her eyes. "Hear no evil," and I dandled her ear in my mouth. "Speak no evil," and my lips were on hers, and there was moistness above and below and around us.

.   .   .

Only once did I almost break the spell. It was our fifth day there, and I could feel our departure beginning to gain substance between us. She had gone into the bathroom, to take another shower—she was taking four or five showers a day then, even in the heat, she was so excited to have hot water—and while she was gone, I got out my camera, and set up the strobe, and when she opened the door to the bathroom, hair tangled, eyes bright, in a perfect state of trust, I ran off a few frames, and her eyes began to blaze.

"So this is how it is, Richard? What do you want me to do for you? Who do you want me to be? You want more images for your magazine?"

"It's just for us, Lourdes. I want something to remember you by."

"Why not take me? Why not make more memories? Why settle for a photo?"

I could feel the impatience rising in her like desire. "It's not so easy. This way at least we can have time together. If you come to America, you'd never see me. And you wouldn't see your family, either. You don't know how it is for foreign women there."

"And you won't give me the chance to know."

"It's not like Cuba there, Lourdes."

"I know, Richard. I'm not stupid. I can speak English. I can teach Spanish. I can work."

"But it's better like this."

"Better for you."

"Better for us both," and she turned and stalked into the bathroom, slamming the door behind her.

She was in there for a long time, and I had a chance to cool off, and I tore out a piece of paper from my diary, and wrote:

Querida *Lula,*
What do I miss when you're not here? Your eyes, your arms, your voice, your face. Your mouth, your hair, your hands. Your thighs, your lips, your tumbled hair. Your heart, your mind, your soul.

I put it under the bed, to give to her when she came out, but something made me forget it there, and when I tried to find it two days later, I guess a chambermaid must have taken it away.

Those days felt like a holiday from life, like a trip into some other kind of self, as if we had stolen away from Cuba, from America, from everything we knew. From ourselves even. And now, with the curtains drawn, we were in some other, unknown land. And it wasn't like any of the other times I'd been on R and R breaks, it wasn't like Ko Samui, or Búzios, or Cozumel, or Barranquilla. There was something different about it, the way Lourdes kept taking me by surprise, and just when I thought I'd got a bead on her, she'd show me something new. Almost as if she were tiptoeing through me, with her candle, down corridors that hadn't been visited for years, and opening doors, and letting in fresh air, and exploring all kinds of forgotten places in this drafty haunted house. It was as if she were throwing open the windows in me and brushing away cobwebs, and somehow, every time she found the key to open a long-locked door, she showed me a new part of herself too, and I saw her in a different light, at a new angle, in the sun. I couldn't even remember now the unknown girl who'd come on to me so strong in the dark Havana nightclub.

One night, I saw her eyes shining as she looked up and ran a distracted hand along my arm. "You know, Richard, it's funny. Before, I was different. I was proud of what we had here. I thought Cuba was the greatest country in the world. Ten million only, but we could make the *yanquis* tremble! When Fidel told us to think of others before ourselves, I thought he was like Martí, like our conscience. But now it is not like that. I think we are just like snapshots; like pictures in the album of *El Jefe*. So he can always remember his romantic youth."

"Are you working for the government?" I said outright. It was late, and we'd let all our defenses fall away, and we weren't even ourselves by then. Everything was possible. "Did you ever?"

"Why? Why are you saying this? Are you a spy?"

"Sure. Why else would I be here?"

"No joke, Richard. Tell me."

"Why do I come here so often? Why so many cameras? What do you think I'm doing here?"

"Don't joke. Tell me the truth."

"I'm collecting information here. On you. For my files. I'm collecting images of you."

"For whom?"

"For me. For history. For the government."

"I don't like this game, Richard," she said, and she got up and walked to the window. I saw the moon, when she pulled back the curtains, I saw the outline of her face. I saw the royal palm behind her, I saw the stars. Her body silver in the night.

After that, it felt as if we'd crossed another threshold, and now there was no way, ever, of going back to the place where we'd been. Some door had closed behind us. I kissed her legs, I kissed the inside of her thighs, I kissed her where she glistened, but still I couldn't find the person I had seen two days before. Some part of her was lost to me, remote.

"I want to ask you, Richard," she said when I was finished. "Where is the trust in our love?"

"What do you mean?"

"What trust do we have?"

"We have each other."

"But how has this helped me? If I trust you, if I love you, it brings us no closer. We are still here, in a hotel, for one week; you are still going to leave. If I open myself to you, if I give you everything I have, what do I get from you?"

"You have to win my trust."

"How? What can I do? How can I ever get you to believe in me? If I am perfect, will you believe it? You will think it is a trick. If I am not perfect, you will not keep me. Or maybe I am perfect, but I am in some other room, and you cannot see me. How does it help me to be perfect? What can I do to win your trust?"

"Come to the airport with me. Meet me when you say you'll meet me."

"How does it help? If I am kind to you, you think it is for a reason. If I am not kind to you, you think I am bad. What can I do? Tell me, and I will do it. I will do anything. I will cut out my heart and give it to you. I will cut myself till I bleed. What do you want?"

"Just be patient."

"How long? How much longer must I wait?"

"As long as it takes. You can't force love. Or trust."

"But you can deny it. It's not fair, Richard: I can't force love; but even if I get it, you will say it is not love. I can't win. It is like with Fidel."

"Of course you can."

"Sometimes I think your job is like a poison. You go to all these wars and make pictures of the girls in the hotels in Manila and Honduras, and you tell me about the "English teachers" and "tour guides" who want to make friends with foreigners, and now you think that every girl is like that. I will be honest with you. The first time I saw you, of course I saw you as a North American. You are rich, you can go anywhere, you can fly away tomorrow. You are living in the Nacional, eating good food, and we are living like pigs. Of course I see that. But I also see you. It is not easy. Yes, you are a foreigner; yes, you are a man who can rescue me. But I see also you have a dream. Not like the Cuban men, sitting on their asses every day, and then handling us like pieces of meat. And you have a life: a job, a future, a purpose. But because I see you as a foreigner, you will not have me. You believe that if a woman has a reason to love you, it is not true love; like if you have a reason to believe in God, it is not true faith. Then maybe you should find a girl who has no reason to marry you. Marry her!"

"It's not like that."

"Why must you try to explain everything? So maybe you meet a girl, and you are pulled by her, and she has gold hair, and a pretty smile, and a sexy dress. But these are not the reasons you love her. There are other girls with more beautiful hair, more pretty smiles, more expensive dresses. It is something else. It is like asking why you like beer. Why your favorite color is blue. Why you eat cheese. You think you can find reasons for anything. But they do not help. There are a hundred reasons for not believing in God; and the reasons for believing in Him are bad ones."

I thought a lot about what she'd said, after she went to sleep, and I could see that she was right in part. Maybe that's why I liked her in the first place, maybe that's why she'd gone deeper in me than the others. But it was harder and harder to get through to her now. Our time was running out. Two days from now, we'd be back in Havana, back with silence and secrecy and spies. It was like the curtains were pulling open, and the light was coming in our eyes.

"You know, Richard," she said, the next morning, lying in my arms, "I think you are like Fidel."

"Thank you."

"No. I am serious. You are always talking about helping people, about idealism and truth. But it is all in your head."

"I don't buy that. Just ask my agent: I make pictures, and they sell."

"But why do you not help the man who is starving? Why only take his picture?"

"I'm not a doctor. Soon he'll be dead. But the picture may save people who are not dead yet."

"But what about this person right here?"

"I help you."

"Yes, you give me bottles of perfume, and a trip to Varadero, and when you leave, you will give me money. But what about giving me a life?"

"It's not easy."

"Sure. Nothing is easy. Taking your pictures is not easy. Coming to Cuba is not easy. But you do it! Why not me? Why not try helping me?"

"I've got a lot on my plate right now. I'm trying to find a balance."

"So while you look for this balance, I starve."

"You never starve, goddammit."

"I never starve for food. But there are other kinds of starving."
Her eyes flashed, and in that moment I felt stripped: like I was in
some flashbulb glare, and couldn't see. With the other girls, it had
been a different kind of game—"You help me, please? For my
mamá?"—and we both knew the rules. But here things were different: like going into a strange country late at night, and going out
into the streets, and finding them empty, and you didn't even know
if there was a curfew on.

"Fidel is in love only with his ideas. With these beautiful abstract
things. With Communist textbooks. They say that he is reading
even when he is making love. That he makes slogans even in a
woman's arms. That he has only one love, and that love is not alive.
It is the same with you, I think: you and your camera. You cannot
look at truth. Everything, you must change—with your filters, your
special lenses, your editing. You say you are showing the truth, but
it is only the truth you choose."

I went into the bathroom then, to cut the
discussion short, and I took a long, long shower. To think this over.
To wake myself up. To recover strength. When I came out, she was
already asleep. I couldn't see much—the curtains were drawn, and
there weren't many stars—but I could see her body rising above the
sheet. I sat on the bed and looked at her. The wisps of hair curling
down her neck. The way she opened and stretched her small hands
sometimes. The occasional groans or cries she made.

I sat there for a long time, just watching her, and looking at the
bag in which she'd brought her things. I saw my camera bag next to
hers, and the small necklace I'd given her from Miami. Her gold
cross. Her faraway smile.

I watched her for maybe an hour or more, and as I did, I made
up my mind: the next night, I would go for it. I remembered something Hugo had said, that night in Cayo Largo: say the words, and
you begin to believe them. Recite the Lord's Prayer often enough,
and you become a sort of Christian. Tell her you'll do anything for

her, and maybe it comes true. The next night, after the cabaret, was the time.

We went to the big show at the Continental our last night on the beach, and we sat through the blackface minstrels and the tinselly mulattas and we watched the spectacle around us: the girls in zipped-up minidresses, bursting at the seams, the Italians looking at them as if they were a kind of dessert brought over by the maître d'. The broken words, the usual exchange. "You're free tonight?" "For you, *señor,* I'm always free."

We danced a little on the floor, and Lula shimmied like she never did in Havana: I could see how she'd been refreshed by her week away from life, how she had a new shine to her. This was a night she'd always remember, I figured: she even asked me to take a picture of her, and another, and another. At our table, with a flash, playing with her cocktail.

We watched the couples form, the hands slipping into hands, the eyes discreetly meeting. She told me which of the guys onstage were gay, she sang along with all the standards. I took a few pictures, here and there, for my "Love for Money" story. And finally, when it was over—it must have been one-thirty, two—we went out onto the beach. No stars, no lights, but the sand beneath our feet was warm. No shards of glass, no trash or tar: a virgin place where none of the usual rules applied.

As we drifted over to the surf, she took off her shoes, and her eyes were bright, and I could see she was giddy from the rum. There were long kisses sometimes, and a hand under her shirt, and her hair was beginning to escape from its comb, one lock falling over her eyes. I would have liked to catch her like that, against the sea, on a Varadero night, her earrings sparkling, her eyes on fire, her lips moistened by the rum. My half-abandoned beauty.

"So what do you think?" I said, after we'd kissed.

"Of what, Richard?"

"Our future. Next week. Next year."

We walked a little back from the sea, looking for a warm place to sit.

"You see, I was thinking," I said slowly, and then, as we walked, she dug her nails into my arm, and I almost shouted, and then I followed her eyes to where she was looking, against the dunes. An Italian—you could tell from his groans—with his trousers down around his ankles, his body moving up and down against something dark and silent.

That put an end to my speech. But that was okay: *mañana*, I figured, was the national motto.

When we got back to town, next day, she told me we could leave our things at her cousin's house, near the Bodeguita, and then she led me along O'Reilly, then right on Habana, past the old Western Union store, and then down again, to the Royal Bank of Canada. We turned again, onto Obra Pía, the Street of Good Deeds, and went up to a dark entrance, and up a lightless staircase. In a back room, in the dark, sat a wiry man in a loose white shirt.

"Encantado," he said, when we were introduced.

"Richard speaks English," she assured him.

"Pleased to meet you," said the man.

"Mr. Tran can help us," she explained, for his benefit as much as mine. "He has friends in Hong Kong, California, here too."

"So you can get her a visa."

"Of course. I can get anything. But nothing is cheap." He flashed his golden smile at me.

"How much is nothing?"

"Thirty-eight hundred dollars, U.S., for Bolivia or the Dominican. You want American, you give more."

"That's crazy."

"That's Cuba."

Sensing that we had reached a temporary roadblock, he got up and went into a little kitchen. I saw his name on a slip of paper. Nguyen Van Tran.

"This guy comes from Vietnam."

"I think six years ago, more or less. He was a student here. He makes this business. He brings cars, batteries here to Cuba. He knows the *yanquis* too. He knows how you guys think. He has fought against imperialism."

"And you trust him?"

"Trust is not important. He is . . ." But the man was coming back now, with a pot of jasmine tea.

"You see, Mr. Richard, in Cuba you must always be patient. It is not like your country. Wait, and you shall be given—isn't that what you say?" The yellow smile again. "If you have dollars, you can get what you need. If you have patience. If you can wait. For the right moment. The right place."

This character was giving me the creeps: it was too much like being in Phnom Penh again, after the "liberation" of Cambodia. I could imagine his smile as he offered you a bargain on his teenage daughter.

"How long must I be patient?"

"If you know how long you must wait, it is not patience. You Americans always want everything so fast."

The old Vietnamese line—except, in this case, he was right.

"Okay, I'll think about it," I said, and motioned Lourdes for us to leave.

"No tea?" he asked. "Too bad." And we left him to his papers and his pot.

I guess that was the second time something broke, and the crack went deeper than before. Out on the street, Lula was mad, restless—why wouldn't I pay, why couldn't I wait, wasn't this her life we were talking about—and I was feeling the way I often did in Havana: like everything was complicated, and behind every transaction there was some kind of shadow deal going down.

"Look, I'm sorry, I've got to think," I said, feeling I had to step away in order to see her again, and I went off to the Havana Libre, which the Spaniards were busily tarting up for 1992.

While I was looking around the lobby, suddenly I felt a hand on my shoulder, and I whirled around, tired of whispers and deals and unwanted friends.

"Jesus, Richard, what's the problem?" It was Mike Alvarez; the last time I'd seen him was when I'd crashed the Magnum party in Paris a couple of years back. We'd worked together a few years before on *A Day in the Life of the Philippines,* and he'd done all these double-truck shots of Olangapo at two a.m. and then they'd canned the whole spread because he'd been shooting in Fujicolor instead of Kodak.

"What the hell are you doing here?"

"Oh, the usual. Baseball. *El equipo del sueño.* Pan Am warmup, Olympic preview."

"Shit, no kidding? I'm here for the *Geographic.* Three months. With Miguel over here." He pointed to a guy standing beside him in the lobby. "Miguel makes sure I see light from dark."

"So how are you spending your time?"

"How do you think? Checking out my roots. Shooting dawn to dusk. Trying out a few friendship offensives. Hey, you want a drink?"

"What about Miguel?"

"Ah, Miguel's happy as long as I'm not talking to Cubans. He loves everyone in the world except his fellow Cubans."

"A true Communist."

"Right." We went to the wicker-chair bar they have over there that's always empty except for a few Ecuadoran trade fair delegates getting blitzed to "Guantanamera."

"So what's the matter?" he said, after we'd toasted the Yellow Book. "You look upset. Not getting any?"

"Kind of the opposite."

"Too many crooks spoil the broth?"

"Just one. And she's no crook. That's the problem, Mike. I'm in, in really deep. I met this girl, like three years ago, took her with me to Varadero, now she's trying to decide whether to wear white or cream at the wedding."

"What about Diane?"

"What indeed?"

"The import duty on this one figures to be really heavy."

"Don't I know it!"

"Just bag it, man! Say sayonara, hasta la vista, stay out of the city for a while. She can survive. There are plenty more where you came from."

"You don't need to tell me that. I know she'll survive. It's me I'm worried about."

"You're really gone on her?"

"Really gone. Far gone. Not like before. You've never seen me like this, have you?"

"Well, there was that one time, in the Camino Real . . ." But it was true, and we both knew it.

"So how about you?"

"I'm great. Come prepared, don't you know?" He pulled out a do-it-yourself AIDS test he must have bought in Bangkok or somewhere. "Doesn't do any good, of course, but it scares away the wild ones. Also, this." He pulled out one of those over-the-counter pregnancy tests. Mike was like a pharmacy on two legs. "Only thing to do here is stay away from the politics. Far away. I remember this one time I was in La Rampa—that bar down near the Sofia restaurant—and I was shooting with a flash, a big one, and these guys suddenly came over from a booth and said, 'You're a North American,' and hustled me out of there. I was shitting bricks, man, seeing my visa getting revoked, watching the boys in Washington freak out. I flashed them a 'dazzler'—you know, one of those official-looking letters with embossed seals the *Geographic* gives out—but they weren't buying it. 'Let's just go to the hotel and talk it over,' this guy says, so we come back here, and they order some drinks, and I kind of tell them how I've set up the thing with the Foreign Ministry guys, and they order some more, and ask me if I'll give them twenty bucks apiece. I do, and then they just stand up, shake my hand, and head off. 'You're safe now,' one of them calls back to me. 'Your friend's back.' And I turn around and see this guy darting behind a pillar. Crazy: like something out of Groucho Marx. That's the kind of Marxism they have here. And they also tell me that everything we'd said had been recorded, which was great since we'd been mostly talking about Robert Redford, and this deal he's got going with García Márquez." He looked around him. "Man, I just love this place; *la situación* comedy."

"Yeah. But how long is it going to stay like this? Things are getting really bad really fast."

"Forget it. It's always been like this: been cockeyed from the beginning. These guys don't know their asses from their brains. Their big celebration is of this coup attempt where ninety of their hundred and fifty guys got wasted in the street, and everyone knew about the surprise attack in advance, and thirty of them had to go to jail. Why do you think they have these statues of Quixote all over the place?

"It's like the Keystone Kops meets Yogi Bear, man. You never know what's going to happen next. You know the night they attacked—twelve men on a boat against the world—they arrived two days late, on the wrong beach, to be met by a welcoming committee who took out seventy of their eighty-two guys? Purgatory Point, the place is called. They're always talking about how they fought against the odds—but who was it who made the odds so crazy in the first place? These guys were shooting themselves in the foot from the moment they got guns. They were making problems for themselves so big they would have to be heroes just to conquer them. Heroes chasing their own tails. At least I'm chasing someone else's."

"But that was their heyday. Fidel giving exclusives to the *New York Times*. Getting carried by cheering students around the Princeton campus. Handing out checks for three hundred thousand bucks. Appearing on "The Tonight Show" with tears streaming down Jack Paar's face. Fidel was the American Dream in action, riding into town with a few *compañeros* and cleaning up the whole place. Rugged individualism with a vengeance."

"Sure. Only thing that saved their asses was that their enemy was even more screwed up than they are. So Washington mass-produces *Fidelistas* as fast as Fidel produces good capitalists. It's great. And"—he swerved around as a couple of *señoritas* displayed their wares—"capitalism with curves.

"I'll tell you one thing, Rick: this is the only place in the world where the hookers pay you. I was driving along the sea a couple of weeks ago—in this rental car, which works on them like catnip—

and a girl flags me over and gives me two twenty-dollar bills. For shopping, she says. So we go across town to the Hyper-diplostore—over in Miramar—and then go to her 'aunt's house' to recuperate. Cute girl—nice complexion, lots of sparkle. So we do the deed in the house—this empty mansion by the sea—and then I'm on my way again. But later I realize I've got two bucks in change we never used. So she ended up paying me two bucks! For humping her! And you wonder why the whole country's bankrupt."

I felt happy just listening to him talk: it was like being on solid ground again. The world I knew.

"So how much longer you here, Ricky baby?"

"Leave tomorrow."

"Okay. See you round somewhere. Long live *la lucha!*"

I left him to his sport, Miguel cracking his knuckles in a chair nearby.

The last thing I had to do that day was check in on José: self-interest, I guess—I needed a reading from him. On the private side of the Revolution.

When I went into his apartment, the place was transformed. In the front room, where the stereo and books had been, there was an enormous *santería* altar, each shelf given over to a different deity, with framed pictures and food at the bottom, and a coconut with a face.

"Let me get a picture of this," I said.

"No, no," said José. "You cannot."

"Why not?"

"For one year after I make saint, I cannot have a photograph. My father tells me—my *santería* father: I cannot give food to anyone; I must only wear white; I cannot have a woman." I looked again at the roses in bottles, and the old pieces of meat, and some handmade swords, and axes all around.

"What's going on here, José?"

"This is my new religion." He looked at me with his broad smile. "Many, many people are doing it. For me, is like a bank. If I need something, if I need anything, I can go to a tree—a ceiba tree—and

I hit the tree two times, and I can talk to the gods. Like a prayer."

"Or a telephone?"

"Sure. And if I need something real bad, I can go to my father: I give him some money, and he talks to the gods for me. He can do anything; I introduce you to him later."

"Fine, but right now, I need you."

"Sure. What can I get for you? When you need it?"

"Your advice only."

He looked a little disappointed.

"About Lula. What do you think of her?"

"She's a pretty girl."

"I mean, beyond that. What would you think if I married her?"

"Okay. If you want. Give her a ticket out." I caught the change in his voice, and knew that some kind of wall had come down.

"The thing is, my divorce hasn't come through yet. To get it through is going to take a lot of paperwork, a lot of time." I'd put it in terms he'd understand. "A lot of money too. Lawyers, trips to Singapore, payoffs, all that. And I'm not going to go through all that if she turns out to be a washout. Or maybe, in the year it takes to do this, things get even worse, and she can't wait, and she's got some other iron in the fire, who can give her a confirmed seat."

"Maybe. So if you want to move fast, you find a guy to marry her."

"What do you mean?"

"You find a friend, a foreigner. *Soltero,* maybe *siempre soltero.* Give him some money if he wants. Then she marries him, he takes care of the papers, and when she's out, you go and get her."

"Sounds crazy. Why make everything so complicated?"

"Is better. Not so difficult. Everyone does it all the time. I have a friend, he can help you."

"You mean we fix up the marriage here, then she gets a visa, then both of us are safe?"

"Sure. It happens all the time. Is easy, no problem. There is a way of doing these things."

"In Havana?"

"Sure. But is better outside. In the country."

"Like Cayo Largo."

"Right." He gave me a broad, and approving, smile. "Not so many police there. Very free. Maybe you go there with Lula, and her new husband, and my friend, he can plan everything. Then they come back to Havana, go to the *yanquis'* Interests Section, show them the papers, and she is free."

"As easy as that."

"Sure. Why not? It is not against the law to make love. Not yet. So I tell my friend tonight?"

"No, wait a little." I thought about what he said when I got back to the hotel; and again, when I went to say goodbye to her; and then again, on the plane home. After a while, I figured that anything was better than nothing; sitting around would get us about as far as it had got the Revolution. It was the crazy ideas that were usually the best ones. So I got out a postcard of the Cameron Highlands—to remind him of his king and country—and wrote.

Hugo: I'm not much of a correspondent, as you've probably noticed, but I've got an idea. How about we meet up again—our third reunion—and go for a drive to Santiago. It's a funky place, and the Carnival there is just incredible: round-the-clock dancing for two straight weeks. Whatever happens, it'll be crazier than Greece. And I have a surprise for you too, to collect upon arrival. What do you think? Yours, Richard.

Ten days later, I got a reply, in his church-mousy little black-pen scrawl.

Dear Richard,

You can imagine how surprised I was to come upon your letter. Not displeased, though, and I really can't see any reason to say no. I can easily organize my arrangements with the travel agent, and might even be able to scrounge some reimbursement from the school. A bird's-eye look at the Revolution, so to speak. With jazz bars in the background.

I do hope that all is going well indeed for you, and that developments—of every kind—are proving fruitful. I imagine that delays in a car can be quite as exciting as those on a plane. With warmest regards, Hugo.

IV

W e planned the meeting for just before the Pan Americans: that way I could get some pictures in my spare time. I knew it was the kind of event I could shoot in my sleep. New stadiums. Fat Fleet Street journalists being bused to distant hotels, where the taps never worked. Razzle-dazzle new billboards and slogans and TV crews, with teenagers outside the arenas begging for bread. Everywhere in the world it was the same: suddenly, everyone is told to stop eating dogs, and to be polite to foreigners, and to refrain from spitting in public, for two weeks. Walls are spruced up, shops repaired, camera angles worked out in advance. Bright colors; Potemkin houses. Even in Beijing, the whole city had been turned into one murmurous haze of hospitality girls, speaking good English in the hotels, filling up your glass every time you took a sip, smiling you in and out of security checks, and every single flight into the city, during the Asian Games, had been met by whole welcoming groups of kindergarten cuties waving fans and singing folk songs. Cuba didn't have it together for all that, but they'd repainted all the houses along the Malecón, dressed up the city in its tropical best.

I took the Iberia flight over that time, from Madrid, the cabin attendants putting on black gloves before they handed out the copies of *Granma*, as if they were scared of contamination. When I went to the immigration booth, they waved me over to the Hotel Reservation desk, as usual, where a sweet young thing with dark lashes asked me where I'd like to stay, and when I said, "Victoria," she said no, and when I said, "Habana Libre," she said no, and when I said, "Sevilla," she said no, and then, smiling deliciously, with that look that all the Cubans have—"Sorry, *compañero*, but we're all in this together"—she told me that I could stay only in the Colina.

"How about the Colina?" I asked.

"No problem," she said, laughing again, and pushing the brown curls from her eyes. I hadn't even formally entered the country, and already I was in some kind of ambiguous exchange.

"Okay, you give me the—"

"I know. I give you the money, you give me the receipt. I give the guy at the desk the receipt. He gives me the key to a room without water. If I want water, I give him more money. . . ."

"You know our country very well."

"Not well enough," I said, and she shot me a glance, and sent me back to the immigration officer, who gave me a conspirator's smile, and sent me off to the customs official, who checked my case to make sure that everything was contraband, chose not to look at the nine pairs of jeans and six bottles of whiskey, and then all but pushed me into his country, with a friendly "Have a good trip!"

"Catch you later," I said to the girl before I left.

"I hope you will," she said. "I have the number of your room."

I grabbed a public taxi then, told him I'd give him dollars, and we drove toward Havana in the dark, darker than I'd ever seen it, pitch black like Africa or Bali, with just a few sudden faces at the bus stops, and then monuments and convention centers and four-story paintings of Che. The Plaza de la Revolución. The shadows around Lenin Park. The broken, lonely bus stops. A city of dancing ghosts.

In the hotel, the policewomen, brown hair tucked under their blue caps, and mouths unsmiling, worked the lobby in pairs, circling around the girls who were circling around them. Female policemen were not subject to temptation, went the thinking. Here and there, display-case mulattas were arranged on sofas, and boys whose smiling eyes caught anyone's who looked. The receptionist thumbed wearily through a huge handwritten ledger, hoping not to find my name. The six-seat bar in the lobby was all occupied, all female.

I walked out past Coppelia, past lines outside the restaurants, past bars slammed shut by shortages. Sunny girls and moony couples; a few fat English guys barreling into the Habana Libre with teenagers under their arms. On the wall near the TV station, an ad for a production of the *Oresteia,* Kabuki style, with chalky phantom faces in black leotards prowling around the stage like spirits.

I crept into a bar, and the smiling guy behind the counter said, *"No hay beer. No hay whiskey. No hay nada. Ron solamente, y aqua minerale."* Because of the Games, the stores and restaurants were even emptier than usual, he explained: food and drink were reserved for authorities and strangers. Glad to have got anything, I drank warm rum out of a dirty tin cup, next to a few old guys sitting before their empty glasses, staring into space. A girl in a pink dress was stretched out on a booth like a corpse. Two kids were strumming love songs in a corner on a guitar. A friend of theirs with a pixie smile was bouncing up and down on the lap of a Mexican with long dark hair and shades who looked like he was on the way to the slaughterhouse. He pawed her fondly, and she threw back her head and laughed.

I bought the guys next to me a round of drinks, and as soon as I did, the two guys from the corner came up and introduced themselves. Ángel and Israel, they said. "Do you like Cuban music?" said Ángel. "Or you like girls? *Mulattas, chinas, qué quieres?"* I looked around to plan my escape. *"Mira,"* said the other. *"Somos amigos. No tienes miedo. Yo no quiero robarte. Somos amigos, entiendes?"*

"Entiendo," I said, and hightailed it out of there, figuring I didn't have the time or the energy for more of this. Outside, on the street, I heard a car honk, and I looked up to see two guys from Canada I'd met at the airport, and I was so tired I decided I'd go with them, and we ended up at a table in the Pompero tango bar, drinking water.

At the next table, a CIA man was talking about his jobs in Venezuela and the University of the Andes, while his willowy punk daughter, in a flowery peasant skirt, was handing round copies of the review her performance piece had got in the *Boston Phoenix.* "You know," said the entrepreneur from Toronto, "they say the story of Cuba is the story of sugar. A story of exploitation. By the Spaniards, Americans, British, even the Cubans themselves." Across the table, his friend, the semiotician from the University of British Columbia, was quoting Foucault on power while his Cuban girlfriend—a slim black beauty with a Sinead O'Connor cut—was talking about her days in Kiev. "For me, Russia was marvelous. Like a dream. For material things they have so much. But for spirit—nothing! They are like ants, like worker ants there. Every man looks out for himself; if you walk behind him, the door will slam in your face. They are so directed. Not like here. In Russia, if I fall down in the street, nobody stops to help me. Here in Cuba, it is the opposite: people catch you before you fall."

Then she joined her girlfriend from Canada—they both lived in the *Granma* towers—in a sweet, soaring rendition of *"Qué Linda Es Cuba,"* their voices alive with hope and light as they sang, *"Con Fidel, que vive en la montaña . . ."* I could hear the CIA man saying, "We're here to have fun," and explaining how easy it was for Americans to come down here—the U.S. had no rule you couldn't visit Cuba, only that you couldn't spend money here. The sweet, honey-haired dreamer from grad school was telling us now about the Salvadoran guerrilla she'd fallen in love with here, and her hopes for working for the FMLNF in San Salvador.

As the night went on, the other four kind of paired off, and there were giggles and exploratory kisses, and the semiotician was buried in the black girl's neck. "Hey," his voice came out at one point. "Conchita wants to know what 'entropy' means." The Canadian girl was saying, "Some people say—though it's a bit too cynical for me—that in Cuba people think of making love as casually as smoking a cigarette." At the piano, some guy in a faded tuxedo was playing "Try to remember the kind of September . . ."

By three in the morning, I figured it was bedtime, so I took my leave of the festive group and set out on the long walk home: there was still music pulsing out of vacant lots, and the outline of groups of figures along the Malecón; CUBA—JOY UNDER YOUR SUN, said the first sign I saw. The Nacional was closed for renovation, though—it was going to be closed during the Games, the only time in thirty years when they'd have a chance of filling it—and a cop on duty in the driveway told me that Alfredo had gone back to Asunción. There were some rickety excuses for samba bands now even in the cheap hotels, and an air of fake laughter and light, like Las Vegas rebuilt in Siberia.

In the hotel, there was a steady procession of unattended girls, like in some police lineup: blondes in flimsy hot pants, ebony women in see-through blouses, teenagers with Oriental features. The joke now, Mike had told me when he came back to New York, was that any place just for foreigners was about 30 percent foreigners and 70 percent Cuban girls.

In my room, I went into the bathroom, and the door locked me in by mistake. *"Qué linda es Cuba,"* I remembered the Canadian girl singing as I set about breaking it down.

When I went down to breakfast the next morning in the hotel, it was the same old craziness. *"No hay."* *"No hay."* *"No hay nada."* Fat old mammies sitting on their asses, and waiters smiling in the hope of getting a piece of spare bread, and girls who snarled when you asked them for some juice. Cuba must have been the only tropical country in the world where all the juice was canned and the fruit tasted like it had been sent over, sea mail, from Pyongyang.

Around me, the local beauties were telling the hippies from Munich and Vancouver how good they had it, while the ponytail brigade was trying to tell them the same. By eleven o'clock, I knew, the guy in the black tie would be back at his piano, playing "As Time Goes By" without a trace of irony, and the waitresses would be looking at you like mothers who've heard their kids tell the same bad joke once too often. Even now, there were people fighting for the seats in the lobby, where the air-conditioning was free and there was a suggestion, a faint hint, of the world outside.

When I got to Lourdes's home, I saw a Havanautos car parked outside, and my heart missed a beat. The main door was locked, so I sat on the stoop and waited. A few kids, a couple of mothers, some guys in shiny guayaberas. Then, at last, a man came out—he looked like a government official—and got in the rental car and drove away, and my heart came to life again. The street hadn't changed at all—it was off the Pan Am circuit: pockmarked walls, gutted windows, dirty clothes hanging out of balconies. Bahia in a shotgun marriage with Bombay.

When finally a woman opened the door from indoors, I raced up the broad stairs and knocked and knocked. The door opened up, and it was her mother, rings around her eyes, in curlers and a white print dress.

"Richard!" she said, kissing me on both cheeks. *"Qué pasa? Cómo estás? Café?"* Cari was sitting at the table, and when she saw me, a warmth came to her face too, and I kissed her, and held her hand, and we sat around the table, talking.

"You have heard the news? Lourdes told you?" her mother asked.

"What news?"

"About the marriage." I looked back at her. "You don't know?" She got up, with a groan, and labored over to the same shelf where she kept her glasses and her souvenirs. She pulled out a photo album—one of those Far Eastern things, from Vietnam perhaps, with smiling pink kitties all over it—and opened it up.

"Mira, Richard. Lourdes's sister. You remember her?"

Inside, there were pictures, of a party mostly, a small, sad party in some tiny kitchen: of Lourdes's mother, and her man, dancing with their arms around each other's waists; and Lourdes's sister, thick and mustached, sitting on the knees of some mobster-style guy in his early forties, with bright balloons behind them on the wall; and some bread on the table, and bottles of cider here and there. Their faces in the flashlight glare looked otherworldly almost, red dots in each pupil, and later there were more pictures, outdoors, of the balding mobster lying on top of the sister on some grass, kissing her on the lips, and more dancing in front of red balloons.

"This is her *novio?"*

"Claro. They will be married."

"I thought it was her uncle."

"Uncle? No. This is Giuseppe. He will marry her soon. He brings us cheese, and wine, and balloons."

"So she is happy?"

"Cómo no? We are all so happy. He is a good man, very kind to her. He works in a factory in Italy, and he comes here already three times to see her. The government says she cannot get a visa now—she is only nineteen. But when she is twenty-one, she will be free."

"And she isn't sad?"

"Look at her face."

It was true: she looked as happy as if she were marrying Robert

Redford. Happier than I'd ever seen her sister. In the arms of this balding mobster.

The marriage kind of took the wind out of my sails, and I could feel the room fill up with expectation. It was as if all the questions Lourdes's mother wanted to ask, and all the things Cari was waiting to say, were everywhere around us, hovering.

"I guess I'd better make tracks. If Lourdes comes back, tell her she can find me in the Colina. Today. Tomorrow I'll be leaving."

"O-ka, Richard," said the mother.

"Richard," said Cari, touching me shyly on the arm. "Can you help me?"

"With what?"

"This."

She motioned me to follow her into the room she shared with Lourdes. She gestured for me to sit on the bed. She walked across the room and locked the door. "It is safe here," she said.

The room was dark and musty; the sheets had traces of the perfume I'd given them. She came toward me on the bed.

"Cari . . ."

"It's nothing. Just this," she said, and I saw her turn toward the dresser, and open the top drawer. From where I sat, I could see a bottle of rum, some old tubes of lipstick, a stash of papers. She brought the stash over. There was a withered snapshot of the day she'd spent in Varadero once, with a Spanish businessman. One of her fifteenth birthday at the Tropicana, a teenage Lourdes smiling by her side. There were scraps of notes, a map someone had given her once of Belgrade. Then she pulled out an envelope and handed it to me.

I saw the *par avion* rectangle of France.

"Richard, will you read this for me?"

"I'll try. I don't have much French, but I guess it's more than yours."

I read it over quickly. What could I say?

Cari was looking at me bright-eyed. "Please tell me, Richard. What does he say?"

"He says he misses you, and always thinks of you, and the times you spent together."

"*Claro.* So do I."

"He says that the weather is very sunny in Lyon, and he is making a trip to the mountains with his friends."

"A trip?" she said, and she sounded worried.

"He says he keeps your picture next to his bed."

"And he will be coming back soon?"

"He doesn't say when."

Cari's eyes were filling up.

"But he says that he loves me?"

"Yes. He says that he loves you very much." I handed the letter back to her, and she folded it up carefully, and put it back in the stack. It was one of the first times I was almost glad that my job had taught me how to lie.

Lourdes found me that afternoon, calling from the telephone in her neighbor's room, and when I arrived to meet her, in her kitchen, she was all lit up like I'd never seen her before. I tried to maneuver her back to Vedado, or into a *colectivo,* or somewhere where we could be private, but it wasn't me that made her excited this time, and it wasn't her sister's wedding, and it wasn't the clothes I'd brought for her. It was something else.

"Richard, I want to tell you something. For your job. Follow me." We walked out onto the balcony outside the kitchen, and then up some steep stairs, tricky as in some old Tibetan monastery, up to her roof.

"*Mira,* Richard. My home!" It was a bare space, enclosed on the roof, with cardboard for walls and a huge straw bag on the floor and a broken wooden table in the middle. "Later, this will be my home. My—how do you say it?—studio. Next time I will show you. The private world of Lourdes!"

I took it all in, and made the right noises.

"I will have videos, I will have music, I will have everything here. My own private Cuba."

"Nobody surrenders here," I said.

"*Exacto.* But, Richard, I want to tell you something, something very important. You can tell this to your magazine. Tell this to

Jorge Bush. You can say you know this from a true *cubana*. Señorita X. Nuestra Señora de los Dolores. There is a group now, a group *clandestino*, and they are everywhere. They are all lovers of Fidel. If you say something, if you say, 'I am not happy' or 'I want a life' or 'Why can we not find food?'—if you say anything, in the street, even in your home, they can hear you. And they can kill you."

"Kill you?"

"Of course. I know a boy who was killed by this group. Anyone can be in this group—young people, old people, my mother, anyone."

"But it's always been like this."

"No. Before, they could only talk to the police. Now they have guns. They can shoot you—right here, in the street! They can do anything, and the police will not touch them!"

"So you keep quiet."

"Yes. But it is not so easy. So sometimes I go to the cathedral and tell *El Señor*. And now I tell you." Behind us, some wild merengue music from the Dominican almost blotted out her words: the whole country seemed blue and white on this scalded afternoon. Blinding light, and cool blue distances. "The police know everything," she went on. "But I tell you only. I tell this to no one else. Not even a stranger. Maybe I tell him, and he tells another friend, and he tells his *novia*, and . . ." She drew a line across her throat.

"But why are they forming now, these groups?"

"Because they are afraid. They know the Cubans in America, in Miami, are going to invade. On the eighteenth, no? So this group is ready. I know this, Richard: my cousin is a member."

"Marielita?"

"No. You remember the boy in Artemisa? In my aunt's house. He is not a true *Fidelista*, but he must join, because of his job, because of his family. I did not know about this group, but he informed me."

"But I thought you said a woman told you."

"Oh!" She slapped her forehead theatrically. "I forgot. That is what I had to say. To protect him!"

Murkier and murkier. "And Fidel knows about this?"

"Fidel knows everything. You remember Ochoa? From 1976, he was sending drugs to North America. For thirteen years. You think Fidel doesn't know? His best friend, a Hero of the Revolution, his old *compañero,* is selling drugs to the *yanquis,* and he doesn't know? *El Máximo* knows how many liters of milk come from every cow in Camagüey, but he doesn't know his friend is making business?"

"Cool it, Lula—someone may hear." I began to think she was getting off on this stuff, or this was what they did to while away the afternoons. I remembered how I'd seen the kids in Prague and Leningrad make dramas of their lives to fill up all the empty spaces. Or maybe she just wanted to make herself more attractive to a sentimental foreigner with a nose for news.

"What can they do? What more can I lose? I have nothing. I have no food, no clothes, no freedom. I have no life, no job, no husband. What more can they take away from me? Only in this way I am free. I have nothing.

"*Mira,* Richard"—she put a soft hand on my leg—"I tried once to sail to America. After five minutes they caught me. They have this trick. Someone—maybe someone from school, or a neighbor—comes and says, 'Today a boat is leaving for Miami. Near Cojímar. At twelve o'clock.' You go there, and they are waiting for you." She made the gesture of a manacle around her wrist. "After five minutes they catch Lourdes. And for thirteen years they do not know that Ochoa is selling drugs?"

"So what about it? Where does that put you?"

"I need to leave, right now."

"You have plans?"

"Maybe. I thought before maybe you could help me. But I understand now you will never marry me."

"Why not marry someone else?"

"No. I want only you."

"I know," I said, and put my arm upon her shoulder, but our lives were not what she wanted to talk about right now. "Look, Richard. Give me your notebook." I handed her the pad I kept for captions, and she wrote down the names of the secret groups on a piece of paper. Then she had me read them out again, read them back to me herself, and made sure I got them by heart. Then she tore out the page and put a match to it. It looked like a lighted joint, this poison for the mind, burning itself up on a Havana afternoon.

In the evening, after a dinner we did not have, we sat on the stoop, taking long swigs from the bottle. I didn't like to see how quickly she fell into this routine: getting a bottle from next door, bringing it down to the stoop, wiping the top before she swallowed. In every gesture I saw a whole trail of nights like this, on and on, in both directions, taking her through ten years in a week.

"My mother told you about my brother?"

"Your sister, you mean?"

"No, my brother, Arturo."

"The one in New Jersey?"

"Yes. She didn't tell you? Maybe she does not want to think of this. She thinks of him, and then she cannot sleep, she goes crazy with these thoughts. So she talks about my sister's wedding, and tries to feel happy. But inside, she is always thinking of Arturo. That is why I asked you for this Tylenol. To help my mother sleep."

"He's in prison?"

"*Muerto.*"

That was all she said, but I could figure out the rest: what happens to a kid without any English, who washes up in America from Cuba, ends up with the gangs, gets into running drugs or hard-line protection jobs.

"My aunt is a millionaire," she said—she still believed that—"and she does not help him. She has two Chevrolets and color TV and swimming pool. But she is an American now. So she never thinks about the family. Only money."

"You Cubans seem to have a good eye on the dollar too."

"Of course," she said, her words already slurred. "The dollar is our god. We make love to the dollar. We suck the dollar. We want to marry the dollar. But we have nothing else to do. Anything we do in Cuba, we are a traitor—or a loser. If we work hard, if we never work, it is the same. *El Caballo* has invited us to a party where there is no music and no drinks. And if we do not come, we will be dead."

"Señor Bush will invite you to a party where there are plenty of drinks, and everyone is fighting for them. And if you're not quicker than the next guy, you get nothing."

"But if you *are* quicker?—if you have a mind?—then the world is yours, right?"

"Right, Lourdes," I said, and stopped the conversation with my mouth.

She put her arm around my shoulder, woozy from the drink, red-eyed, and looked at me in a kind of blur.

"I love you, Richard," she said.

"I love you, Lourdes." And then I figured it was the moment. While she was soft like this, defenses down. Not exactly the proposal I'd planned in Varadero, but something a little more practical.

"Listen, Lula, I have a plan."

"I know," she said, eyes sparking a little.

"No, not like that. A plan for us. For our future."

"Your next trip?"

"*Your* next trip. How would you like to get married?"

That stopped her in her tracks. "I think I am drinking too much rum. Say it again."

"Do you want to get married?"

She looked at me again, her eyes more in focus now.

"Not to me. I mean, to me, in our hearts, but on paper, to someone else."

"What are you saying, Richard?" She felt my forehead. "You are sick, I think. Too much rum?"

"Listen: it happens all the time. I choose a friend—Hugo, maybe—and we go to Cayo Largo, with you. You marry him. Then he gets you a passport—and a visa. You go to join him in England, and I meet you there."

"But why? Why do you not marry me?"

"It's not so easy. I'm American. I'm here on a different kind of visa. And I'm still married."

"You can divorce."

"It's not that easy. Divorce is something your government is better at than mine."

"So you want me to marry Hugo?"

"For one day only."

"And we go to England?"

"Right. And I pick you up there. It is a way for us to be together. For you to see New York."

"And Hugo? He likes this idea?"

"I haven't asked him yet. I will tell him this weekend in Santiago."

It wasn't the way I'd planned it, to be asking her like this, on a stoop, with a bottle of rum between her legs, her breath stinking, I on my way out of town. It wasn't Varadero. But it was practical.

"So, Richard," she said, taking another long swig. "You will make the wedding photograph?"

"Of course," I said. "But all the pictures will be private ones. And the groom will not be in any one of them."

She kissed me then, mostly on the lips, and she waved her bottle blindly at the dark.

I hadn't managed to hook up with José that day, to square away the details of our honeymoon, but the next morning, when I went to the Havanautos office next to the Capri, as soon as I sat down in the *cola*, next to some Swiss granola kids, I heard a voice behind me. "I think you get the '54 Plymouth. Is better for you."

It was José—who else?—working some Irish guys, and when I turned round, he flashed me his smile. "So what are you up to, my friend?"

"A little this, a little that," he answered, leaving the Irishmen to their calculations. "*Capitalismo, más o menos.* Look, I tell my friend to give you his best car—you would like a Mercedes?—and we go and have a drink in the Capri."

Half the hotels on the island were being tarted up, or closed off, for foreigners, so we sat in the lobby, among the Vegas statues, and ordered Taoro mango juice.

"So the car's no problem?"

"No problem, Richard. Look, you want an Oldsmobile, I can get for you. My friend has a friend who sends them to Ja-my-ca. Thirty thousand pesos. Only five thousand in your money. If you want, I tell him, he shows you the car, you give the money, and it's yours. Or, if you want, he keeps it here, drives it every week, keeps it clean, until the old man goes. Then you can come and get it."

"It sounds like your plan for Lourdes."

"Sure. Women and cars, that is what everyone wants from Cuba now. The cars are old, the women are young, both are worth much money. But anything, if you want, I can get for you."

"Thanks."

"So what is happening with Lourdes?"

"That's what I wanted to fix up with you."

"Sure. No problem. My friend can do it. Twenty-four hours, forty-eight hours. 'While you wait,' as you say in America."

"So what's the deal?"

"You have a friend?"

"Yeah. He doesn't know the whole plan yet, but he flies in today, from Shannon. He has a reservation at the Inglaterra, but we're going to bag that, drive down to Santiago as soon as possible. A couple of days alone on the way to talk things over. Then we come back here on Monday, and there's still five days for Cayo Largo."

"Is good. Look, I make the plan for you. When you go to Santiago, you visit my father, okay? You will like him. He speaks English, I think. I have never heard it, but he learned from his father in Jamaica. He was in the hills with Fidel. So you stay one night at my father's house." I wondered how many fathers José had, strategically placed around the island.

"Okay."

"Then you wait, two months, three months, I think. You don't see her, you don't talk to her. Then she gets her papers. And it is the same as you are husband and wife."

"How about you?"

"Me? I'm fine. Today I make a party at my house. Lobster and champagne. You come at eight o'clock, okay?"

"No time. I've got to make more pictures before I go to the wedding. But what about you in the future? When are you going to leave?"

For once, José looked taken aback. For once, he paused before he spoke. "I will go when the time is right. For now, I wait. My friend makes your wedding in Cayo Largo, I help him, maybe you give him fifty dollars, and a hundred dollars for me. That will help. Then I make business."

"Here?"

"Sure. I tell you something, Richard." He leaned in closer, and put his hand on my back as if he were telling me a dirty joke. "I go to the American Embassy before, maybe three months before, and I tell them I was in prison, four years: a graduate of Combinado. So now I want to leave. Political asylum. This guy there—a fat guy, a Chicano, speaks good Spanish—he tells me, 'You stay here. We need more guys like you. You stay here, you watch the streets, then later we'll take care of you.' "

"And your passport from Bolivia?"

"Sure. I can get it anytime. Dominican too. But I want to make more of a dream: maybe I go to Barcelona, open up a coffee shop, a library—no, a bookshop, right? Is like what Pepe—Martí—says. 'It is a torment of man that to see well he must be wise. And then forget that he is wise.' "

I fixed up a car then—a Nissan, less conspicuous than a Benz, and less likely to attract unwanted friends from both sides of the fence—and headed for the airport. Hugo's plane was due in at 7:50, and I wanted to get going as soon as possible, we had so much to do.

It wasn't hard to spot him on the sidewalk: the only guy I knew who'd come to Cuba in a cricket sweater and an old boy's tie, with a Marks & Spencer suitcase in his hand. He looked like a district officer sent out to check on the natives. But when he saw me, he smiled so broadly, and waved at me so warmly, that I almost felt bad, to be thinking of these clothes as his wedding dress.

"Very good to see you again," he said, shaking my hand.

"Here too. How was the flight?"

"Oh, not too bad. Russian service is not so different from British Rail."

"Are you wasted?"

"No, I wouldn't say so. Slept quite well on the plane, actually. Ready to go anywhere."

Even to your altar, I thought, and then I started up, and we drove back toward town, and then hit the Autopista and drove along the sea as the sun began to set. Later, when it got dark, we cut inland, toward the interior. The small country roads, after the main highway to the beach, were black, pitch black, no lights along their margins, no lights on bicycles or trucks, nothing but a line of fields, and sometimes, out of nowhere, a figure all in white standing by the road. Who were these people, standing by an empty road, at dead of night, alone? Hitchhikers in a country without private cars? *Santeros* out to placate the spirits at a crossroads? Taxi girls working the back roads? "Highwaymen," is what Hugo decided on, ready to perform some kind of nighttime robbery.

I didn't want to drive too far that night—I needed time to talk to him, especially while he was still a little out of it—so we stopped at a hotel in Trinidad, a big gaudy place by the sea, sleepy, haunted by absences, its bright corridors and party-colored dining room waiting for tour groups that would never come. Outside, near the pool, some Italian boy was singing "It Ain't Me, Babe" to a guitar, while his girlfriend lay back on a deck chair. A Euro couple or two were in the bar, listening to a canned version of "Surfin' U.S.A.," while the locals gathered in one corner to watch Spanish porno movies on a VCR. We had a room overlooking the sea—like Varadero again, or Cayo Largo—and when we checked in, Hugo opened the terrace door, and stretched out his arms.

"Can hardly believe it. Woke up this morning, and I was in my flat in Winchester, after a night at the Wykeham Arms. Now here I am next to the Caribbean. Doesn't feel quite real."

"You feeling the flight?"

"No. It's not too bad, actually. I'm rather coming to life."

"Let's hit the town, then," I said, and we went down to the pool for a drink, the faint sound of "Girl from the North Country" and "Blowin' in the Wind" carrying through the night toward us.

"So what prompted you to decide so suddenly on a reunion?"

"I don't know. Impulse, I guess. And the fact I can't get the place out of my system."

"By place, I suspect you mean Lourdes."

"That too."

"In fact, I'm rather surprised you're not spending the time with her."

"I'll see her. She'll probably meet us in Santiago in a couple of days." I decided to play things quiet right now, just to plant a seed or two.

"She's such a sweet girl."

"Yeah, I guess you could say that." I waved away a couple of boys who were about to offer us their friendship. "You really like her, don't you?"

"Well, there's no denying her charm."

"I know. The thing is, charm can be used to good effect."

"Better that, I should think, than its opposite."

"Yeah, I guess."

"Don't you ever think of marrying her?" This was all going way too fast.

"What do you mean?"

"It is, one gathers, the usual thing."

"Yeah, but I'm married already. And with my job, it isn't easy. Traveling all the time, I hardly have a home, and I'm not pulling down what you'd call a steady income."

"Hardly insurmountable obstacles."

"You're the type she should marry, Hugo."

"Oh, of course. Mr. Glamour and Excitement."

"No, I'm serious."

"Thank you. Here's to marriage." And he raised his glass of orange juice and toasted me.

"To the Queen."

"The Queen," he said solemnly, and we toasted again.

On the next day, it was more of the same. We drove through avenues of sugarcane, through long, dusty roads empty of cars but swarming with cats and chickens and dogs and kids on bicycles. Sometimes we stopped at broken gas stations with ropes across their aisles under signs that said OPEN 24 HOURS, and sometimes I felt I was in New Mexico or somewhere: the squat pumps, an empty office, a sign on the road, ESTAMOS CONTIGO.

We passed through provincial towns that morning, with long lines of yellow and green and sky-blue houses, lined up along shuttered cobbled streets, like in Bolivia or Honduras, except the people here moved with a slow and sensuous African gait. There was something Nigerian about these towns: the bouncing-ball rhythm of the boys, the black girls with their sultry Yoruba walk, the giant florid palms. And there was something Spanish about the African rhythms too: something gilded and inert, in the churches and the lines. The way everyone hurried slowly, and moved in place with laid-back fervor.

On the road, the signs were almost too good to be true. SOCIALISM TRANSFORMS OUR LIVES, said the billboards, presiding over empty fields and dead, deserted, one-lane roads. ALL ROADS LEAD TO VISA, said a newer one, and I remembered how, the one time I'd managed to use a Visa card here, I'd been hassled for months by registered letters from some bank in Mexico. Sometimes the signs said: SANTIAGO 969 KM. Then we would drive for ten minutes, toward Santiago, and they'd say: SANTIAGO 973 KM. The whole country moving backward, further and further from its goal.

"Aren't you going to take any pictures?" Hugo asked. "I would have thought these would be perfect."

"Too perfect," I said, and it was true: that was the problem with the place sometimes. The symbols came too easily. Everything was just too ready-made. There was a girl on a balcony at dusk, looking forlorn, and the sign across from her, half broken, was for the Imperial Hotel, and next to it another sign, in neon, with some of the letters blinking on and off: XX SIGLO—Twentieth Century. If I sent that to my editors, they'd think it was a setup. The ironies here were too much to believe.

Innocence, blindfolded, in a city of the dead? Give me a break.

We stopped for lunch at a small town, wooden cash registers in the stores, like in some forgotten frontier town, and salty old dogs in John Lee Hooker glasses sitting on park benches. A bus, with PIONEROS on the side, sat along the square, not moving, and the little girls—young Communists—by the windows combed their hair by the reflections. The signs around them said: VICTORIA DE PUEBLO. TE SIGO PORQUE TE QUIERO.

Outside, in the plaza, *campesinos* in black gaucho hats, and skinny, shirtless boys, and the girls gathering in the street to look at the foreigners, while the horse-drawn carts clopped by. A line was already forming outside the Santa Fe Confectionery door, two hours before it opened, and in the Blue Sky shop, there was, above two dusty cans, and a row of empty shelves, a sign that said: SOCIALISM IS THE ONLY WAY, AND I AM A SOCIALIST—FIDEL.

A couple of policemen stopped by in a Lada to have a chat, and when they saw we weren't trading any dollars, they drove away, disappointed. A young waiter came up to ask us about Bush's beliefs, and the latest developments of perestroika. Then came the daily downpour, a hot wind blowing through the open doors, and the darkened rooms where men were sitting at empty desks, and then the supermarket, where all the shelves were bare except for four bottles of baby cream, and along the verandas where the *abuelas* sat and rocked back and forth on their chairs. A girl—the local beauty, I guessed—with acid-washed jeans and a bare, golden midriff, came out to us in the rain, cradling a puppy in her arms. "Hola," she called, her sheer black top clinging to her cocoa skin. "Where are you from?" "England." "I like England," she said, and looked up at us from where she stood, showing off her downcast eyes.

Then, as suddenly, the rain stopped, and the wind took over. The trees bristled and shook in the gusts, and the people scattered back to houses like leaves. The plaza was empty again, and soon it was dark, and our lights caught the eyes of goats as we passed, or sometimes a lone bicyclist. We stopped in Camagüey, in a hotel where the guys in the lobby were watching video nasties from Hong Kong, and the hard-currency lovelies were taking turns walking across the lobby, shooting us saucy, languid looks.

Dinner would be a three-hour wait, we heard, and besides, there was no food, so we took to the road again, in the dark. Occasionally, very occasionally, we were blinded by the headlights of an oncoming jeep; sometimes we passed burning torches in the back of horse-drawn carts. The road signs were impossible to read now—no one knew where anyone was going—and, in any case, the roads were completely unmarked, so we were like blind men in an unlit house.

When we got to Holguín, we stopped at a hotel on a hill, a huge luxury hotel full of no one except a few Argentine guys on the look-out for girls and maybe a Spaniard or two dreaming of condos. The restaurant was open, the man at the desk said, but it didn't have any food; there was a party by the pool tonight—lots of music.

I don't know, maybe I was tired then, of seeing the country slowly winding down, and losing its luster and energy, and maybe I was tired of hearing the people talking more and more of Franco, and waiting out the long, painful death of a dictatorship. And some-times, when the country sparked back to life, it was saddest of all: like an old man who just won't let go of his bravado. *"Caramba!"* he shouts to all the *muchachas.* "How about a dance? You know, not many years ago, all the *chiquitas* called me *El Sabroso, El Tigre.* I had more girls than you've had beers. I was the king of the city then." But now, when he talks, he gets red in the face, and loses his breath, and you can see where he puts shoe polish in his hair. "You know this Ava Gardner: even she wanted to go with me when she was here. Ay, how can I tell you? The way the girls lined up then, over in Miramar, to get a dance with me. I could have had anyone I wanted—*rubias, chinas. Mulattas* too." And now people laugh in embarrassment when he's around, and find excuses to slip away, or let their eyes stray around the room as he talks of all his conquests.

Maybe it was all that, and the long drive, and the dark, and the sense that we were about to hit something, but something in me snapped when we got to the pool and the whole chorus of *"No hay nada"* started up again. "You know, that's what I love about all these Communist countries," I said, and I could tell my voice was too loud. "They have all these Three-Year Plans and Five-Year Plans and Ten-Year Plans, and they can't even plan tomorrow after-noon. They're just making it up as they go along. They're treating Marx the way the Southern Baptists treat the Bible. I mean, here you are, you've got a funky tropical island in the Caribbean, hot, spicy, all sex and rum and color, and you try to get it to dance to some ideas laid down by a nineteenth-century German in the British Museum. Might as well tell you Brits to go Rasta."

"But you've got to concede that the people here are terribly warmhearted."

"Sure. But warmhearted also means hotheaded. It's the one thing the government has achieved. They've got the whole island united, just the way they want it, but they're all united against the government. Every *compañero* helping out every other *compañero* to find a way to beat the system. They're all lined up against a common enemy, but the enemy isn't the Yankees, it's Fidel. He's made a whole island of Revolutionaries against the Revolution. It's like the island is up against the system."

"Cuba and the night, so to speak."

"That's right. You've been reading Martí?"

"Well, it's a funny thing. You remember I was telling you about my uncle?"

"Kind of."

"Used to be here in the fifties. Well, I rooted around some more in my aunt's house. Turns out he was working for the guerrillas."

"Fidel and Company?"

"Exactly. When they were still just starting. I suppose he was one of those imperial types who'd been trained to go forth and do good deeds for the provinces. And with the Empire gone, he came over here."

"And . . ."

"Well, I think it all ended rather badly. His girlfriend turned out to be a government informer. And so he rather left with his tail between his legs. But it did get me to rethink things a bit. And I found some books of Martí among his papers. He really was quite an extraordinary character. You know he went into battle armed only with a revolver and a collection of speeches by Cicero?"

"Sounds like one of you guys."

"Maybe so. But I do think there was something terribly stirring about him. Look, I've got one of the books here. 'His whole life was like the dawn of a wedding night.' " It was the tribute to Emerson again. " 'What raptures filled his soul, what visions swam before his eyes!' " I saw where he had made some of his black hieroglyphics next to a line about how friendship, for Emerson, "had the solemnity of twilight in the forest." "And you know this one?" he was going on. " 'The desire to rise above oneself is an unrelenting human longing.' "

"That's great, Hugo. But where did all that get him? Where did all the noble sentiments end up? The first time he went into battle, he got shot."

"But his memory is all around, his precedent."

"Sure. Giving Fidel a rationale for more heroic blundering."

"The thing is, he completely believed in all these things. He really had conviction."

"A typically Cuban conviction." I thought back then to the talks we'd had those first nights in the hotels. It sounded like we were on opposite sides of the table now: that was how Cuba worked on you. Suddenly you found yourself taking up the same position you'd been arguing against the day before.

I watched him sip his beer. "I mean, after all the pretty words, what comes next? What about the reality?"

"Well, I'll grant you that the main problem for Castro is that he did so much so early. So dramatically. He pulled off so many miracles when he took over that everyone expects him to keep on doing it all his life. Even he expects it, I suspect. Having seen lightning strike once, he can't believe that it won't happen again. So he keeps trying to pull a new rabbit out of the hat."

"And while he's playing with his hankie, ten million people are starving."

"I know. It's always easy, don't you think, to sympathize with people who are victims of circumstance? But much harder to find sympathy for those who are the victims of themselves?" He gave a sharp laugh.

"Like you and Carmen, you mean?" and I don't know why I was trying to hurt him.

"Not really. She's probably married to a solicitor now."

"But you have no one to blame for all that except yourself."

"I know. It's not as if I haven't realized that."

"And now you're back in school, just the way you started."

"In a manner of speaking. I did actually try to be an antiquarian bookseller for a while, but it wasn't really my thing. So I thought I might as well go back to Winchester, and do some teaching there while I was making up my mind. Path of least resistance, so to speak."

Just then something in me, and it wasn't the best part, just wanted to shove his face in it: to bring out my black portfolio and show him all the pictures I'd taken that the editors wouldn't run. Because they were too powerful. The refugees in their burned-out shacks in Somalia, their babies two or three days from the grave. The girls in the ruins of Smoky Mountain, not yet past puberty, offering blow jobs for their dinner. The kids in the townships getting necklaced for choosing the wrong girl to date. Here he was, worrying about Latin adverbs, while half the world was starving, or living amid war and poverty and oppression. I don't know why I suddenly felt like that: maybe I was angry Hugo wasn't more like me. Maybe I was angry I wasn't more like him.

The next day, when I got up, it was as if the storm had passed, and blown through town, and I felt as open and cloudless as the sky. On the last leg of the drive, I decided just to pass the time with war stories: about the time I'd done acid on the beach in Thailand, with a girl, and we were making love in our hut, and then I'd heard helicopters overhead, and I thought I was freaking out, and I ran out to the beach, and there were all these Hueys, and a beach littered with the corpses of dogs. About the time I'd been on patrol with the Tigers in Sri Lanka, and been reported missing at sea for two weeks. About the time I got kidnapped in the Bekaa for six hours before they decided I wasn't valuable enough for them. I guess I was talking to myself as much as him.

But soon the stories ran out, and the rain started up again, and somehow I got to thinking about what was waiting for me back home: a couple of contact sheets, a few carousels, some images of war. A suitcase packed for emergencies and a Radio Shack beeper. A pile of unanswered mail. Last year looked like next year, and the year after that, and the next. The images stretched on and on. Like Lourdes with her bottle, in a way; like Fidel with his textbooks.

"I don't think I ever told you," I said, as we drove through the downpour. "The last time I went to see my friend José. There was a girl there, in the kitchen, called Myra. She laid out some tarot cards on the table, to tell my destiny. I was living in a big house, she said. With a girl. I had found the partner of my dreams."

"I expect she was thinking of herself."

"I'm sure she was. But still, you know, I think she might have been onto something. Because after a while you get tired of this job. Feel like you'll go crazy if you keep doing it, living for the moment, swallowing lithium by the handful, waiting for the next disaster. The last guys in the world shooting stills in the age of motion pictures."

Outside, the rain had let up, and the light was silver and blue above the fields. Like the whole island had been washed clean, and returned to its infant self.

"So you're thinking of a career change?"

"I don't know. I don't know what else I could do. But I see some of these guys, and they become such adrenaline junkies, there's no way out for them. And some of them get out, and then they can't make pictures anymore. Because suddenly every starving kid in Ethiopia is your kid, and you don't want to be away too long from your wife, and you've got to look out for yourself because you've got a family to protect. No way I could do that: for me, I've got to give it everything, or not do it at all."

"So what have you got in mind?"

"I don't know. Maybe try to hook up with the *Geographic* for some three-month jobs. Or go into advertising. Maybe try videos." We passed a group of boys smiling by the road, and a village of bare houses, with people sitting on their porches; we passed small parks with ice cream stalls, and empty stores, and lines.

"I ever tell you about the girl in Paraguay?"

"I don't believe you did."

"Well, she was really from Brazil. And Brazil with a big *B*. You know, that wild, sun-bleached hair; sweet, lush mouth; golden skin. And a way of whispering those sexy Portuguese gutturals so that everything sounded like a come-on. Brilliant too, in her way."

"Sounds ideal."

"She *was* ideal. One of a kind. I met her at the Presidente Hotel one day. She told me she'd been living up in Ciudad del Este for four years, with some Lebanese guy, into import-export, if you know what I mean. He'd had to return to Lebanon to take care of business—liquidate the assets or something—so she was on the loose. So anyway, I lost no time, gave her a ticket to come to Rio with me, kind of set up house there. Two blocks from the beach, in this Ipanema apartment complex. I started working for one of the newsmagazines—I knew the bureau chief from Southeast Asia—and she just worked on her tan. Went like a dream. Weekends, we'd go to Búzios, Parati, Foz do Iguaçú; the rest of the time we'd spend on the beach, or in the golf club at Gavea."

"Very nice."

"It was. And then one time I was on assignment, and I called in for my messages, and I got a man's voice, saying she wasn't there right now. And then I ran into a guy from the Intercon, who said he'd met her over there one night, in the disco. And then I found these boarding passes in her drawer."

"Had you been planning to marry her?"

"Maybe."

"Did you tell her that?"

"I was waiting till I was sure."

"Could have been a long wait, by the sound of it."

"How can I marry someone who's always flying off? I've been through that already."

"Why should she not fly off when you're not going to marry her?"

"So what do you suggest, Dr. Ruth?"

"I suggest you marry your Cuban lady."

"I suggest you do."

He looked at me blankly for a moment, and then laughed. A little farther on, we picked up two girls by the side of the road, a blond beauty and her friend. Dolores and Esperanza, they said their names were. Sorrows and Hope. Too perfect yet again.

When we got to town, I dropped Hugo off in Céspedes Park, and told him we'd meet up again at seven in the Casagranda: there was still a lot of daylight, and I wanted to use the light after the rain. I parked the car in the plaza, and then I began working the streets, the samba bars and cobbled alleyways around the cathedral, the houses along the slope, the place where Frank País used to live. I got the two girls to pose in front of the Venus Hotel, and asked them to come back at sunset, and I'd pay them for their time. I rode the buses, shooting blind with a wide-angle lens, pretending I was just another local returning from Miami.

I walked the streets till they were imprinted on my feet and I could have found my way with my eyes closed. Sometime around noon I took a break in the Casa de los Estudiantes, downtown, and a woman came out to talk to me, a woman with a gray bun and a kindly face. "Where are you from?" she began, in English. "Do you like our country?" But before I could answer, she was going into her spiel. "Before, it was all poverty. Beggars, prostitutes, people who lived in the street. We had money, sure, but there was nothing we could buy. Now I have in my room TV, a refrigerator, an air conditioner. We do not have money, but we are rich." As I got up to leave, she asked me if I could spare a present for her kids.

In the main plaza, the old guys were sitting on benches, not smiling, not talking, just watching the world go by, though there wasn't much world, and it wasn't going by. They'd canceled Carnival this year, some guy told me, because of the Games, and they needed the money for the foreigners: Cubans were reminded again that the only thing there wasn't a shortage of was sacrifice. A true egalitarianism: everyone had the same amount of nothing. At the best restaurant in town—the only restaurant—the one thing on the menu was "Roast Feef," and when I ordered that, the waiter brought me a burned-out piece of water buffalo.

I went to the Casagranda for some coffee, and the waiter told me there was no coffee today. No milk. No water. No tea.

"Hey," said a man in a white guayabera at the next table. "No salt, no sugar, no pepper, no bread. But we got dancing girls!"

I looked back at him, and he wasted no time.

"May I join you?" he asked, in perfect English, and he came and sat down at my table. "Pleased to meet you." He extended a hand. "My name is Faust." I guess he'd gauged his audience already.

"Faust can tell you everything, my friend. Whatever you want to know, Faust will tell."

"The first thing I'd like to know is what you're doing here."

"Business, pleasure, a little conversation. Cuba is not easy for the Cuban, my friend." He ran a nervous hand through his thinning hair.

"Where did you get your English?"

"In the old days. Guantánamo. Used to fly for the Cuban Air Force. Way back, the good old days. Everybody used to speak English then. Before, I used to live in Florida. You know the Club Number 4 in London? You know the Copa in Coconut Grove? Sure. I know all the places. Get a look at this."

He pulled out, from his wallet, an old black-and-white photo of someone dressed as a devil in some long-ago Carnival. "Me." He chuckled. "Faust must always come as the devil, no? Santiago, 1957. What a party we had! With the Yankees. All the guys from Guantánamo, me, what a week!"

He put the photo back. "Used to be married to a Dade County girl too. A model. A beauty queen. My mistake number one was to divorce the girl by proxy in '67. That was how I got stuck over here. My mistake number two was to lose her address. I tried to contact her family, but, as they say in America, 'No dice!' "

He sat back, and then pointed to the huge holes in the ceiling, and let out a terrible toothless cackle.

"So what do you think of Cuba, my friend?"

"Interesting. Real interesting."

"You are a diplomat, I see, as well as a photographer. My friend saw you taking pictures in the street. Who do you work for? *Miami Herald? New York Times?*"

The guy was coming on too strong: whichever side he was on was the side I didn't want to be on.

"*Turista.*"

"Sure. A tourist with a 1947 Canon. I don't think so, *compañero.*"

"And you? What kind of work are you in?"

"Work? Who works in Cuba? Only the stupid and the blind. Me, I just try to get by. I deal in poison." He waited for a reaction. "In contamination of the mind." He picked up a pocket transistor, and pressed a button. I heard the ads on Radio Martí. I figured the guy was so far gone, he had nothing to lose. "You see this? Poison! Contraband! If they see this, it is worse than a gun. A radio Revolutionary!" He threw back his head and laughed.

"So, my friend, what would you like to see? Faust will show you everything. Faust is at your service. You want photographs? Photographs of the true Cuba? Photographs of the country that nobody ever sees? What say we drive? You got a car?"

"You work for the government, right?"

"Heh-heh, not so fast, *compañero*. I work for myself. Who does not?"

It was like playing chess with a blindfold master: he had the whole game in his head.

We got into the car, and I began driving.

"Hey, I tell you I had a ticket out in 1962? But I told myself I'd wait a little. Look at where it got me! In a pickle, as you say."

He laughed and laughed, dementedly. "You see, my friend, I am Catalan! That is why I am so strong. If you call a Catalan a Spanishman, he will call you the worst names in the world! Sure. We Catalans are tough and wily. You cannot fool us. Not us. Not me. There's no fooling Faust!" Again, the ratchety laugh.

"Just like your leader, then?"

"Sure. You know, when our friend was young, he read Nietzsche, Robespierre, *Mein Kampf!*" There was silence; I wasn't going to make it easier for him. "Sure. Listen to Faust! Faust knows everything! You know that time our friend was in the cornfields in Alegría del Río, with only two others? And they had to lick the dew from the leaves to stay alive. That time when he said, 'Nobody surrenders here!' You know the names of his friends, my friend? They were Faustino and Universo. Not this Faust, oh no! But the same name!" He went on and on, like a record that was jumping. "When he was young, you know, our friend was reading *Mein Kampf.*"

"And yet you admire him?"

"Of course, my friend, why not?" He looked around the car hungrily. "I say many things, many things. More things than you can know. You cannot stop me. Faust knows everything. And in Cuba, it is always best to have many points of view. Just like a girl needs different dresses for every day of the week." He cackled horribly. "To some we say Fidel is a god. To some we say he is a Hitler."

"And to yourself? What do you say to yourself?"

"I say, 'Be quiet.' Walls have ears."

"Shit!" A bicycle came out at me, and I swerved the car off the road, into the grass. With a shrieking of tires, the car rolled up the incline again, and we went on.

"Be careful, my friend," said Faust. "You need more patience. Chinese patience."

"That's the trouble with you guys," I said, angry with myself for taking on this guy and thinking it might lead somewhere. "Too much patience. Everyone is patient with everything. Waiting in lines to wait in lines. Waiting for someone else to spring the trigger. This is an island of goddamn waiters."

"You are wrong, my friend. That isn't the problem. What Cubans have isn't patience. It's a lack of something—call it balls." He looked around. "Hey, you got a McDonald's hidden away in here? You got a hamburger in this car? How about we stop and eat?" He started foraging under the floor mats.

It was horrible to see, more horrible in its way than the kids in East Africa or the Sahel: the hunger had made him desperate, craven, and instead of just a kind of slow withering and silence, there was this terrible speeding up, and this chatter, like the feverish death throes of some animal. Toothless Faust was grinning as he whored for bread.

"Give me the McDonald's," he shouted. He was losing it. "Give me some food. Faust needs food. Faust hasn't eaten anything today!"

I turned the car round and headed back to town.

"Look, my friend," he began again as we passed some buildings. "Look at the apartments. They aren't homes. They aren't houses. They are carton boxes. That's what they've given us. Shit and then more shit. When do we see a black in power? When was the last time we saw a black with any power?"

I stopped the car where I was, and opened the door to let him out. "The ride ends here, *Señor*," I said, and gave him a couple of dollars. He grabbed at them hungrily, and opened up his little transistor, and took out the batteries, and stashed the money away in the battery compartment.

"Okay, my friend," he said. "I'll see you later. When the shooting starts, I'll meet you under the bed." And then, weaving crazily, he veered off into the distance.

I got back into town in time to shoot the girls, and then, in the long twilight, I picked up Hugo and drove up to the Las Américas, to satisfy anyone who was watching us. It was Mad Night that night ("Here you will have chance to Sing, Dance, Jump, Cry Out," said the notice on the bulletin board), and there were some old ads—maybe they'd been put up only yesterday—for Happy Hour and Blind Night ("with your Accustomed Participation"). Blind Night seemed pretty much the story every night in Cuba.

After we'd filled out all the forms, and left the key in an envelope for José, sweetened by ten bucks for the guy at the desk, we followed José's directions to his father's house, a few blocks away, on Avenida de los Libertadores. We parked around the corner, as he'd told us to do, and then followed the brass plaques till we came to the door: the same as all the others, an ancient Spanish-style numeral by a bell that didn't work, a door that had lost its paint. Inside, one big dark room, a couple of icons on the wall, and a small passageway, leading through a courtyard past a series of rooms.

"Señor Cruz?"

"Great to see you," said the muscular old man, shirtless, who greeted us at the entrance, his close-cropped hair gray under his cap, his body still sturdy and firm. "My son told me you were coming. Hey, Luis." He turned and shouted back into the interior. "Run along to Raúl and see what you can get in the way of rum. Maybe we'll have a party tonight. I'll tell Pastor to rustle up a pig."

The man spoke Spanish to his sons; to us he spoke the kind of English I'd only heard in sitcoms, a kind of jaunty, Rotary Club English that came straight out of "I Love Lucy."

"Here, come and see the palace," he said, and he led us out into the courtyard and past the drab and darkened rooms. Inside the first of them, a pudgy boy all in white was methodically arranging offerings around a kind of altar. "You see," said the old man, in a low voice, "Pastor has gone the voodoo way. He knows I don't like it, but what can I do? You've got to have something to believe in when things are hard. So he talks about it to his mother. I don't like this voodoo thing, but for him, that's where the hope is."

He led us back into the main room, and Hugo sat in one corner of the sofa, I in the other, checking it all out for light. "Here, let me get you guys some beer," he said, and pulled a few cans out of the freezer. He handed us a couple, then sat back in his rocking chair and popped open his Labatt.

"I guess José has told you my story. You probably heard more stories in this town than you could read in the *Reader's Digest*. Enough stories to fill a book. Mine's not so different. Used to work with the Yankees on the base over there: listen to the Dodgers on the radio; catch some shows on TV; just havin' a good time. Then one day my commander says to me, 'Hey, Peter. Give me some guns.' So I do, and he says, 'I've given them to the guys up there in the mountains.' And a few days later—maybe a couple of weeks—I get this message, 'You better join us.' My mother says to me, 'Son, don't join them. It's only trouble.' But what do I know? I'm twenty-five years old, it sounds like an adventure."

Hugo was sitting spellbound; I was getting restless.

"So anyway, I go up there, work with Fidel, grow a beard, train with a gun: the whole thing. Then, when they take Havana, one of the guys say to me, 'You're a captain now, you can have anything you want. What'll it be?' They give me a job, high up, runnin' everything, tell me I can take any car I want, any girl from the cabarets too, and pretty soon I'm findin' that it isn't so much fun anymore, not like in the mountains. Like with a girl, y'know? When you're after her, everything is romantic and exciting, and you're always thinkin' of the girl. Then you get her and—kerboom: it's back to the same old routine.

"I was young then, like I say, but I could see where things were headin'. They give me a big house in Miramar, anything I want, any position in the government, any food and drink. And after a while I say, 'No, sir. I'm goin' back to Oriente, where I can live in peace.'

"That's the way for me now. Just keep quiet, keep your head low, don't talk back to no one, don't ask for nothin'."

"Till what happens?"

"Till you die, I guess. Or he does." He laughed. "See, I can talk to you. With you guys, I can say anything—it's like a vacation for me, speaking English. José tell you I was born in Jamaica? Never spoke a word of Spanish till I was fifteen. Now I never speak a word of English. Never speak a word of truth, either. 'Cause maybe one day I'm mad, and I say something to the wife, and she doesn't like it and she tells her sister, and the sister tells her husband, whose brother's in the Party, and next thing you know, there's a knock on my door. 'Mr. Cruz. We hear you have a complaint against the Party. Come with us.' So you can't talk to no one here: not your wife, not your kids, no one. Why do you think Fidel ain't got no wife?"

He sat back and rested and drank the beer. There was a photo of Fidel, thirty-five years before, on the wall; a picture of Camilo. There was the sound of the fat boy mumbling something to his gods.

"I tell you something," the old man went on. "It ain't so bad for me. I'm old; I've seen worse; I'm not goin' anywhere. But it's the kids who suffer. And when they suffer, I suffer twice. So I figure the best thing is not to tell them too much. It's better they don't know about the past. Because the more they know, the more they suffer. Already, they suffer. They say, 'I want a T-shirt.' But to pay for it, I got to get my hands on eighty bucks. They say, 'Father, give me an ice cream cone.' But I can't get ice cream. You got a hundred dollars, but still you can't get a pound of rice around here. You got a thousand dollars, but still you can't buy a chicken. So they cry. And when I see that, I want to cry too. But I can't. Can't let them see how I feel. Can't tell them I still have nights, even now, after thirty years, dreamin' what those guys could do to them. You know, I still wake up sometimes, and my arms are all shakin', and it's because I'm thinking what they could do to my kids."

He went out to take a leak, and I tried to see what Hugo was doing. I could hardly see him, it was so dark, but he was sitting very still, and I wondered if he was thinking of his uncle. I was thinking with one part of myself of a picture here; with the other, of our host.

"Don't get me wrong," he said as he rolled back in, with a sailor's kind of walk, and settled back into his chair. "I ain't 'gainst Communism. I ain't 'gainst nothin' that will bring some food and good livin' for my kids. Kids need ideals, somethin' to believe in. Communism's the only hope for guys like me—black, not too much education, never gonna be rich. But I'm not for fightin' five years in the mountains for the same thing we've been killin'. It's like killin' a snake and then goin' off and drinkin' a gallon of snake juice. Where's the sense in that?

"Those guys at the top, they ain't so bad. I know them; I fought with them. Maybe they do want to help us sometimes. But they've got their minds so full of Gorbachev and Pan Am Games and pere-stroika shit, they don't have any room for me and my kids down here. They're thinkin' 'bout pesos next year, and how their cousin's goin' to get a job. I don't blame them; I'd be the same myself. But they ain't helpin' no one but themselves.

"See, Jackie Robinson was always the one I loved," he went on, and I saw the man from next door coming in. *"Bueno. Sientate! Son Ricardo y Hugo. Amigos de José."* We shook hands, and the conver-sation turned to Spanish. "I was just tellin' 'em about the old Dodgers. Best team I ever saw. Saw Gil Hodges once, in Havana, and Duke Snider, in spring training. Heard Campy used to go to the Tropicana."

The conversation went on to the national team, and Luis Tiant, and José Canseco, and then the neighbor must have figured his curiosity was satisfied, because he stood up and walked out.

The old man leaned toward us in the room. It was pitch black now. "See, I just talk like this, to you guys, for an hour, and already the hair is crawlin' on my arms."

"I guess you wouldn't be comfortable with my taking some pic-tures round here?"

"Why d'you need pictures? Maybe this time you just keep the images in your head, okay? Remember them. Because pictures won't show you anythin' in Cuba. Everyone here is wearing a mask. In the house, in the family, everywhere. For me, there's nothin' more important in life than your family. But even in the family here, you can't talk. Maybe somebody believes one thing, somebody else believes the other thing. It's like a civil war."

His voice was coming to us out of the darkness.

"Look, my friends." He lit a match. We could see only the outlines of his face. "Look. I'm lookin'. I'm searchin'. But I can't see no hope anywhere. Can you? Can you see hope? Even with this light, can you see any hope? Where is it? I can't see it."

He shook us back into the dark.

"Like I say, I don't need so much. For me, it's not important. But it's my kids: what have they got to look forward to? José, he's crazy, talking to foreigners, speaking English, all that. But how can I tell him not to do it? It's the only thing he's got. What else has he got to hope for? More voodoo? A job with the Party? We needed change before, sure. Before, during Batista, there was plenty that was hurtin'. But they changed it too much. Now it's crazier than Batista's time. Then, if you had money, you could get something. Now, even a millionaire is broke." He laughed again, a tired old man's laugh.

"So it was lousy during Batista too?"

"Sure. It was shit. Real bad. Prostitutes and drugs; gambling, everything. No question Fidel made things better. But right now, you can't talk about better or worse. It's like choosing between death by gunshot and death by starvation. Maybe the gun's better 'cause it's quicker. But seems to me like we got liberation from craziness so we could get nothingness instead. Many more bargains like that, and old Fidel's gonna be more broke than he is already."

He looked back, and said nothing for a while. "Okay. That's enough politics. Let's eat. Have a fiesta."

Somehow, after all he'd said, I didn't have the heart to go through with the pig: it was like eating the guy's savings. "That's okay," I said, shooting a glance over at Hugo. "We ate at the hotel. Maybe we'll just stay and have a few more beers."

"Make that rum at least," he said, getting up and asking Pastor to hustle up a couple of bottles. "And from now on we speak Spanish again. Become innocent again."

. . .

Hugo went to bed maybe thirty minutes later, and after the last bottle of rum was finished, I let the old guy show me to my room. Hugo was already asleep in the bed, so I just found an open space on the floor and lay down. But there was no way I could sleep. I was wired, head buzzing, like on one of those nights when I had to go out with the guerrillas on patrol at four a.m., and I was so on fire that I'd wake up at two-thirty, and just lie there in the dark.

Outside our room, the pig was snuffling, and rooting around in the grass, and closer to home, I could hear Hugo tossing and turning. Then a sigh, and the sound of the sheet being furiously tossed aside.

"Can't sleep?" I whispered.

"Not really. I think it must be the heat."

"Or the drink. Or something in the air. Or the story we just heard."

"You think it was a story?"

"Sure. You could tell the guy had it all ready for foreign consumption. Why do you think José sent us here?"

"You mean you don't believe it?"

"No, I believe it. The fact he's got it down so perfect doesn't mean it isn't true. When I listen to José and all the others gripe about the Revolution, I figure they don't know anything else. They've lived all their lives with the Revolution, so everything that's gone wrong they can blame on the Revolution, and everything that's not the Revolution, they think is great. But this guy's seen it both ways. I trust him."

"I never thought I'd hear you confess to that."

"Doesn't come easy. Trust too many people in this job, and you wind up getting set up by every group around. Becoming a mouthpiece for anyone with an ax to grind."

"So you believe only what you see?"

"Right. Only what I can catch in my camera. It's not the whole truth, maybe, but it's true at that moment. Right then, it's what's happening."

There was silence again, and a groan from next door. "How about you, Hugo? What do you believe in?"

"Well, that's not the kind of thing one usually talks about."

"That's why I'm asking you."

"I have things I believe in."

"But, being English, you can't say what they are exactly?"

"I'm a member of the Church of England."

"Sounds like one of your clubs."

"I suppose it is."

"Sign up, pay your dues, and you're in for life. Only difference is, you don't need someone to recommend you."

"Maybe so. But I believe in something. I believe in fairness. In the rules of those clubs, and the fairness of those rules. It's the same as with the boys: as long as one lays down some rules, and enforces them without partiality, the boys realize that they will reap the benefits of what they sow. That there's some kind of mechanism of justice in the world. That if you do good, you'll be rewarded, and if you don't, it's no one's fault but your own. Without that, you've got nothing."

"So you believe in your clubs? In a sense of responsibility? To something, at least." I had to get going; somewhere, in this city, Lourdes was sleeping.

"Yes. Insofar as I am able."

"And you believe in God? In love?"

"Yes. Not in the abstract, perhaps, but if I feel it, I believe it."

"Well, I have a proposition for you, Hugo. You remember I mentioned a surprise in my letter?"

"Of course."

"Well, this is it. I know some people would consider it a jackpot."

He was silent. The pig snuffled and rooted. There were murmurs, soft voices from next door.

"This is it: why don't you marry Lourdes?"

"What do you mean?"

"Not for real. But for her sake. To help her escape. Then I'll take over."

"You can't be serious."

"I am. It happens all the time here. It doesn't mean anything; it's just an answer—a convenient answer—to a difficult situation."

"That's absolutely absurd. You're the one who loves her."

"I know. But it's not easy for me. I'm American, I'm married already, I'm here all the time. If you marry her, no one will suspect a thing. You're as clean as a baby."

"And what about her? You talk about her as if she were a piece of property."

"She's the one who gains most out of this. Anything's worth a ticket out. Can't you see that's what she's living for? Dying for? This is your chance to do something, for a change. To help out."

"And then?"

"Then I come over and take her off your hands. This isn't going to be any big hassle for you. Anyway, she likes you."

I could picture him going through options in his head. His glasses on the table beside him; his pajamas collecting sweat.

"Why don't you live, for a change? Do something daring, something dangerous. W. H. Auden did it."

"I don't believe W. H. Auden had many other matrimonial options."

"No, but he did it. Stood up for what he believed in. Put his life on the line."

"More like 'put his wife on the line.' And besides, what am I going to do when I really do want to get married? Later on."

"No problem. Lula'll be long gone by then. It'll even give you some extra glamour. Add some spice to your name. Hugo who rescued the Cuban beauty."

"Just what a nice girl from Hampshire wants to hear."

"You'd be surprised. A woman in your past could lead to women in your future. Just think how the boys at the school would take this. The other teachers too. You're putting yourself out to help a young woman who wants to be free."

"As well as a not-so-young photographer who wants to be free."

"Well, maybe that too. Why hesitate about something where everyone stands to gain?"

"Thank you, Richard. Perhaps I'll think about it."

"Do that. I don't expect you to decide immediately."

"Sleep well," he said, and turned on his side. From the next room, we could hear the old man relieving himself with his wife.

I had a strange dream that night. I was walking through the streets of Vedado under a canopy of trees. The city was bathed in apricot light. There was the sound of voices from the buildings, sometimes faint and then remote. The cars standing motionless along the streets. A few black birds scattered through the trees.

I walked into a room. There were men only there, crouching on the floor. Small cups of coffee at their feet. Somewhere, from inside, I heard her voice. High-pitched and screaming. In ecstasy or pain, I didn't know.

When I awoke, I saw Hugo, in the early light, lying on his back, and staring up.

"So what if I say yes?" he was saying. There was the sound of a rooster outside, and the pig waking up: kids of various ages walking shirtless past our door.

"Then we can set things up right now. José has a friend in Havana who can make the whole thing go two days from now. In Cayo Largo. The sooner the better; you don't know when we'll all be here again. Then we go back to Havana, you take care of the paperwork. I know a guy in your embassy, a cultural attaché, who can help."

"And that's it?"

"That's it. Easy as one-two-three. They do these all the time. It's not a real marriage; just an easy way of keeping the authorities off your back. I pay the whole thing up front, and José's buddy closes the store. All you've got to do is show up."

"And then?"

"You just go back to England, the way you're planning to do. She comes over there as soon as the papers are processed. I wait around until the coast is clear. Then we have a big reunion at the Dorchester. My treat."

"You still won't be able to marry her."

"Not yet. But I have ways of getting round that. As soon as we're together, it'll be plain sailing."

"It just doesn't sound right. Or even very possible."

"Just live for once, Hugo. Come into the real world."

"I appreciate your solicitude."

Before we left that morning, I took the old guy aside.

"You mind if I ask you something—something private—before I go?"

"No problem. Fire away."

"You know Lourdes?"

"Sure. That pretty girl from Havana? José brings her here sometimes. I know her."

"You think she's on the level?"

"She's a nice girl. Pretty, goodhearted, speaks good English. What more can you ask?"

"I'm thinking of marrying her."

"Sure. Why not? Where are you going to find better?"

"You trust her, then?"

"Trust?" He chuckled hoarsely. "Don't ask me about trust. I don't even trust my own wife."

A couple of kids came out then, and I could tell it was time for us to go. "Good talking with you guys," he said. "First time I'm speaking English in maybe two, three years. If you see any of those baseball magazines at home, maybe you could send me a couple? I got a sister in Boston, an aunt down in Hialeah, but they don't never send me nothin'. Take it easy," and then we were out the door, and he was back in his room of shadows, speaking Spanish.

We met José and Lula at the hotel ten minutes later, and as soon as she saw Hugo, Lourdes came up to greet him.

"Look," she said excitedly. "Look what I found in my altar!" It was a clipping, from some old American magazine, and there was a picture of an English guy called Ogilvy, and there was a long story about how he'd been framed in some liaison by the Communists.

"You understand?" she said.

"My uncle," said Hugo, reading it more closely.

"So we have another historian here," I said. "Another thing you two have in common."

"Set up by the guerrillas," he repeated to himself.

"Look, Hugo, José has something he wants to talk to you about." I steered him off in the other direction, so I could take Lourdes aside.

"I think we're on," I told her, as soon as they were gone. "This week."

"He's so kind to me."

"I guess."

"It's true. *You* wouldn't do this for someone. Not unless you got money for it."

"Sure. I guess this is the only way he'll get to spend a night with a woman."

"Very funny, Richard," she said. "You are a comedian."

"Just imagine him on the wedding night," I went on.

"I won't have to. I'll be there with him. Keeping the police occupied. Proving to them that this is a true wedding."

"Yes," I said, "I guess you will," and went up to collect my camera case.

W e drove out of town then, all four of us, past the cashew trees and the trucks loaded with date palms, past the ancient sugar mills and the lookout posts, standing lonely sentinel on the hills, and up into the sun-baked village of El Cobre.

Lula was looking glamorous—she'd worn her best pantsuit for the visit, the one she'd worn our first time, on the way to Artemisa—and she'd brought a ring, she said, to give to the Virgin, to bring good luck to her marriage. It felt strange for me, her saying it like that: as if her wedding was real, as if she needed good luck for it.

Up in the famous Sanctuary, it was again like the Southwest: charged, elemental, with that kind of supernatural, underground force like you feel in Anasazi country. Blue skies, empty spaces, a spire reaching into the heavens. A sense of strength, a hint of magic. *"Virgen de la Caridad. No me abandones,"* read a message on the wall. Virgin of Charity. Don't abandon me. By the altar was a Cuban flag.

The room where they kept the Virgin was one of the most crowded places in Cuba: it was as if the emptier the rest of the island got, the fuller this space became, as if the more real life faded, the more the faith in magic got worked up. The place was packed with every kind of gift and offering you could imagine. Pablo records, eggs, a model Citroën. A ship in a bottle. A life jacket. A pair of spectacles. A Mickey Mouse pendant. A meal voucher.

There was something too much about the room, so I put away my camera and just looked at all the heaped and abandoned hopes of Cuba laid before its patron saint. Stuffed animals, and dolls, and dancing figures of wedding couples. Military hats, models of Jesus, and, along the walls, clutches of keys. A castanet too, and yellow clippings of Ernesto Hemingway receiving the Nobel Prize, and dark flowers, in this small room lit by candles.

It was like all the rooms in Cuba combined in one, all the private altars and glass cases pooled to make some communal appeal. There were bright medals from Angola, pre-Revolutionary coins, certificates belonging to kids who'd studied in Ethiopia. There were boxing medals and medals given to soldiers who died. And, from Fidel's mother, Lina Ruz, the maid who'd married the boss, there was a small gold talisman.

Lourdes left her ring by the altar, then went into the nave and prayed.

I watched her from a distance, kneeling on the cool stone floor, eyes closed, muttering some kind of prayer, and then I got tired of waiting and went outside, into the sun.

"What did you ask the Virgin for?" I asked when she came out.

"That will be my secret," she said, and linked her arm around my friend's.

.   .   .

Dear Stephen,
I expect this will come as something of a surprise, but I wanted you to be the first to know: tomorrow I am getting married. To a lovely girl, very intelligent, very sweet, a friend of a friend, in fact. You may think this abrupt, but things happen very suddenly here, and, what with the political uncertainty and the economic chaos, I thought it best to act decisively this time. So we are preparing the paperwork at the minute, and then shall be planning our return to England.

Rather romantic, don't you think? Rather like Daphnis and Chloe? With warmest wishes, Hugo

Dear Stephen,
This is my first letter as a married man. I don't know that I feel entirely different, but I imagine something in me must have changed. Rather like when one gets confirmed: it seems an empty ritual at the time, but later one realizes that something in one has turned, or been transfigured.

To tell the truth, the wedding itself was rather a sorry affair. We couldn't find any witnesses, and Cubans aren't generally allowed on the island, so Richard, the photographer I believe I mentioned before, simply went out into the hotel lobby, and persuaded some German tourists to come in. We said our vows, though it didn't really feel like that at all, not least because they were all in Spanish; and since I couldn't exactly follow what the man was saying, I just said "Sí" whenever Lourdes—my wife—nudged me. When it came time for me to kiss her, I found myself a little at sixes and sevens, and mostly watching Richard, who was standing behind her shoulder, giving her away.

All the same, though, there was something special about it. For one thing, Lourdes looked transported that day, in a long white dress they keep for these occasions, and her happiness seemed quite unfeigned. And for my part, when I said the words, I could feel I was committing myself to something: rather like those times at school when, simply by saying something, you feel it. Like saying "God save the Queen" to give yourself strength in an emergency.

There was also a rather lovely poem that Richard had chosen to read, by José Martí—you know, that extraordinary Napoleon-Churchill figure they have here, the George Washington of Cuba, as he's sometimes known—who was the country's greatest fighter and its greatest love poet. One of those extravagantly romantic Spanish kind of verses. "El corazón es un loco/Que no sabe de un color: / O es su amor de dos colores,/ O dice que no es amor." The heart is a madman that never knows a single color. Either it is a love of two colors. Or it says it is no love at all.

That struck a suitably ambiguous note, I suppose. Afterwards, we just walked over to the hotel—the only one on the island, as it happens, and, in fact, the one from which I wrote you before, when I spent the night with Richard. We had a slightly desultory reception around the pool, and then, to avert suspicion, Lourdes and I proceeded to our room, while Richard went up to his.

I shall spare you the details of our wedding night, but suffice it to say that one has more or less to go through the motions here, to keep the police at bay. They're highly suspicious of these unions—visa marriages, as they're called—and there are stories of their breaking in on couples on their wedding night and, if they're occupying separate beds, taking them off to prison. Chastity's always something of a taboo here. So we had to go through a charade at least, and when some of Lourdes's exhortations grew more urgent, I couldn't help wondering whether she was addressing them to me, or to the microphone she assumed to be somewhere in the room. It felt a little like being in the school play again—remember The Duchess of Malfi, *when I had to pantomime passion with that Bettina girl?*

Now, to recuperate, so to speak, we shall go to Varadero for four days—passionate lovers in the spell, as it were—and then the plan is for me to return home while the embassy processes the papers.

I suppose much of this will seem very strange to you. It seems a little strange even to me: a once-in-a-lifetime adventure, at the very least, and something of a dramatic act. But I think the fact of my agreeing to this may have something to do with that letter of which I once wrote you, the love letter someone gave me in the cathedral. I don't quite know how to explain it, but somehow, reading that letter, in that way and in that place, struck me as an augury of sorts.

I'm not superstitious, as you know—the dean's always talking about my "agnostic muddle"—but this whole episode has a kind of rightness to me that I wouldn't presume to deny.

I do hope that your forays in Delphi were as pleasant as ever. With warmest regards, Hugo

Stephen—
This is our honeymoon hotel—not exactly the Connaught, as you can see. But the sea is nearby, and the food is tolerably good, and there aren't many holiday-makers around. I shall have quite a bit to tell you when we meet. Please do give my best to everyone; and, if you wouldn't mind, please keep this latest development to yourself. Yours in holy matrimony, Hugo

That must have been the worst night of my life, just lying there, in that room, alone, wondering what was happening in their room, wondering what was not happening. Sometimes, when I heard a footfall in the corridor, I half expected it might be her. Breaking the rules, and honoring a higher law with me. But then the steps would pass by, and I'd remember the situation I'd set up was way too precarious for that, and so I was left alone with my thoughts.

I tried all the tricks I knew—imagining points of blackness, practicing the yoga exercises I'd learned in the monastery in Saigon, even thinking my way through the checkpoints in Beirut—but still I couldn't sleep. I got up and tried to write some postcards to the agency. And as I rummaged through my bag for cards, suddenly I came upon a hair, a long, black, silky hair, that must have been a relic from that last night in Varadero. And I remembered how she'd looked along the beach; the feel of her mouth on my legs; the way she'd smiled, and put her hands over my eyes. I saw her turning the pages of her book of poems. I heard her cry, the way she'd never shouted out in Havana. Soon it made me feel like when I was in Davao, and the NPA set off a bomb, and a couple of kids got blown away, and when I moved in for the shot, and saw their girlfriends weeping, I hardly had the will to go ahead. But I did. And that shot got syndicated around the world: "Pretty Filipinas Torn by Grief."

The next day, back in Havana, I was walking toward the hospital—to get some pictures—when I saw Cari in the street, and as soon as she saw me, she came up to me with her warm smile, and hugged me, and asked me how things were going. I decided not to say anything about Lula's marriage, so I just told her about my trip to Santiago, and how I'd got ripped off by the woman at Havanautos. I guess I'd always liked Cari, especially after that time with the letter from France. And right then, in any case, it just felt good to be talking to someone, anyone, and free, for a while, from my thoughts.

She asked me if I wanted to come along to the Malecón with her, and I thought it was better than being alone. We walked past the new industrial beach, where teenagers were swimming among the garbage and debris at the foot of a few stone steps, while half the trash of Cuba floated past. "El Condom Pasa," I said, but she just looked at me and smiled, and it was one of those moments when I wished Lourdes had been there. She'd have got the joke.

Cari, though, was always good-natured, even though she still hadn't heard from France, and she didn't have much English, and she probably couldn't find a way out. Along the wall, she looked at me with her blue eyes, and smiled with that creased expression, as if she were going to cry.

"Richard," she said at last. "Will you take some photographs of me? For my *novio* from France? Maybe if you take some photographs, he can keep them by his bed. And remember to come back to Havana. Lourdes told me that you took some special photographs of her, in Varadero, and you sent them to a foreign magazine—*Vogue*, no? You can do the same for me?"

No harm in that, I thought; at least it would use up the time. And maybe fill up my lens with something other than the shadow of Lourdes. Might as well use the camera in a good cause: I'd looked at Cari before, in the street, and figured out how I could light her, how she could show off her colors and her curves, how to bring out the gold in her hair, and her bittersweet eyes. I'd even worked out the jokes I would tell her to make good on her glittery smile.

"Okay. We'll go to the beach. Get a hotel room. Do it really nice and stylish: tripod, strobes, filters, the works."

"You will be careful? Make them big. Not like those small things." She'd looked disgusted once when I'd pulled out some contact sheets from the shoot of Lula on the beach; she didn't even go for slides. "You will make them big, okay? Like this?" She pulled out a photo of her sweetheart from France.

"Sure. Big like this: no problem."

She looked at me as if I were some kind of miracle worker. *"O-ka, Richard, un momentico."* She walked—she almost ran—back to her room (to Lourdes's room, I thought), and told me to wait a moment in the street, while she decided which clothes to bring and collected some lipsticks and eyeliner, and then tried to remember what her mother's shoe size was, and what kind of clothes her aunt had requested for her boy, and then what kind of coffee Lourdes's mother liked the most.

Then she came running out into the street, all her things in a bag, and we found a car to take us to the hotel—for me to pick up my equipment—and then all the way to the Internacional. I got a room to serve as our base camp, just the way I would if I were shooting fashion, and I got into the whole thing like it was an assignment: at least it got me out of myself.

For most of the morning, I just took standard pictures to warm her up: Cari in a bikini, Cari next to the rental car, Cari in front of the religious statues, the blue-green sea behind her. We stopped for a drink in the lobby, and I took a few more pictures there, but the sun was too high, and so I figured we'd shoot indoors until dusk.

So we went back to the room, and she pulled out all the clothes she'd brought along—the black T-shirt dress, the halter top I'd seen before, the Victoria's Secret thing the Spanish guy had given her.

"What do you think?" she asked, changing in and out of outfits in the walk-in closet. "How does it look? This is pretty? This is nice?"

"Stay there," I said, as she was changing. "Like that. Like that. Again."

Cari in bra, Cari in panties, Cari unfastening. Cari reclining. Cari lying on the bed. Cari . . .

Somewhere in the middle of all this, I thought I saw Lula coming into the room. But it was only Cari, I guess, sobbing, and whipping her head from side to side, and holding my head between her knees, and saying, "No, no, no, Richard. No, no, no."

V

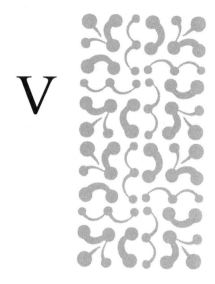

I still couldn't sleep when I got back to New York. We'd agreed that the code for my coming over would be the fourth letter I received, and before that, I wouldn't get in touch with her or Hugo: we didn't need a code, perhaps, but habits like that were hard for her to break. So I went down to the mailbox every day, at nine o'clock, at ten o'clock, at eleven, and always there was the same Cuban silence: a huge amount of nothing. I spent long afternoons in the apartment, just in case she'd call, though I knew it wouldn't be safe, but there was nothing: only silence. I wondered if she was waiting but couldn't get through, if she'd sent four already, but they'd all been confiscated or lost en route, if something had happened after I'd left. I stayed awake all night, and thought of her sitting in her room, wondering why I never came.

I called up the agency, and asked them to send me anywhere, on any gig, as long as I could get out of New York, and I found myself in Panama, then Mindanao, then stopping off to see some friends in Delhi: when I was working, at least, I was back in focus. But then one day, in Manila, I went into the Spider's Web for a drink, and a girl—a really pretty girl—came up to me and said, "You're so handsome, honey. You want to come dancing with me?" and then her friend said, "She's a good girl. You can do anything with Lourdes," and I felt sick, sick to my stomach.

I came back to New York, and still there was no letter. I tried to call José in Havana, I figured that was safe, but always it was the same: static, and a crackle, and a faint, underground voice, saying, "Dime, dime," as if casting lines into the deep. I could have chanced a call to Hugo—who ever checks on telephone calls between England and America?—but still I couldn't face the thought of hearing his recriminations. Or, even worse, his enthusiasm. And then saying, "How's your wife, Hugo, the great love of my life?"

Finally, I could stand it no more. I called the travel agency in Montreal, got on their next package tour to Varadero, leaving the following Sunday, and arrived, with a group of blue-rinse vacationers, at the Internacional. I went to the Havanautos desk—run as usual by the only person in Cuba who understood economics—and got her to give me a Sentra for two hundred bucks a day. I pulled out onto the highway and drove toward Havana: even two hours in Varadero was like a lifetime in a haunted house.

I drove fast down the long, empty road, so empty it looked like it was set up for some fashion shoot, with a thin line of lipstick down the middle. The night riders were out in force, like poppies in the spring, extending their brown arms, laughing and giving me the eye. Above them, there seemed to be more billboards than ever: ONE OPTION ONLY: THE FATHERLAND, REVOLUTION, SOCIALISM.

I passed Cojímar, and remembered the café where I'd gone for lunch my first week in Cuba, many years before, in search of Hemingway ("Sorry, we don't know that name here," the old man in the street had said). I came closer to the Malecón, and saw all my previous trips all jumbled up. There was the place where we'd gone after Maxim's; there was the place where we'd kissed and kissed; there was the place where I'd almost popped the question. Down by the U.S. Interests Section, where the government still flashed a neon caricature of Uncle Sam every night, I could see the place where I'd sat, my last morning in the city the year before, and thought: If I never, ever see a sight as beautiful as this one, I'll die happy.

It was late by now, and I was in that half-drugged, emotional state brought on by jet lag—when you feel wide open, and your mind is on cruise control, and you open up your heart to the first person you meet. I peered into the Nacional, but it was all glitzed up now, sparkling with empty conference rooms and chandeliered bars and computers in the lobby, showing you the sights of Havana in seven different colors. There was a rooftop bar now, full of gold-chain Don Juans, and cops outside the entrance to make sure that the only people who wanted to come in could not.

There were more people than ever among the bushes outside,

and skinny girls posted in the Habana Libre as solemnly as guards: Semper Fidel, I thought. Eternal Vigilance.

Outside in the street, the signs that used to say, "We Are Happy Here," now said only, "We Are Here." Old men were selling books—liquidating their assets—along the streets, books with titles like *La Promesa* and *Whither Mankind?*, edited by Charles A. Beard. Along La Rampa, some of the old stores were turned into new "Tourist Information Centers," open twenty-four hours a day and full of workers crowded round a black-and-white TV; outside, people were still waiting for buses that, every few hours, labored, like fat Habana Vieja mammies, off into the dark.

THE FUTURE OF THE FATHERLAND WILL BE AN ETERNAL BARAGUA, said the new sign outside the cinema, and as I read it I wondered who the signs were aimed at. At the Americans, who weren't allowed to come here in the first place? At the traitors, the ones who'd already left? Or at the people who still remained, and were the last ones who'd believe them? I thought of a guy who says "I love you" after his girlfriend has slammed the door.

I walked, walked, walked, just tracing the hill down toward the center of town, and everywhere I turned, I saw José Martí: his statue here, his words on that plaque, his book *Ismaelillo* number one on the current best-seller list. A hundred years dead, and he was everywhere; and Lourdes, the one I wanted, I couldn't find. I decided there'd be even more guys trailing me now than the next day, so I didn't even stop at Concordia, but just kept walking, the slogans tumbling slowly through my head like choruses from a Top 40 song. *Siempre es 26*, I heard, and thought of the night in Artemisa. *Resistir para Ganar*. Not every time, I figured. *Estamos contigo*. Don't count on it, good buddy.

That night, in the Colina, I dreamed of a knot of men, in robes, by the banks of the Nile. I saw them pounding drums, chanting, clapping, saying things I couldn't understand, these men all in a circle, by the banks of the Nile. I saw the dust rising from their feet, felt the pulsing of the ground, sensed this throbbing group of men, in dirty robes, chanting something terrible. I felt a sense of menace, of being on the outside of some circle, intruding on some sacred rite. A knot of men, chanting all together, shouting for my death.

· · ·

When I woke up, I took a shower, and headed out to find her. The still blue morning seemed almost a mockery to me. The big guy's sex appeal was almost down to zero now, but still he wouldn't take no for an answer. Once upon a time, he'd seemed the romantic hero of every politico's dream. The ideologue with a passion for baseball and cigars. The only guy who could play footsie with Barbara Walters and Brezhnev and find a way to charm them both. A Revolutionary straight out of the Radical Chic catalog. Now it was as if he belonged to a teenybopper group that hadn't been heard of for ten years. And yet, I thought, the Ortegas had come and gone, Gorbachev was history now, the dreaming kids had moved from Managua off to Prague, and the other Communist cities—Beijing and Saigon—were famous for their free markets; but Fidel was still in control, thirty-three years and going strong.

Lula's door, when I got there, was locked. Every now and then, some neighbor came by, heard "Lula?" and then said *No sé* and walked on down the peeling street. Finally, I heard steps inside, and the door opened up behind me. Her mother was in the kitchen, as if time hadn't moved at all, wasting cigarettes and waiting for the news, and when she saw me, she came up and kissed me, and said, "Richard, Richard." A cousin was doing her makeup in the next room. There was no sign of Lourdes, or her life.

"Sit, sit, Richard. How have you been? How are things with you in America?"

"Fine." It always seemed the safest answer down here.

"My mother in Miami—you saw her?"

"Miami is a long way from New York."

"But she sent you the money?"

"No. No money."

"*Ay!*" She shot off something to the cousin, and the girl peeped out and smiled, and then some neighbor came in and said, "*Oye! Qué pasa?*" and then everyone in the building wanted to hear about how her mother had not sent the money and how in the land of plenty people forgot about their families and how this stranger from New York had come to give presents all around.

"And Lourdes—have you seen her?"

"No. I only got here last night. That's why I came here."

"In New York?"

I didn't follow this. "I guess I'm often not there."

"She said she would call. You didn't hear nothing?"

"Maybe she tried and couldn't get me."

"Oh, that girl! She said she would call. New York is not so far from England, right?"

"England?"

"*Inglaterra, no?* That is her new home. With that English boy."

"Hugo?"

"*Claro.* Every week she sends me money. In England, you can have anything, she says. Here"—she spat out—"nothing."

"You have her address?"

"Sure. Somewhere here." She got up and went to the cupboard.

"And Cari?" I asked, while she was fumbling through her papers.

"She's gone."

"Where? To her mother's?"

"Where? I don't know. After Lula got married, she left. I never heard nothing from her." She muttered something to herself as she went on sorting. "I can't believe you never got her letter. She wrote to you, I think." Then she found what she was looking for, and came back with Hugo's address. "You know, Richard," she said, as I copied it down again, "before, I thought it was you that would be her husband."

"You're not the only one."

She took the address back from me, and put it back in the coffee can where she kept a couple of wrapped-up Alka-Seltzer tablets someone had given her years ago, and a card from some acupuncturist in San Francisco, and a couple of tiny photos, taken in machines.

"That's funny," I said. "I came here to find Lula. And she's away in England."

"Sure," said her mother. "But now you are here. Stay, have lunch. Maybe we go to the Tiendas this afternoon."

"Maybe," I said, but my mind was already out the door.

I didn't know what to do then: the charter flights only left on Sundays, and I had six days to kill, in a city full of memories I didn't want. I got out my camera, and thought I might go to work, but I wasn't seeing anything, or else seeing only things that weren't there: maybe I'd finally become a true Revolutionary.

I went down to the Prado, but the place felt like a swirl of ghosts, a whole *cola* of spirits, some mine and some the Revolution's, and sometimes I didn't know which ones I was seeing, and which ones imagining: that figure on the staircase, that olive-skinned girl with the smile, that couple in the plaza. The band was still playing, but the dance floor was all empty.

Down near the British Embassy, I remembered the time I'd come down here with Hugo, on our way to the Sevilla, and he'd pointed out to me how you could see the original writing on the sidewalk, which said "Mann, Little Co." right outside the boarded-up Hotel Siboney, and that, if you looked real hard into the dark, you could see, way, way up in the gloom, "The Happy House, Open Day and Night. Prado 331." And the NO HAY BAÑOS sign in the window of the Hotel Packard, and the Martí slogans scrawled across the walls.

And then we'd taken in the other phantoms of the Prado: the outline of the old Cine Shanghai, famous for its shows, and the building where the Casa de Negros had been. There was the shadow of the Blue Moon, with its high-priced dancers, and the famous gambling houses, La China, La Central, the place where President Prío held his infamous nights of white powder and tall showgirls. Beside one doorway, you could see where Superman had per-formed his stunts before half the guys in Skull and Bones, and along the Paseo de Martí, you could still imagine all the sailors walking beneath the laurels to the Marriage Palace.

A little way on, in the park, I felt her by my side again, tucking her hair behind her ears, and giving me her slow, sly smile, and leading me up to a room where I couldn't make out the shapes, and the sound of our things as they fell to the floor.

I went off into the refurbished Hotel Plaza, where there were four times as many waiters as customers, and every time I moved, a couple of them came forward, and bowed, and said "Excuse me," and showed me all the other tricks they'd learned from their Spanish masters. A band was playing *"Cielita Linda"* in the next room—the fancy dining room—before an audience of empty chairs. "Excuse me," said the waiters, "I'm sorry," as I waited fifty minutes for a beer.

I walked up the street again, and I saw her coming toward me, breaking into a smile. She was leading me now toward the Hotel San José, and she was taking off her earrings in a side street. I followed her up the grand triumphal steps of the university, and through its heroic columns, and past the tank, where groups of pretty students twittered away like students anywhere, and then down into the backstreets of Vedado. At one point, I heard a whisper from the bushes, and turned to see a dark-eyed girl beckoning me toward her: Lázara, I thought. She must be eighteen now, out to help her mother.

Around the parks on Calle 19 and 21, the cars with empty sockets for headlights looked like sightless men, and the dull shells of buildings like bodies whose souls have long ago departed. On the grand, white-columned monument above the Avenida de los Presidentes, the young were still pouring out their hearts, and commemorating their own private acts of Revolution. But the counterrevolutionary messages were as full of bravado and desperation as the ones they were rejecting, and it was like seeing one mirage replaced by another. "Any idea that isn't dangerous isn't an idea," someone had written, and "Purity of the head doesn't come without sterility of the heart. A person rich in ideas is always poor in virtue."

At the bottom of one column, I read, in a girl's careful scrawl, "Sometimes the stars come down and walk among us as people. Since I've known you, life feels happy and full of possibility. These words were written after meeting Carlos."

I felt I needed to be anchored then, brought down to earth and reality, so I sought out José, and went along Calle J till I came to his house. I could tell from the picture of Che outside his door that things were getting harder.

I rang the bell, and it was the same as ever: the yapping dog, the heavy footsteps, the sudden swinging open of the door. Inside, though, the place was almost empty for once: just his *santería* altar in the front room and, at the stove, a grumpy-looking woman making beans while a curly-haired girl, with a cataract in her eye, played with a broken doll.

"Come, Richard," said José. "Meet my wife and child."

"*Mucho gusto,*" said the woman, and the girl looked up at me from where she played. "Vilma, give Richard some coffee. Strong and sweet, right?"

"Strong and sweet."

"So how are things, José?"

"Great."

"Fiddling while everything around you falls apart?"

"Why not? You know what they say: we got good news and bad news. The bad news is that everyone's got to eat stones. The good news is that there aren't any."

"But, José—"

"You know, Richard, before I was always talking of going outside—to America, Spain, the Dominican. Now I see is better here: we don't have to work, we can drink and dance and make love. Is good. The other places are not so good. On TV, they show pictures of Peru, Guatemala: there are people starving there!"

"But, José, as long as I've known you—"

"Look, Richard," he said, leading me out onto the terrace. "Let me show you my city."

He maneuvered me out onto the roof, and said, more quietly, "Is better we talk here. Vilma is the daughter of a general. I had some problems with the government, and so now I am a married man. We were married before one time—a long time before, when we were in college—but then we were separated. Now is better for me like this. Like you too, no? Her father is a Hero, very high in the army; he fought with Fidel in the mountains. A good man; he likes me, he gives me his poems to read."

"And he looks after you?"

"Sure. *Más o menos*. He looks after her. She looks after me. Is good."

Just then, the woman came out, and touched me, smiling, on the arm. "José, let me talk to your friend. For a moment only. *Un momentico.*" She watched him go back inside, and then she took me to the very edge. It felt like something from the Bible—"All this I will give to you"—in reverse.

"I have heard much about you, Richard. I feel we are friends already. José is always talking about you. His best stranger friend. A true *compañero.*" She gave me an imploring smile, this woman I'd never met before. "I do not want to ask you for your help; I am not like the others. You are our friend. But I want to tell you we have nothing in our kitchen. If you want to give us anything, we will always remember you in our thoughts. It is not for me; it is for the *niña.*" She ran her fingers along my arm. "I never ask for me. Only for my daughter. She is so young."

"I'll think about it."

"For her, Richard. Not for me." She smiled again at me. "But don't tell José, okay? He will not understand."

"Richard," he called out from the kitchen. "Come and see my photographs." He was seated before the TV, the paterfamilias tuned in to some program from Miami with the sound off. He had an old photo album in his hands. "You see? This is my brother. My mother. Me." As usual, the pictures were all blurred, and the identities even more so. The one José called his "son" looked exactly the same as him, the one he called his "father" looked nothing like the old guy in Santiago. I remembered how writing captions in Cuba had always been a bitch.

Then the little girl came out and showed me her box of condoms—the only kind of balloons they had left—and a stack of photo albums stuffed with scraps of foreign papers: torn pieces of Carnation labels and Nescafé ads and stickers that said "Knorr's Soup," status symbols in the local elementary school.

"That's really nice," I told her, smiling. "But I need to see the house where Abel and Haydée lived."

"Sure," said José quickly, taking the hint. "I show you." And we went out into the street and took a taxi to the Inglaterra, where we could talk. The stained-glass windows in the refurbished lobby dappled the tables in color, bathing the faces of Irish boys in red and blue and yellow lights, turning the German professors' hair purple, dropping circles of color around us like petals.

"This is like something from *Our Man in Havana,* no? From the time of Batista."

"When Cuba was the Land of the Almighty Dollar."

"Sure. When the *yanquis* were king." I looked around at the cooing couples at every table. "You know, Richard, one week before, I found a book on Obispo, from twenty years before, about the Revolution. It was telling us all that Fidel had achieved. Now there are no prostitutes, it said," and he motioned with his eyes around the lobby, filled with girls. "Now there are no tips, it said," and he looked toward the waiters, angling for gifts. "This is the only country without any alcoholism, it said, and I thought, That is true, if you do not count the drunks; this is a country where telephones are free, and I thought, That is true, if you do not want to call anyone. Everyone goes to work, it said, though nobody here has a job; everyone has vacations, it said, but there is nowhere to go."

"I know. They say every son comes to resemble his father; I guess every Revolution comes to resemble the one it overthrew. Reminds me of that old joke they tell in Moscow. You know, 'Capitalism is the exploitation of man by man. Communism is the opposite.'"

He gave me his wry smile. "Sure. Is crazy now. The ones who think too much about the future, they go crazy. They are like the Apostles around Jesus; for them, if Fidel dies, Cuba dies. There is no after. So for me, I just make love and stay quiet."

We went on drinking our beers.

"So anyway, Richard, how is Lourdes?"

"I don't know. She's not here."

"She's with the Englishman, right?"

"I guess. You've heard from her?"

"No. When a Cuban leaves Cuba, Cuba leaves the Cuban. After they leave, they never think of us."

"It's like that everywhere."

"Sure. Is better like this. Is better for her. You remember Myra?

She is working in the *cola* now. Every day, she gets in the line, and she gets ten, twenty pesos. And Rosita? Lourdes's friend? She is now married with a North American. A criminal. He was on this TV show—'America's Most Wanted,' right? Because he killed a guy up there, and so he comes down here for a quiet life."

"And you, José? You can eat?"

"Sure. I can always eat. Now, the government says, is the *Período Especial*. Time for heroic sacrifice. In one month, one piece of meat. One box of matches. Three hours a day, no light. But for me, I make business, is not so bad. You have seen the new fifty-peso note?"

"Don't think so."

He pulled one out. "*Mira*. Before, fifty pesos was too much money. Now, is nothing. So Fidel makes new fifty-peso notes like promises. If you look at this note, you can see, like a ghost, a picture of Célia. Célia Sánchez. This place is crazy now."

Crazy indeed, I thought: a whole nation holding banknotes up to the light to see the silhouette of its president's long-dead girlfriend.

"Before, I had some problems. Big problems. In the Habana Libre. The police catch me. I was in Combinado before; if I go again, is not so good for me. So I find a lawyer, and get out."

"And a wife."

"Sure. A wife helps too."

"You were buying stuff?"

"Sure. As usual. I was with a guy from Panama that time. But he gets scared, and then he says he does not know me, and I am taken to the police office."

"What were you buying? TVs?"

"No. Only shoes."

"How much?"

"One hundred."

"A hundred bucks for a pair of shoes? No wonder the cops came down on you."

"No. One hundred shoes."

"Come on, José."

"Is true. Why not? Everyone does it. That's the way here. Usually is no problem. I go to the store, I talk to the guard.

Everybody knows me. I give the girl five dollars. Then, when I am finished, I go into a Turistaxi, and speak English. If the guy doesn't understand, I say, very slowly, *Yo quier-o ir a emba-jada.* Then, if anyone sees me get out, they think I am a foreigner."

He grinned. Life was a crossword puzzle that José solved every day over breakfast. "But this time they stop me. And the guy from Panama says, 'It's for him.' "

"So why don't you do the buying yourself?"

"Sometimes I do. At the Diplotienda, where my brother works—my religion brother, not my prison brother—is easy. But with a foreigner is better. There are many foreigners here. You give them a hundred pesos, they do anything."

"That's a hell of a lot of money."

"No. Now, for one pair of shoes they pay four hundred pesos. For jeans seven hundred. I make good business. Some people say to me, 'Why don't you go to America?' I say, for me is better here. See, if you work for the government, you get one hundred twenty pesos in a month. One dollar thirty. But if you got dollars, you can live like the president."

I bought him another drink. A girl came over, and set my beer before me with a smile.

"See," he said, and I caught the edge in his voice again. "For her is easy. She can meet foreigners, she can meet policemen. If the policeman stops her, she says, 'I'm sorry. What can I do? Why go to court? Why give money to the government? Maybe you and I meet tomorrow, in my room. Drink some rum, have some fun.' Then the policeman is like a doll she keeps in her pocket."

"That's why Cuba's losing all its beauties."

"Sure. Everyone is leaving."

He paused to sip his drink. "You remember my cousin? She is not my cousin; she is my wife's sister. She meets this man from Spain, very rich. Every time he comes to Cuba, he takes her everywhere, like his wife. Brings her TV, camera, anything. He tells Fidel, 'If she don't come with me, I don't sign the contract.' "

"And what does she think?"

"She thinks it's good. He is old, he is sick—maybe he won't last so long. So what is the problem in giving him some happiness before he dies?"

"And inheriting all his cash."

"Sure. Is better like this. Everyone is happy. Who is hurt?"

"Only the truth. Trust. That kind of stuff."

"Richard." José looked pained. "You are talking like a Communist. What are these words? Who can eat truth? Who can live on trust? These people are human, they need to live, to love, and you are talking only of ideas. If you love these ideas so much, go to a library and make love to a book. Take your trust to a love hotel, and do it up the ass."

"Touché," I said, and then I thought that maybe I wasn't in the best position to be talking about trust and truth.

Being with José reminded me that there was nowhere I could turn: everything took me back to her. I tried to concentrate on nothing but my work, but everything was weird and jumpy now, like an old machine slowly winding down: the whole country was like one of its ancient cars, stalled, or hardly moving, a dinosaur jalopy running on empty, and being coaxed by patience and resourcefulness and sheer willpower alone to bump and stumble along a street where all the lights were down.

René Arocha, the star pitcher, had defected. The Russians were all gone now, replaced by South Americans here to polish up their name as Latin lovers. The mannequins in the former Sears downtown were all naked. And the worse things got, the more talkative the streets became. THERE ARE NO TRAITORS HERE, said the signs now, all around, and THE REVOLUTION IS WITH YOU FOREVER, just above the Quixote, where men were selling hand-painted birthday cards. Downtown, one whole wall showed the many faces of the Revolution, beginning with Pride and Jealousy, and moving to Upset and Disenchantment. The last space showed THE BEAUTY OF SACRIFICE. The less the people had, the government kept telling them, the more they had to be proud of; they were the world leaders now in self-denial.

Outside the National Museum, I saw they were planning a Festival of Monologuists. The government might be sinking, I thought, but it hadn't lost its sense of humor.

Finally, I could take it no longer; could take no more of the dead cats lying along the sidewalk, and the long lines of kids, in the dark, going into nightclubs that didn't have any drinks; could take no more of the strains of "La Cucaracha" drifting across from the Rincón del Feelings and the waking up at dawn to find bloodstains on the sheet. Everywhere I looked, it seemed like I was seeing lovers, pressing themselves against walls, or murmuring fierce promises, or taking themselves off into the dark; lovers who looked the way that we must have looked. Maybe that was the definition of love, I thought: to feel yourself so different, and so blessed, that you hardly knew you looked like all the rest. To be so taken out of yourself that you hardly cared that you were living inside a postcard, or a cliché. To forget about the filters and the light meters.

There should be a law, I thought, against long kisses in the street.

The next day, as soon as I got up, I went into the Cubana office and showed them the letter I always carried from my doctor, explaining how the malaria was recurrent, and how, at its outbreak, everything must be done to get me to the nearest hospital. They talked and fretted over the letter, but I knew that there was no malaria treatment left in the local hospitals, and finally, shaking their heads, and muttering, they put me on the next plane out. A few hours later, I was back in Mexico City, among fake *rubias* in furs and with plastic all around.

It was really late by the time I got back to the city, and in the dark, in the cab in to my apartment, I could hardly see the portrait of Martí up on 116th Street, in Harlem, right near the Hotel Theresa, where Fidel and his friends used to stay, carrying live chickens and shocking the country with their voodoo *houngan* tricks. I could hardly make out the Salvation and Deliverance Church next door. I could hardly read the Spanish signs.

I rifled my mailbox as soon as I got into the lobby of my building, and there was an airmail envelope there, from England, and I tore it open where I stood, and took in the page of neat, curled writing.

Querido, inolvidado *Richard,*
Free at last! All my life I have waited for this time, and now, thanks to you and to Hugo, I am free. How can I thank you? When will I see you? When will I hold you between my legs?

Hugo is so kind to me, like a father almost: a true gentleman, like some knight from Quixote. *We laugh together often and we often talk of you. But where are you now, Richard? I never know. And when will you come here and take me to your castle in New York? I wait for you, I wait. My body waits, my mouth waits, my darkness and my silence wait. Even the spaces between my toes wait. I am free now, Richard; free to be your Lourdes.*

Su propria *Lula*

I didn't know how that made me feel; I checked for the postmark, and found it had been sent three weeks before—must have arrived just after I took off. I read it in the elevator again, going up; I went into my apartment, and put on the light, and read it again. It was everything I wanted and had been hoping for; but was this the first letter or the second? Why had she not written before? Did she really know nothing of Cari?

I tried to sleep, but the sleep wouldn't come. My head was electric, full of light; it was buzzing like the streets of Vedado in the old days, with a kind of juiced-up, revved-up, open-all-night buzz. I got up and turned on the light again, and all around the room I saw the pictures I'd taken of Cari: Cari sitting on the beach, Cari with her back to me, Cari with her blue shirt slipping off her shoulders. Cari like a Playmate of the Month.

I couldn't take much more of this—I always liked to develop some prints and put them up around the room before deciding which ones to send the editors—and I figured it was easier for me to leave the prints than for the prints to leave me. So I walked out into the streets of Manhattan in the dark, and walked and walked, almost like I was in Cuba again, along Tenth Avenue, past bars and all-night diners and black transsexuals tottering on their heels outside the leather bars. Rough stuff, not shown on TV Martí. The steaming potholes, the cafés where the cabbies went, the rough-voiced come-ons of the Korean girls.

When the sun began slanting through the concrete canyons, lighting up a window here and there, pinpointing panes of gold, I headed back and tried to sleep again, but still I couldn't do it. I got some Valium, and emptied them on the counter, but my system wasn't taking them right now. I could see all the images around the walls from where I lay, and they went round and round in my head, like a carousel on automatic fast-forward, out of control, jerking on and on, and I couldn't stop its turning.

I tried to count shadows, or to remember acronyms, or to go over every long night in my life, but all I could recall was the night on the beach when she said, "Tonight I will show you a different way of making love," and making love that night was like walking through the streets of Miramar in the dusk, the trees caught in the last of the golden light. Slow and sinuous, a long, slow walk, past dark, shuttered houses, and underneath old lampposts, and down empty avenues, to the sea. All night, the two of us, with all the time in the world, walking through Miramar in the dark.

But that got me to thinking of what she might be doing with him, and how she might be showing Hugo the same kinds of love, and then, when I couldn't control the thoughts any longer, I got up again, and started talking to her in my Sony, imagining her next to me, pretending I could whisper to her, and hear her voice beside me, and call her by all our secret names. But somehow it didn't work. The more I talked, the more I waited for her to say my name. I waited so long it hurt; it was like calling a lover at home, at two a.m., and just hearing the phone ring and ring and ring.

Around noon, the day's mail arrived, and there was another letter from her, sent ten days after the last, and I picked it up, and looked at the stamps, and smelled the envelope, and imagined how she looked when she was licking it, and how she ran her tongue along the back of the envelope, and how, perhaps, she'd spray a little Charlie on the paper. This time I couldn't smell anything.

Richard,

England is so different from everything—different from Varadero,
different from what I have seen on TV, different from everything I
imagined! All old and gray, old and gray, red brick and gray stone,
till I think I go crazy. Even the rain here has no feeling, no passion.
Even the women here, I think, are old and gray, made of red brick
and stone.

At first, when Hugo took me to the Tandoori Centre, I stood outside in the street and waited. "No," he told me. "There's no line
here. We can go in." And the stores, my God, the stores are like
something from the fairy tales, like nothing you can believe! They
have everything here, in a hundred colors, in every size and shape,
and everything you want, all brightly lit like a carnival. At first, I
could not stop visiting these stores. For two days I walked in them,
breathing the smells and the colors. I cannot believe I used to think
the Diplotiendas were a paradise.

But sometimes, I think, it is as if the stores here are all full, and
the people are all empty, like the opposite of Cuba. Like all the
color is in the boxes, and the people are only gray and old. They
have this thing called "fog" here—maybe you have seen it—and
this "fog" visits and you can see nothing, nothing for miles. For
me, this is how it always is in England—like seeing nothing. Like
all the colors are wiped out. Like all the hearts are slammed shut.
Like all the music is turned off. Hugo likes this, he can live in it;
sometimes, when he sits in his chair in the night, and reads a book,
I think the fog is inside him too. But for me it is not so easy: I am
a cubana.

The house where we live—an old house, a very small house, not
like the houses of my cousins—is like a museum, Hugo says. But
how can you live in a museum? Have you seen this place, Richard?
Sometimes I call it "Losechester." A flower would weep if it was
placed here; even the sun is ashamed to visit. Hugo says it will be
better in the summer: there are schools for learning English here, and
many girls from Spain come to these schools. I can meet them in the
pub, he says, these sixteen-year-old girls from Valencia and Madrid.
But what is there for me? Instead of schoolboys, schoolgirls! What is
this place I have come to, Richard? Where the boys have no girls and

the tables are from the Spanish times and the students wash in tin baths.

Hugo is always kind to me; he takes me in the car on Saturdays, and we see old churches and dead bodies. Fidel would be at home here: all the martyrs of Girón and Moncada are nothing to these Englishmen! On Sundays, we go to the chapel in the college. The first time I went there, and saw the light through the big purple windows, and all the lamps, and the people there, so many of them, in different colors, so dignified, I could not believe it: it was like something from the ancient Spanish days. So beautiful, so romantic, so full of feeling. But then the music started, and I caught the tune, and I started to sing, and all the boys looked at me—all these little Nigels and Geoffreys and Ruperts, these boys like old men, in gray suits, with love poems under their pillows—they looked at me like I was una loca. As if they had never seen a woman before, or a woman in a woman's dress. I wanted to cry, Richard. I stopped singing then, and started looking at the floor. I could not look at these boys' faces. But Hugo was kind to me, as always. He held my hand, and the way he looked at me, I wanted to cry in a different way. So proud, so calm. As if he were looking at a Madonna. I have never known a man who looks at me this way. And after, he said that it was not me that was crazy, it was the boys. Sometimes, Richard, I think Hugo is all I have. Sometimes, I think that is enough.

Yo te quiero,

L.

My head was reeling then; I didn't know whether to laugh or to cry. I tried to steady myself by getting out the contact sheet from the day in Varadero. I went over her pictures again and again, but they were different somehow, they had gained more shadows: maybe she was smiling at someone behind me, I thought, as I looked at the first, or maybe she was wearing this dress because she had worn it here before. Or maybe she was thinking of some Spanish businessman. Maybe, when she asked me to bring a friend along, she'd known I would bring Hugo; maybe when she kept on talking about marriage, she'd known I'd fix things up the way I did. And anyway, that had been not my plan, but José's; maybe the two of them—maybe the three of them—had been in it together all along.

Maybe, maybe, maybe.

I picked up the letter again, and read it and read it and read it, and every time I read a different letter, and all I could remember was the ending. I thought maybe I should go over right now, settle the thing quickly. But then I thought back to our plan. And I had a big assignment coming up for Time-Life in L.A.

That night, when I went to bed, I saw him holding her in his arms, in that steady way those English guys sometimes have, and I saw him telling her how he'd never be away from her, and meaning it. And I saw her unbuttoning her shirt, her lips wet. I saw her face moving under his, calling out his name. I saw her saying the words she'd never said to me. And then—and this was the part I couldn't take—I saw her lying in his arms, content, with a future she could hold.

And then, around dawn, just as I was getting to sleep at last, the phone began to ring, and after that, it rang and rang and rang, off the hook. The agency knew I was back in town, and they wanted to get more prints of Cari from me. Somehow, those images was selling like crazy. The Europeans were eating them up, the Argentinians were bidding for a whole series, some French magazine was talking cover story. The pictures were dynamite. I don't know what it was—"It's because of the way you look at her," one editor had said, "and that way she has of smiling, as if she's just about to cry"—and so I went back to the darkroom: Cari, drying her hair as she came out of the bathroom; Cari, in the earrings I'd brought down for Lourdes, as a wedding gift, from Mexico; Cari stepping out of her white dress, with the light behind her. I guess it was maybe just the lure of the Revolution with a pretty, smiling, tearful girl. They used to say that Nora Astorga won more friends for the Sandinistas than Bianca Jagger ever could; in the Marcos days, there wasn't a think magazine in New York that wouldn't go for a picture of a pretty NPA guerrilla with a gun.

Lourdes smiled too much, I thought; Cari looked sad enough to buy. And I lay down in my bed again, and the images went tumbling through my head, and I changed the way I'd planned the story, so that the images that were meant to come last would go first, and the opening spread became an elegy.

That was when the next letter arrived.

Dear Richard,

I cannot tell you how crazy is this place of Winchester. Everything so heavy, and all the men in ties, and I can never feel the sea. They say this is an island, but where are the beaches and the palm trees and the sky? Everything is so tired here, and the streets are small and curved, but not like in Habana Vieja; it is like they are all weighed down by stones. And nothing happens, nobody laughs, nothing changes. The streets are gray, the buildings are gray, the people go from one place to the next. Hugo is at home here, with his books and his jazz records and his sherry. But I, I feel that sometimes I will explode.

You remember, Richard, the postales you showed me once, from France and Germany and Hungary, the ones you always carry with you? From that French man who you love. Sometimes I feel I have entered that same world here, as if I am living in black and white. Where are the colors? Where is the music? Where are the hopes? Hugo tells me that later I will understand; every day, he gets up and puts on his gray sweater, his gray jacket, his gray trousers. He goes out into the gray, and joins the other men in gray.

And you know something else, Richard? There are people here living in the streets! Like animals! Like pieces of dirt. Old people, young people, sick people: people without arms, without jobs, without homes—it is like something from the end of the world. From the time of Batista! Hugo took me to a play—a Soviet play—in London, and after, we walked to the station, and everywhere there were these people, so sick you could not tell if they were dead or dying or only sleeping. It was like something from an article in Granma; *but if I read it in* Granma, *I would not believe it. I wanted to talk to these people, to give them food for their babies, to invite them to our house. But Hugo says it is not safe. "They like it like this," he says. "It is* our way." And the other Englishmen walked past, or looked in the other direction.

Last week, here in Winchester, I saw an old woman burying her head in some garbage—in the middle of the High Street! I asked her if she had lost something. "Bloody lost my mind, haven't I?" she shouted at me. "Bloody lost it all. Fuckin' Margaret Thatcher. Go and ask her what I've lost! Ask the bloody witch!"

I remember, Richard, when I was young, my mother told me stories of the Isle of Pines. If you talk loudly, she said, if you do not think who you are talking to, if you do this, if you do that, you will go to this place where there is no dancing, and no brightness, and no air. But now I am there, I think, in this world of closed doors and closed faces.

But Hugo is happy, happy like you cannot believe. I cook him rice every night, and I make him strong coffee, like in Cuba, and sometimes I tell him stories of when I was a girl. I can talk to him so easily, and always he listens. Always he remembers. To see him so happy, Richard, to feel I am the reason for this happiness, I cannot tell you how it makes me feel. This has never happened to me before, to make someone happy in this way. Maybe this is what being free means: to give someone happiness. I think I will stay with Hugo; he tells me I can bring my mother here too, and my sister, if she wants. It is strange—sometimes I do not understand my heart—but I am happy with him, and I do not want to leave.

I think of you sometimes, Richard, and I do not know where you are, or what you are doing. I hope one day you will look at yourself like you look at the world, through your lens. Do you know what are the times I miss? Maybe you will think I am crazy. When you were asleep beside me. I used to look at you, and I could see the face your boss, your compañeros, your friends could never see. And I knew that then, in that moment, you could never leave.

Con cariño,
Lourdes

I didn't know now whether it was better to get the letter, or to get nothing at all; I didn't know if I should go over right now, or wait her out. Maybe she was only writing this for the people she thought would be reading it; maybe the whole thing was a ruse.

I picked up the phone and called Alvarez. His machine picked up on the first ring. "All telephone numbers gladly and gratefully accepted. If you aren't in my black book already, you could be soon. Price of admission: one naked picture."

"It's me, Mike. Richard. Pick up, will you? I need to talk to you. It can't wait."

"Talk away, *compañero,*" I heard him saying, on the other end.

"Look, Mike. I need to come and talk to you. In person. Right now."

"Okay. Just give me forty minutes, huh? There's some little business I've got to attend to."

I knew what the business was: pretty and just shipped over from Korea. It made me feel kind of sick to think of him like that—and then I thought that maybe that was how Lourdes thought of me, and all the rest of them. Casanova with a camera.

Thirty minutes later, I buzzed him at his place near Limelight. He looked kind of groggy, but it was still Mike: the only guy I could talk to, the only one who knew the place like I did.

"What'll it be?" he said, opening up the closet where he kept his stuff: Mike was probably supplying half the photographers in New York. "You know what they say: where there's a pill, there's a way."

"I need something more than that right now."

"What is it? Same lady?"

"Right. She's gone."

"Where to?"

"England. Fucking red-brick, rainy England."

"That shouldn't be hard to fix." That was the thing about Mike: he always looked on the bright side of things.

"It's not that easy. She's married. To an Englishman. I set the whole thing up."

"You made the bed, and now they're lying in it."

"Right. Poetic justice. A taste of my own medicine. What goes around comes around. I know all the easy morals: just tell me what to do."

"Why don't you come with me to the P.I.? I'm going there next week. 'Faith Healing in Negros,' or some crap. You know what it's like over there: an all-night agony column with beauty-pageant legs."

"It's not like that, Mike. I want her."

"Nothing else will do?"

"Nothing."

"Okay. I guess there's no cure." He picked up the phone, and I saw him punch his way through some options, and then he was saying, "One seat. Smoking. Next Thursday. Upper Class. Picking up from West Broadway. Coming back Tuesday the seventeenth. American Express. Just a minute."

"Your number, Richard?"

I got out the plastic and gave him the digits.

"Seven-fifteen p.m. Thursday," he said, putting down the receiver. "Virgin 004 to Heathrow."

The L.A. trip came up just then, and I thought it would take my mind off things to be back in the middle of the bang-bang: South-Central was the hottest story outside Liberia and Sarajevo. A nice civil war in the comfort of your own home, as some of the guys were calling it. It was like Manila or Jo'burg, they used to say: all day shooting AK-47s, and then you could go to a restaurant or a nightclub, and forget the whole thing was happening. The only trouble was, L.A. just then was Havana all over again. The hot, lazy, clear blue days, the light as sharp as a knife, the sense of suspended motion, the faint scent of jacaranda and hibiscus: sometimes I felt I was in Vedado again.

I took myself up the coast one day, to the little tract house near Santa Maria where a pretty Filipina fixed up three thousand marriages a year, her mother licking envelopes in the next room: the largest mail-order-bride service on the mainland. That story was booming now: the end of Communism had meant a flood of new bodies into the West, many of them ready to market themselves as such and not used to regular employment. Soviet girls were all over the Middle East, Czech girls were cashing in on new markets, East Germans were working Hamburg. The countries that were still committed to Marxism were going stronger than ever: three hundred thousand girls in China, so they said, and Saigon back to its Nixon-era prime. The Philippine woman in the California suburb even accepted Visa cards.

But it didn't clear my head for long, and some nights, instead of going out, I just went back to my hotel and talked and talked into my tape recorder.

"Sometimes," I told her, "I am back in Havana again: the quiet mornings in the sun, the sea ahead of me, the bay beside me, the sense of being in a world without movement or horizon. Alone on a wall, in a world without noise, a few listless cars curving around the sea, a couple of boys throwing stones into the water. And then the night and the music and the long walk through the dark to Concordia.

"I see you at the top of the stairs when I arrive, putting a finger to your lips, and I lead you by the hand into the room next to the kitchen. The room is dark. The child next door is crying. Your mother is sitting at the kitchen table, with her rum and cigarettes, alone. I feel your lips on mine, your hand around my back, the shiver of your hair against my skin. I kiss your arm. I hear your sighs, and then your muffled shouts, and then we are on your bed, and your mother is next door, alone.

"Afterward, you bring me a pad of paper from your drawer. Write something, you say, write anything. Something for me to keep when you are gone. Something for me to remember. Something that will be a little piece of Richard when I cannot touch you. So I tear out a piece of paper and write, 'For Lourdes García Milan. This voucher entitles the holder to a free trip anywhere in the world, at any time, with the photographer of her choice. All expenses paid. Valid for all eternity. Redeem with a kiss.'

"When I leave, you say, 'Shh, Richard, shh,' as I mumble things in your ear. I kiss you once before I go, and, halfway down, I look up to see you close the door behind you."

W hen I got back from the Coast, there were two letters waiting for me from England. I picked up the thicker one first, a fat blue envelope addressed in that precious, spidery scrawl that all those high-class Brits affect, as if making their words hard to read gave them some kind of historical importance, or just helped them keep their secrets to themselves. Two snapshots fell out from the tidily folded pieces of blue stationery with a crest on the top: one of a typical English house, red brick, with milk bottles outside the door and a scruffy garden in front; and another, which they must have taken with a self-timing mechanism—the composition was all wrong—of the two of them, smiling, his arm around her shoulder, in front of the cathedral.

My dear Richard,
You will doubtless have heard from Lourdes already about how she has settled down here, and how she is finding her exotic new home. Actually, I think it is a trifle exotic to her—and even to me, seeing it through her eyes. Sometimes I feel as if I've never lived in Winchester before. Never really lived, that is. All the old places have a different texture now, a different timbre almost, now that she's among them; it almost feels a little like Havana.

I dare say you have intuited much of this, but Lourdes is so happy to be out. I don't think she expected England to be quite so different, but I do think she's well on her way to adjusting. We lead a rather quiet life, very domestic, and to you it must seem terribly dull and mundane. But Lourdes likes it, I think. After all those years of uncertainty in Havana, I suspect she's glad of some stability.

As doubtless you know, too, the visa part went quite without a hitch, and the authorities seemed more than ready to accept us as a man and wife. I suppose the £500 they get from every departing Cuban reconciles them somewhat to the prospect. I can't pretend that Winchester is entirely to Lourdes's liking—she wears a heavy coat even in the daytime, and her requests for papayas have not invariably borne fruit. But I do think she is ready to appreciate what Hampshire has to offer, and will make a good life here once her initial homesickness subsides. She is an extraordinary woman, as you know, in her intelligence and poise: as you may have gathered, the two of us have grown quite close, and I find there is a great deal she can teach me. This intimacy is nothing I've encouraged—and, naturally, I feel rather awkward about mentioning it to you, especially at this dis-

tance—but it does seem to agree with both of us, and I'm happy to support her, whether her affection is for me or for her new life.

We both think of you often and, though perhaps it would not be easy for you, agree that it would be wonderful if you could find a way to visit. The house itself is too small, I think, for guests, but we could easily arrange a room for you at the college, and there's quite a lot to do here: not least, as you'll recall, the Quiristers. I enclose the photographs as a kind of vade mecum. But really, to lure you here, I suppose we'd probably need a civil war. Or a minor insurrection at the very least.

We'll see what we can do.

Do stay well, wherever you are; Lourdes joins me in giving you very best wishes for the Easter holidays.

> *All the best,*
> *Hugo*

The other letter, on the same blue paper, was very short.

Richard,
I saw the picture of Cari in the beauty shop here: in the same hotel we used in Varadero. Maybe even in the same room. I think I always hoped that you would change. I thought that if I loved you enough, you would learn to love and trust. I thought I could make a new Richard. But I was wrong.

I hope one day you will see yourself in a picture. Then maybe you will understand why I will always stay with Hugo.

> *Lourdes*

There were still three days before the flight. Three days to wonder why I'd done it: did I go with Cari in order to get the pictures, or did I get the pictures in order to go with Cari? Was it release or revenge—or both? Had it been because Cari was waiting for me? Or only because I couldn't wait for Lula? I had three days to go through all the possibilities, and none of them was flattering.

.　.　.

It was raining—of course—when the plane touched down, and the Tube into town took us past rows and rows of tired, washed-out houses, with overgrown weeds in their gardens, and dirty lines of clothes. The Industrial Revolution had never died here; it hadn't even grown up. I got out at Victoria, and found myself a bed-and-breakfast near the station, one of those rock-bottom places full of Eurailpassers, and Japan Travel Bureau types who've paid two months in advance, and girls who didn't even make sure the toilets flushed. Just a place for the night, to freshen up and get some sleep before I met her.

When I woke up, late at night, out of sync, I went out to a phone booth and made a reservation for two at the Dorchester. Called Virgin too, to get another seat next to mine, on the seventeenth; bought some flowers at Covent Garden. One time I even tried their number, just to hear her voice. "Eight-double one, four-nine-three," she answered, and I could hear his voice in hers as I hung up.

I didn't want to sleep—it'd only be worse if I slept and dreamed, or tossed and turned all night—so I found an all-night café and filled myself with milky tea until it was light, and I thought of all the things I'd say to her. I had a few lines of Martí prepared—the ones she'd taught me on the beach—and I thought I'd tell her she could use her voucher now. We had a room, I would say, we had two seats on the Tuesday flight to New York.

Then I went to Waterloo and bought a day return to Winchester. I made the 9:05, got off at a sleepy country station—as mild and motionless as all those British places—and then I walked down the hill toward the school. Winchester's not a big place, and it wasn't too crowded. All the signs show you how to get to the "College."

I walked down the pedestrians-only thoroughfare, the medieval areas, past the kind of buildings that must have made her think she'd never left Old Havana. I looked out for the Wykeham Arms, and tried to guess which shops she'd use. One time I thought I saw her, but it was just an au pair, laughing as she came out of an off-license.

I imagined her walking the aisles in Sainsbury's, sipping rum in the pubs, going for runs across the playing fields at dusk.

Under the arches, everything became much quieter. The college had a secluded air, as if it belonged to another century. Not many visitors were around. The little lanes were generic English quaint. A few candy stores. A post office. Some little houses with pots of flowers on their windowsills.

I threaded my way through lanes and streets, and followed Kingsgate down Canon Street to Culver Road. I looked around for a phone booth: I thought he'd be out now, so I could invite her for a drink, or even get myself inside. Just long enough to show her the ticket and give her the flowers and tell her the lines from Martí. No problem with the visa, I'd explain: now she was English, she could go anywhere she wanted.

And then, as I walked past number 18, I saw them, through the window. Hugo was sitting at a piano, in the same sweater he'd been wearing in the bar that first night, but something in him had changed. He was singing along, for one thing, sort of quietly, and when he played, it sounded nothing like the kid's tinkling I'd expected. Nothing fancy, to be sure, but it had the sound of someone who knew what he was doing, and wasn't shy.

Lula was sitting in a chair across the room, a stuffy kind of professor's room with framed pictures of cathedrals and even one of a soccer team. On the coffee table, there was a picture of the two of them together, at their wedding, the one I'd taken to keep the witnesses happy. Her eyes were bright, and she was smiling as he played. Her skin had lost something of its healthy color, and she wasn't wearing any makeup. Her clothes were as drab as the English designers could make them. But she looked calm, and settled.

Then he stopped his playing, and looked over at her like a man who'd just come out of church, and she looked back at him and smiled. It wasn't much, and I couldn't hear what they were saying, but it was a different smile from any I'd seen in her before. Not the one I'd caught in the hotel that night, not the one I'd taken in the plane. Not any kind of smile I could have gotten in my lens.

She leaned down to pick up a book from the table. From where I stood, it looked to be Martí.

A Note About the Author

Pico Iyer is a longtime essayist for *Time*
and a contributing editor at *Condé Nast
Traveler, Civilization,* and *Tricycle: The Buddhist Review.*
His books include *Video Night in Kathmandu,*
The Lady and the Monk, and *Falling Off the
Map.* This is his first novel.

A Note on the Type

This book was set in Monotype Dante, a typeface designed by Giovanni Mardersteig (1892–1977). Conceived as a private type for the Officina Bodoni in Verona, Italy, Dante was originally cut only for hand composition by Charles Malin, the famous Parisian punch cutter, between 1946 and 1952. Its first use was in an edition of Boccaccio's *Trattatello in laude di Dante* that appeared in 1954. The Monotype Corporation's version of Dante followed in 1957. Although modeled on the Aldine type used for Pietro Cardinal Bembo's treatise *De Aetna* in 1495, Dante is a thoroughly modern interpretation of the venerable face.

Composed by ComCom, a division of Haddon Craftsmen, Allentown, Pennsylvania
Printed and bound by The Haddon Craftsmen, Scranton, Pennsylvania
Designed by Anthea Lingeman